Evan,

BLIND TRUST

Book Three of The Rector Street Series

The BNP scandal
I spoke of. Hope
you enjoy.

JOHN NUCKEL

Second edition 2018

Published in the USA by *thewordverve inc.* (**www.thewordverve.com**)

eBook ISBN: 978-1-948225-13-7
Paperback ISBN: 978-1-948225-14-4
Library of Congress Control Number: 2018900618

~~~~~

Blind Trust

A Book with Verve by *thewordverve inc.*

Cover design by George Muller
grmuller12@gmail.com

Paperback and eBook formatting by Bob Houston
http://facebook.com/eBookFormatting/info

ACKNOWLEDGMENTS

Thank you all for your help: Glenn Burgos, David Lender and Jeff Laffel.

As always, thanks to Lindsay, Sarah and the fabulous Vicki for the continuing inspiration.

CHAPTER 1

Ben Hirsh had heard the shot ten minutes before. He put a cigarette to his mouth, cursing himself for picking up the habit again, then lit it. He was waiting for his phone to charge in the rental car. He wanted to get into the house and get a photo. He had just arrived when the shot went off. He thought it might be a hunter. After all, he was in upstate New York, three hours north of the city. He had heard that people did such things up there. He thought better of it. The shot had come from the house he was headed to.

It was a perfect early summer night. The sun had set less than an hour before, and there was still a red glow on the horizon. He could smell the lake and a hint of pine over the fumes of his idling car. He reached in through the open passenger window and picked up his phone, accidentally pulling the cord out from the base. It said 10 percent. Ben thought it might be enough for the job. He pulled his head out of the car, phone in hand. He didn't hear the girl until she was at the end of the long driveway.

She was young and thin with long blond hair hanging to one side, covering half of her face. She was wearing a skin-tight purple dress. It was far too revealing for a girl he took to be fourteen or fifteen. It looked as if she was at a party and had tried to imitate her idea of what sexy was. The effect was to make her look skinny and sad. She was barefoot and crying, the gun in her right hand hanging limply at her side. She was shocked to see him. Ben positioned the phone in his hand to take a shot.

The girl seemed to be looking past Ben, over his shoulder, when she spoke. "You, you fuck. You. You killed him."

Ben raised the phone and looked into it to square the picture, frame it.

Through the floating image he saw her raise the gun. It was as unsteady in her hand as a forty-pound dumbbell. Rather than feeling threatened, Ben felt sorry for the kid. He lowered the phone then walked over to her. She lowered the gun, and Ben put an arm around her and took it. He set aside the idea of pictures for now and dialled 911 with his thumb.

CHAPTER 2

August 8, 1972, New York City

This would be the last one, William Brogan thought as he looked through the scope. Jesus Christ, he was thirty-eight years old with over fifteen years of service. Couldn't they find a younger guy?

The target was walking briskly, headed west on Fifty-Third Street. The team had picked him up outside his building. He spotted them, as planned, and they steered him along. The team choreographed the target's path perfectly, funneling him down Eighth Avenue to Fifty-Third. There were seven pedestrians on the street, all Brogan's men. The "movie set" barricades were set up on Sixth. The street was under his control. The target approached the truck, and Brogan tightened his grip on the rifle. Only now did he put his finger on the trigger and aim at the back of the target's head as he walked over some two-by-fours lying across wet cement on the sidewalk. The men following the target started running toward him.

As the target turned to look forward again, Brogan pulled his finger toward his right cheek and felt a gentle snap. The bullet went through the target's head and lodged into one of the boards now five feet behind him. The angle from the office building was lower than Brogan had calculated, and the shot almost missed the last board.

Two of the men caught the target before he hit the sidewalk. A third bent down quickly and picked up the two-by-fours, awkwardly balancing them horizontally across his arms. The back of the yellow rental truck opened with a rattle that was too loud for Brogan's liking, and the man was thrown in the back, the boards thrown on top of him. The door was closed by the unseen agent in the back, and the truck pulled away.

Brogan spoke into the walkie-talkie. "Pull it."

A man on Sixth Avenue said, "Got it" into his unit, removed the sawhorse barricades, and started waving traffic through.

Brogan disassembled the rifle in sixteen seconds, by his count. *Getting slower*, he thought to himself. He placed the parts into the slots of the foam-filled briefcase and bent down to pick up the lone shell casing. He waited until he got out on the street before taking off his gloves, then headed west toward the Hudson.

August 23, 1972, Park Row, New York City

Hank Johnson knocked twice. As he closed the last box and reached down for the tape roll, Brogan hollered, "Come."

Johnson opened the door and swung his upper body into the room, keeping his grip on the doorknob.

"There's a Mr. Handley in the lobby wanting to see you. He says you'll know who he is."

Brogan knew. Handley was the source, the tipster for the last three assassinations. His first panicked thoughts were to wonder how Handley knew both him and where this office was. Brogan wasn't the one who had turned him. He merely followed orders on this one. They came from high up the chain of command. He quickly registered what he knew of Handley, at least what he had been told: some oil guy from a family business with strong Mideast ties. A rich kid who worked in finance. He left the family oil business after falling out with his father, who had stayed in Saudi Arabia, likely with a woman. The family was rich, old rich. Handley's mother drank herself to death after his father left.

It wasn't a particularly unique case. The mother's death caused the resentment that the agent Handley had gone to exploited. The relationship led to tips on men Handley's father knew or did business with. These men, Brogan's targets, were organizing groups to attack America's interests. "Terrorism" was the term used. It was a new movement, one that was best snuffed out early.

Johnson was waiting at the door. From across the room Brogan could smell

Brylcream and Listerine. Johnson was fresh out of Yale, an eager new agent. He was good. Brogan saw a future for the kid. He liked his demeanor and his grooming. He was always pressed and starched. Johnson cleared his throat to get Brogan's attention for a response.

Brogan picked up the tape roll to seem preoccupied and said, "Send him up. Is the audio still rolling?"

"No. They shut it down this morning with the phones."

"Okay. Fine, yeah, send him."

Brogan lifted the box and put it on the stack with the other three. The office was now shut down. Men were coming to take the boxes away in a few minutes. He sighed as he looked at the final box. He had packed it two minutes before, and it was supposed to symbolize the closing of the case. *Perhaps not now*, Brogan thought. Handley should not be there or anywhere around him. For the informant to make contact with the shooter was highly unusual. This was a turn he hadn't anticipated. There was nothing else to do but deal with it. He was made, and it was time for damage control. He thought he should call his superior before Handley came into the office but then remembered what Hank had said about the phones. He'd have to wing it, try to keep a record in his head. He reached inside his jacket, took the safety off his revolver in the holster, just in case, and sat back in his chair. He put his feet up on the green metal desk.

Handley walked through the open door like he owned the place. He walked briskly to Brogan's desk and extended his hand. He was sharply dressed, though his hair was a little long for Brogan's taste. Other than that there was absolutely nothing of note about the man. He was average height, weight, and demeanor, a man who would be lost among a crowd. Brogan thought he was the type that would make a good FBI agent or secret service man. He was younger than Brogan, maybe thirty.

Brogan didn't stand but put his feet squarely on the floor and pointed toward the chair in front of his desk rather than take his hand. Handley sat, and Brogan immediately took control of the meeting.

"Who do you know in the agency?"

Handley was surprised by the question. He tried to tap dance. "Mr. Brogan, is it? I don't know what—"

"The phones go down this morning, you shouldn't know who I am or where

I am, and you happen to stroll in here? Today? No, that doesn't work. Who do you know?"

Handley crossed one leg over the other. His bell bottom flopped over awkwardly. He took the end of the cuff and neatly folded it to make a clean line. He started to speak then halted. Brogan saw that he was contemplating his answer, sure now that he would be lying. It would be his task to decipher the truth. Handley spoke in a high-pitched voice with a bit of a lisp. His words were measured. No doubt he had some sort of speech impediment that had been schooled out of him.

"I'm here to thank you."

Brogan leaned forward. "Bullshit."

Handley chuckled. Brogan's rare outburst of profanity seemed to encourage him. He wasn't at all intimidated.

"You seem to be a man who appreciates bluntness, so I'll get to the point. You're about to become a wealthy man."

Brogan thought of his wife, her fortune, and the fact that he hadn't seen her in over a year. In that brief moment he thought of the back of her neck as he kissed it, the smell of her clothing. Then, as always, he thought of how quickly he had come to hate her.

Handley hadn't gotten the response he wanted, so he continued. He uncrossed his leg and leaned in.

"There will be a takeover of a financial services company tomorrow. Axis Financial, symbol AXL. You own quite a few shares. You've been accumulating them for the last six months or so."

Brogan figured that the guy was crazy. Not too uncommon for this type. Most snitches had some form of a defect. He thought that perhaps Handley might have to be dealt with. He shook his head and chuckled then rose to call Hank to get this crank out of there. Handley ignored the act of dismissal and kept on.

"I do know someone in your agency. He unfortunately got himself into a bit of trouble. You see, he has a penchant for young girls, some rather young—a detail that allowed me to get this meeting, but that is not really the point. I wanted to introduce myself since we will be tied together for some time. Partners in crime, so to speak." He smiled a creepy grin with his left upper lip frozen and drooping, the speech impediment a physical thing. "You'll find out soon, so I thought I would have the courtesy to let you know beforehand. The first two men you eliminated so expertly at my behest were indeed very bad characters. Terrorists, they call them. A nasty business. Mass killings, beheadings, all things you were no doubt told. The third was a selfish bit of work on my part. He was the CFO of Axis Financial. He was quite uncooperative, and it is better for all parties that he has been removed."

"You set me up?" Brogan was incensed. He stopped in his tracks and turned to hover over Handley. Who the hell was the guy up the chain of command that got him into this? Put him in a room with this creep.

"I prefer to think of it as a mutual benefit. The shareholders will make a profit, my business will grow, and you will be rewarded all because of the elimination of one difficult little man—whose motives, I'll assure you, were not pure."

Brogan paused to look down at him then headed for the door. He thought he could just leave the room and take a few minutes to regroup.

"How will this read in the papers, Mr. Brogan?"

Brogan stopped before the door with his back to Handley, not giving him the regard to speak to his face.

"Are you out of your mind? Do you think this will fly? I don't care about perception. You're going to jail if one word you have said is true. No one—I repeat, no one—plays me." He reached his hand inside his jacket, around his holster, and grabbed his badge from his inside jacket pocket. "You have the right to remain silent. Anything you say—"

Handley interrupted. "You have a sister and a brother, is that right? She's a professor at Columbia. Your brother's a doctor. Wonder what they would think of their brother the assassin? Oh, that's right; perception doesn't matter to you." He shook his hands as if swatting away his next sentence. "Let me dispense with the theatrics. I've met both of the men you shot previous to the assassination in dispute. They were indeed terrorists. Fanatical murderers, religious zealots. I've heard the hatred they spewed during travels with my father. I think I'm correct in assuming that you are very capable of fending for yourself, but this could be very bad for your family. You see, these are men who take vengeance—I guess they would consider it justice—very seriously. If any of these terrorists were to find out that it was you who assassinated their brothers in the cause, well, I'd rather not go into details of what they might do."

Brogan turned to Handley. He tried to keep his composure, though every instinct he had was to crush this bug, stomp him out. Instead he took a breath and put his hands in his pants pockets to keep them from Handley's neck.

He leaned into Handley and whispered, "No matter what happens from this moment on, I will kill you."

Handley was visibly shaken, and he leaned back in his chair to get away from Brogan's Irish red cheeks and predator eyes.

He continued. "Your sister leaves her apartment on First Avenue at approximately seven thirty-five a.m. on Monday, Wednesday, and Friday for a jog along the East River. The other days she goes directly to the university and parks in an underground garage, space number eleven oh seven. This is not a bluff, Mr. Brogan, and you will not kill me. If anything happens to me, there will be consequences. I don't think I have to go into your brother's schedule or where his sons play hockey. I'm a serious man, Mr. Brogan. I would not have walked in here unprepared."

Brogan was not defeated. He had to play for time. "What is this stock you spoke about?"

Handley smiled again. "The purchase was made in a blind trust. The account will show that you have been buying stock in Axis—very cautiously, mind you—for over six months. Before you ask, yes, this has been ongoing for quite some time. You were specifically chosen not only for your expertise as an assassin but because of your family and the logistics of their vulnerabilities. You really should have them use more security in the future with what your profession exposes them to. You're too easy to bribe, Mr. Brogan. Not unlike your superior." He clasped his hands together, gathering his thoughts. "The trust is set up with one of my financial executives as the manager. We have copies of your signature thanks to our mutual friend from the department. Any future transactions will be made by my man. I assure you all due diligence will be used. The trust can only be accessed upon your death. It should be a tidy sum to leave behind to your children or whomever." He waved his hand, making a brushstroke.

Brogan figured it out as Handley was finishing up. "Who came to you with this? Was it CIA, NSA?" He could tell from Handley's face that he had hit on something. He continued. "This is too big, too deep for you. This is a nice little act here, but, no, this is too big."

"Mr. Brogan."

"No, no. Not you. I'm guessing CIA. Not terrorists with a scope on my sister but maybe a marine sniper. There's no superior with little girls; that would have been sniffed out long ago. They know when you go to the bathroom around here. They came to you with some kind of Saudi oil thing. Your old man has the contacts. I'm sure that there is some kind of national security component to this. I'm thinking maybe you snuck that last guy in. They're embarrassed now that the stock takeover is happening. You played them, and this is the backup story." He stood again and started pacing. "Yeah, that plays. Lots of oil...this country runs on oil." Pacing, he cupped his elbow in his hand and put his fingers to his face. "The question is, what's your take from this?"

"I assure you that there is an account in your name. The terms are as I stated, and there will be dire consequences if you break this agreement or speak to anyone."

"I have no doubt of that. I don't like the idea of being used. I will figure this out, and you will be very unhappy when I do. I can't put together why you bought this stock in my name unless it was the department that bought the stock then backdated it."

"That answer is really of no consequence. The stock purchase is a bonus, or maybe you consider it a price to be paid for your silence. I'm sure you can see how it will play out: rogue agent looking forward to profiting from his clandestine work. I wasn't sure whether you felt a sense of loyalty to your career or your family, so I covered both. I have met men who are more motivated by money than any sense of family."

"Like your father?"

Handley was stoic in silence, but Brogan knew the dig had cut.

Brogan continued, more to make this out to himself than to grill Handley. "If you did originate this plan, you've been buying this stock for six months. I was only given the assignment four months ago."

"Well, I've found that it is best to be prepared. If it eases your mind some, your superiors weren't aware of the stock position until recently. I have some friends at the SEC who backdated the purchases once I obtained your signature. I have figured it out. This is what it is. You lost. It's done. No one in your agency is going to cooperate with you on this. It's been shut down already. I did use you for my purposes, but from this point on the justice department will take over. Face reality; you kill people for them. Do you think this hasn't happened before? That you haven't killed a man unjustly? You go back to your world; I go back to mine. You'll have a great deal of money to leave behind. Besides, you'll kill more men before you are through. You're a company man; you'll do what you're told. All this won't matter a few years from now. Yeah, you'll kill again. I can see it in you. You enjoy it. You can go on killing people, and I'll go back to my big new financial company." He smiled and held out his arms. "It's good business. We both win."

He stood up and walked past Brogan out the door. He turned back a few steps down the hallway. "You won't see me or hear anything of this again unless you talk. The money from the account will go to your heirs. I give you my word."

He smiled at the irony of the statement and walked down the hall. Brogan had nothing to say because he knew Handley was right on all counts.

CHAPTER 3

July 8, New York City

Ben Hirsh sat on the bench, sweating through his shirt. It was another hot one. The breeze coming across the Central Park Reservoir provided no relief. He had been contacted by his main client, Sol Landsman, that morning to push up their monthly meeting to this day. Ben had been working without a contract for Landsman for over three years. He had other accounts, but Landsman was far and away his biggest client. Perhaps the most powerful man in New York, Landsman was the chairman of Prime Equities. He was at least eighty years old but, if anything, was more influential than ever. Prime was the top private asset manager in the world. Ben was aware of who was on the client list, having done quite a bit of research for the firm. The roster of clients included some of the most influential businessmen and politicians across the globe.

Ben's first meeting with Mr. Landsman was on this very bench, as were the rest. Ben had opened his private investigative practice only a few weeks before Landsman called. After quitting the SEC, Ben was a little concerned that he had acted too hastily, but he couldn't take it anymore. Busting those scumbags in suits only to have them not admit or deny any guilt and walk away with a wrist slap was too much for him to take. The shit he saw, the fucking way those guys skated, it was too much for him. Ben was making about seventy grand a year and watching thieves walk away with millions, hundreds of millions, after he busted them. The last straw came when they busted an entire hedge fund for insider trading. There was one guy who walked free and clear. He made around seven or eight million a year and never did anything. He literally never signed anything or made a trade or negotiated a contract. The best the agency could figure was that the guy had lunch with rich people. He walked away clean. Hirsh heard that he owned a catamaran outfit in Saint Thomas now. Ben had opened his firm with the sole intention of rooting these pricks out and making them pay. A man like Mr. Landsman could make these front-running, insider-trading Wall Street scumbags pay. To hell with the laws and politicians and their payback favors—Landsman used Ben's information to swoop in, to skin those bad actors and leave nothing but bones.

Landsman approached from behind as always. His driver was waiting on Ninety-First and Central Park West. Not one for small talk, Landsman sat slowly and began. He was dressed impeccably and had taken to wearing sunglasses that covered half his face. It was a sign to Ben that he was starting to fade a bit. He kept his posture rigid, formal.

"A dear friend of mine will pass away soon." He stared out to the water. Ben could tell he was upset since it was the first note of emotion he had detected from Landsman since they met.

"I'm sorry to hear that."

"Thank you, Ben."

"What can I do for you, Mr. Landsman?"

"Ben, must I keep telling you to call me Sol?"

Having just turned thirty a few months ago, Ben couldn't help but defer to the older man. It didn't feel right to call him anything other than Mr. Landsman.

"I can't help it. You're going to have to get used to it."

Landsman smiled, and his face cracked in a thousand places. "The friend is William Brogan. I believe you have heard of him."

"Who hasn't?" Ben recited what he knew. "His work was cited a number of times during my initial training with the SEC. Commissioner Johnson was under him for years at Justice. Brogan was the top guy at Justice for years, married into high society, very wealthy. The word is he's a hard man, not one to have as an enemy. He owns some security firm, works out of that big townhouse on Sixty-Seventh off the park. Who's the guy that I'm thinking of, the one who does most of his legwork, runs the shop for him?"

"Frank McGinley."

"Yeah, that's him. I met him once at a conference. I'm sorry about the news. What do you need me to do?"

Landsman hesitated. He seemed to want to change the subject, avoid the topic that he had brought up. It was not normally his style, and Ben could tell that he was broken up over Brogan. Ben sat silent and looked out at the water. He noticed a white egret about fifty yards south and twenty feet into the water. Landsman sat back and exhaled.

"Is the girl okay?"

The question took Ben off guard. He took a second to think about what was asked. "Oh, the girl. Yeah, she's fine physically, I guess. She came down the driveway with his gun. She waved it around a little bit but was too shaken up to lift it, let alone use it. You saw the photos? I don't know why I sent them. I always send everything, you know. No, she waved the gun around a little, but I took it off her hands. I sent the originals—the photos, I mean—to the local cops. Who would have thought the guy would shoot himself? I did press him hard that afternoon, but the SEC was going to move in eventually. I can't for the life of me figure why he wouldn't just tell me who he was working with. I feel bad for the kid, finding him like that, but then he probably should have thought about the kid when he was skimming millions from one of your clients. Not very smart."

"No, not smart at all. I will find out who he was doing this trading for. I always find out; you know that, Ben. I'm concerned about the child. She will be provided for financially, but it is a messy business with what she saw. I do abhor the violence. I'm afraid that business and the imminent loss of my dear friend have set me back a bit. Yes, yes, it has." Ben waited, not wanting to interrupt. After a moment Landsman said, "Egret."

"Yeah, I saw."

"I'm sure you did."

Again Landsman was silent for a long while. He pulled a piece of paper out of his breast pocket. He unfolded it and stared into it as if he was making one last attempt to solve a puzzle. He gave up and dropped his hand with the paper to his lap. He looked out at the water then finally spoke.

"William Brogan changed his will a few months ago. I'm not his attorney but the executor of his estate. I also have control over his healthcare proxy, which gives me the obligation to make health decisions along with financial decisions on his behalf. He was put on life-sustaining equipment three days ago, therefore obliging me to take a fresh look at his financial affairs. This is an account statement among his files that I was not familiar with. I've managed his assets for over thirty years, and this is the first I've seen of the account. There's just a statement with his latest balance. The statement is dated over forty years ago. I had one of my associates try to track its origin, but there is nothing to find. No record of the account being opened or closed. It's a blind trust in his name. He must have hand delivered it when I was out of the office."

"When would that have been? Do you ever leave that place?"

Landsman smiled, appreciating the subtle humor from Ben, the attempt to lift his spirits, and he thought again that he was a good kid. "There is no named beneficiary. As the executor to the estate, I have a fiduciary responsibility to disperse it correctly. What is most troubling about the account is the handwritten note across the bottom of the statement. Not a note, really, just a name: Carter Handley. That's all."

He handed the statement over to Ben. Ben noted the name on the top of the page. "E. F. Hutton? They've been out of business for a long time."

"Yes, since early 1988."

Ben noticed the handwritten name on the bottom of the page. The handwriting was extraordinarily neat. He thought that Brogan must have had a good Catholic school education.

"Who's Carter Handley?"

"This had to be important to Bill for him to slip this into his files without my knowledge. I can only assume that he was referring to *the* Carter Handley, the chairman of the board of Axis Financial."

"Axis, Jesus."

"Exactly. Why would Bill leave this behind and the name of the chairman of the biggest financial firm in the country? I haven't spent much time looking into it, although I am intrigued, as you would imagine. The entire estate is my concern. Bill had many charitable interests, and I believe it would be best to focus my energies on them. They were very dear to his heart. I would like you to look into this for me."

"How much is there?"

"The statement shows an opening balance of two hundred thousand dollars. You can see that there was one credit to the account. We haven't determined the source of the credit. I had my compliance officer look into it, and it looks like the account was closed or, at the very least, hasn't been active for over thirty years. There is no current sign of the account with any registered firm. To be honest it's not something I want to spend my personal time on. I want to be able to spend a few last moments with Bill and make sure the charities are provided for. Still, it's a mystery to me, and, as you know, I don't like loose ends."

"I don't know, Mr. Landsman. I'm not interested in hunting down buried treasure. This doesn't seem to be my kind of thing. What about his man, McGinley? He seemed like a pretty sharp guy to me."

Landsman sighed. "No. I'm afraid Mr. McGinley is no longer someone who can be counted on."

"Why's that?"

"He has his own issues to deal with. I'm afraid he has taken the imminent death of Bill rather hard and has fallen into old bad habits."

"What is it? Drinking, drugs?"

Landsman, discreet as always, responded carefully. "Don't misunderstand. Frank McGinley is a brilliant man. Brogan is quite fond of him, but he's troubled."

"Okay, but, still, I don't think this is for me."

"Ben, I feel strongly about this and would take it as a personal favor. William Brogan would not have left that note if there wasn't some type of criminality involved, which makes this the type of work that you excel at. Bill had—has—a strong sense of justice. My feeling is that an injustice was done and he wants to set it right. I think you can relate to that since you seem to be very much alike. One of the traits I admire about you."

Ben looked over to where the egret had been and noticed that it was gone. He thought it odd that he hadn't seen it fly away. "All right. I'll look into it. I'm assuming that I have access to your database for this."

"Not on this, Ben. I think this could become quite complicated, and I would rather not have any links to my office. If there is a hint of conflict, it could compromise the execution of the estate. You're going to have to research this on your own. We will meet here next week, same time. We'll discuss your fee when we meet next. For now bill at the normal rate."

"Yeah, sure, no problem. You okay? You need me to do anything? Lighten the load for you?"

"No, thanks, Ben."

With that, it was done. Ben was on the job. Landsman rose and looked for the egret himself. Ben waited as usual for him to leave. As he walked away, Landsman spoke over his shoulder.

"Stop smoking."

Ben smirked and reached into his pockets for his smokes. Only three left. He would finish this pack and be done with them for good, he thought. He folded the statement and put it into his hip pocket.

CHAPTER 4

C arter Handley was not used to having terms dictated to him, but, then, it was not often that he spoke to an assassin. He stood with both hands on his desk, leaning into the speakerphone, waiting for the killer to speak.

"Just give me the name of the target, the time, and the place. It's two hundred thousand. When the transfer takes place, I will complete the job. It shouldn't be more than a couple of minutes for the money to hit; you have the routing number for the account."

"Yes. I have a confirmation on my end that the funds have been sent."

"There it is now. Okay. Name, time, and place, please."

"Sol Landsman, Trinity Church in downtown Manhattan, day after tomorrow at around three p.m."

"Day after tomorrow? Not much time."

"I realize that. The security level is such that I was unable to get the time and location until recently."

"How high of a level?"

"The highest."

Simmons paused, and Handley could hear him shuffling some papers from his end of the line. "Send another hundred."

"Mr. Simmons, this is hardly—"

"Mr. Client, I know who Sol Landsman is. I know what will be required. Since the timeframe is short, payments will have to be made on my end. You want the top guy? This is my fee. I don't bullshit. I don't bribe. I don't negotiate or retaliate. You have the number. Transfer the additional hundred thousand now, or I hang up, return your money minus a small fee, and walk away. I'll wait."

Handley took a deep breath and punched some numbers on his laptop. There was silence on the line, and he briefly thought that Simmons had signed off and walked away with $200,000 of the firm's money. When Simmons spoke, it was brief.

"I got it. Okay, it's done." He hung up.

Carter Handley placed the phone gently in its cradle. He took a deep breath and looked across his glass desk at Walter Peterson. Peterson was lost in thought, staring at the Picasso across the room with his legs crossed and his fingers forming a steeple against his chin. Handley wondered again if Peterson had the spine to finish the tasks ahead. He sat at his desk and turned to the window facing New York Harbor. He spoke with his back to Peterson.

"This man, Simmons, his real name is John Leandro. His address is 844 Jefferson Avenue in Miami. He's listed as a freelance artist. I've seen some of his stuff. Not bad. He's ex-military, very hard-core."

Peterson was not only the president of Axis Financial but an ex-army ranger himself. He knew before Handley told him that Simmons/Leandro was either a former SEAL or ranger from the quality of his reputation. He had a plan in mind for him. "I'll handle it."

Handley sat back and spun a little on his chair and smiled, his top lip sagging in that creepy way of his. Peterson thought about what a ruthless prick he was even at seventy years old, but the man had made him a lot of money over the years. Handley turned around and started to spit out his agenda.

"I'll call Senator Marche, let him know that Brogan died yesterday, if he doesn't know already. I recall that Mr. Brogan and the senator didn't see eye to eye on much."

Peterson smirked. "Of course not. Marche is a putz."

"Yeah, but he's our putz. We'll have his and Landsman's records sealed after Landsman is gone. Marche can say it's for national security reasons. Both men had extensive foreign-client listings. That should give us the means to get the statement out of either of their files. Speaking of which, did you track down the rep that sent it?"

"Yeah. He's dead. Over two years ago. After Hutton collapsed, he did local insurance somewhere in Iowa. I don't see where you're going with all of this. The trail has been dead for decades. The Landsman business, calling in our chits with the senator, it's all a little overkill, isn't it? I mean Brogan had more money than the two of us. Maybe he just went on with his life after that meeting with you. Shit. It's been over forty years. From what I know of the man, that might have been a typical afternoon for him."

"Well, Walt, from what I know of the man, he very well may want to stick it to me from the grave. You're right. I mean he's gone on to many great things in his life, but, you see, I bested him back then. I'm sure that stuck with him. No, he did something, I'm sure. Someone knows about that day; I can feel it. On every statement there is a representative's ID number. If, for some reason, we can't get that statement back, it will be traced. I don't know what Landsman knows or if any statements are in his possession." Handley calmed himself as he often had to do when dealing with Peterson. The man had a brilliant business mind but too much of a conscience. As always Handley turned his appeal to tap into Peterson's greedy nature. "How many shares of company stock do you have, Walt?"

"A little over ten million."

"What do you think happens if it gets out that this very company was built on bribes to public officials? That I had a man killed to gain a tactical advantage? I know it was over forty years ago, but you have known about this for going on twenty years now. The stock closed at thirty-four yesterday. This comes out, where does the stock go? Down five points? Ten? You want to risk fifty or a hundred million on this old business? What would this news do to our ability to influence legislation? No, this has to be done. It will be over in a couple of days, Walt."

Walt stood and flattened his suit. "I'll have someone on Leandro in a couple of days. I know someone in Miami, 844 Jefferson."

CHAPTER 5

The black SUV was waiting for Frank McGinley when he stepped out of the lobby of his building. It was another hot one. They had said it would be one of the hottest summers on record. It felt like it that morning. There was a man in black wearing sunglasses and a white wire running from an earpiece down into the collar of his shirt. Secret service. He raised his arm and whispered into his wrist. McGinley strode toward the vehicle, and the man opened the door. Frank stepped in and plopped onto the seat. The action of bending and then sitting back, along with the adjustment to the air conditioning, was disorienting, and for a moment he thought he might lose his lunch. He tasted the vodka tonics on his breath as he belched discreetly. Kat Wells had been picked up before him, and she was seated next to him. She smirked in disapproval as she smelled his breath. The man got in the passenger seat and nodded to the driver, and they headed down Central Park West.

William Brogan had died three days before. Kat and Frank were with him at the end. Brogan went fast. Less than two weeks prior, he was clomping around that townhouse of his, barking orders. One day he didn't come downstairs for the morning meeting. Less than an hour later, he came down on a stretcher, heading to the hospital. It was a stroke in the middle of the night. Until then he was in perfect health despite his eighty years. The lawyer explained the terms of the living will. There was no brain function, so they were instructed to turn off the machines that were keeping him alive. Frank knew that he wouldn't want to die in some sterile hospital, so he made sure he died with dignity, in his home. Despite the trouble, they had all the machines and tubes and wires installed at the townhouse. His brother and sister came and left then Kat and Frank had their time with him.

It happened so fast, Frank thought. One day he was chatting with Brogan about the Mets, and the next day his mind was gone. Frank thought now, on the way to the funeral, about their last conversation. Brogan had proposed a trade of Marlon Byrd for someone; Frank didn't remember who. He did remember his last words to the man: "Ah, you're full of shit."

The SUV made a right on Eighty-Sixth to get over to the West Side Highway. The funeral was in Trinity Church at Broadway and Wall Street.

As they passed the *Intrepid*, Frank turned to Kat. She had been crying, from the looks of her, most of the day.

"No Willy?" he asked, about her husband and his best friend.

"No, security is too tight. I think we're the only two besides his brother and sister. I was on our system last night. There have been some extensive background checks on us since he passed." She started to weep softly then turned her head away and looked out the window. She uncrumpled the tissue she had been squeezing in her left hand and put it to her nose but didn't blow; she dabbed at it. "Besides you, me, and his family, I expect that there will be some heavyweights attending."

It didn't surprise Frank to hear this. It also didn't surprise him to hear that Kat had been working while he was home drinking. That seemed to be the pattern for a while now. Frank knew quite a bit more about Brogan than Kat did. He knew the level of the field he played in and that the game was often rough. Although most of the rough stuff had been behind them for quite some time, Frank was sure that more than one heavyweight would be glad to hear that William H. Brogan had passed, taking some of his secrets with him. Frank turned away from Kat and gazed out the window himself. His eyes started watering for the first time. Having never respected his old man, he had thought of Brogan as his father since soon after they met, something he wished now he had said to him. Now he was gone. There was no present or future with him, only the past.

Frank didn't think much anymore about how they had met. It had been years, and his time with Brogan, and later Kat, had been so intense—they were so closely knit—that it seemed like they had always been together. Frank thought about how life seemed to go from stage to stage. At least for him it did.

One door closed completely then another opened. He put his head against the window and looked out at everything and nothing. Frank thought about his journey: a poor kid in Queens, broker on the trading floor, getting involved in a scam and meeting Brogan, watching him kill a man, the years they were apart, and the horrific events that had led to that separation. Although a grown man, Frank had a fleeting thought, an emotion that he was on his own now. There was no one to take care of him. It was silly, he knew, a fifty-year-old man feeling this way. But that was what he was feeling; it couldn't be helped. He couldn't let go of it. He was alone now. The finality of it was devastating. He'd never see Brogan again.

The man in black opened his window and put a flashing red light on the roof of the vehicle. They picked up speed after Twenty-Third Street. He spoke into a cell phone. "ETA, seven minutes."

They slowed down as they approached the work site at Ground Zero. One World Trade was up, but the site was still a mess with construction. Two cop cars on each side of West Street blocked traffic in both directions at Liberty Street. They made a left and weaved their way through the southern end of the World Trade Center site. They went west on Liberty, past Zuccotti Park, and made a right on Broadway. The entire avenue was clear. Having worked downtown for years, Frank was amazed at the sight. Broadway cleared on a Wednesday afternoon made it look like an empty New York City set at a Hollywood studio lot. They pulled up in front of Trinity Church.

Frank waited for the men up front to open the doors. Kat reached her hand out to him, and he took it. They sat in silence as the men got out and looked around, up and down the street. Frank heard a helicopter above. The men opened the doors, and Frank and Kat slid out of their respective sides of the vehicle. The men took each of them under the arms and escorted them directly into the church. Frank glanced down Broadway to see a barricade and an armored vehicle on the corner of Broadway and Rector Street, where he'd stood when the South Tower of the World Trade Center came down. It seemed like a lifetime ago, and for Frank it was.

The church entrance was a wall of secret service agents. Outside, soldiers took position around the perimeter fence of the churchyard. The agents parted as Frank and Kat were left at the doorway by the agents from the drive down. One of the men whispered into his wrist, and organ music started to play. Something Irish, it sounded to Frank, but he couldn't place the tune. He put out his arm, and Kat took it. He heard her gasp, and he followed her eyes to the front pews of the church. There were only seven people in attendance.

From the center to the end of the front pew were Presidents Bush, George H. and W., President Clinton, Secretary Clinton, and Sol Landsman. In the second pew were Brogan's brother and sister. The rest of the church was empty.

Frank swallowed hard and could hear Kat do the same. They walked down the aisle, arm in arm, and slid quietly onto the third pew. The tune came to him from a long-ago funeral as a boy. He didn't remember if it was for an uncle or an aunt. The tune was "The Strife Is O'er."

The ceremony was brief. Frank sat stunned throughout. He had always known that Brogan was an influential man and had a legendary career as a government agent, but he was obviously bigger than Frank had ever imagined or that Brogan had let on. Frank felt like a boy whose old man had played for the '69 Mets or centerfield for the Yankees and then walked on the moon but never mentioned it. Frank shook his head and looked over at Kat. She was stiff as a board being in such company.

"Fuckin' Brogan," Frank whispered to himself.

When the organ started again, an agent seemed to appear from nowhere next to Frank on the aisle. He put a hand on his shoulder and waved his head toward a side exit of the church. Frank slid out of the pew, and Kat followed. He glanced at the first pew to see that the dignitaries stayed where they were.

The light outside was blazing, and the heat felt like a wet cloth. Kat and Frank were escorted to a small shaded portico. The soldiers were all still in place, and the helicopter was directly over the steeple. It occurred to Frank that he first met Brogan not twenty yards from that very spot, right out in front of the church fence. It made him think how far he had come. They met when Frank was escorted to the back of Brogan's car and taken to a spot under the FDR. His life was spiraling downward in a haze of booze at that time. The great man had pulled him up, in his way. Frank felt like shit for having those drinks this morning and at lunch, but then he felt like shit a lot lately.

Kat nudged Frank's arm and nodded over to the graveyard. There was a short, well-dressed guy walking toward them. He followed the path that led him to the walkway adjacent to the church wall and nodded hello. As he did, Sol Landsman came out a side door and joined him. Landsman patted the man on the back, and they both strolled over to Kat and Frank. Landsman took charge.

"Frank, Kat, this is Ben Hirsh, one of my associates."

Kat observed that Hirsh was very handsome but short. It had the effect of seeming like his head belonged on a bigger body. An ex-cop, Kat had a knack for sizing a person up fairly quickly. Hirsh moved gracefully, athletically, and he had a confident air to him. She liked him, for the moment, but then he hadn't opened his mouth yet.

Frank, as was their custom, looked over to Kat for a nod of approval or a disparaging smirk. From her look, he could tell she approved. Frank took Hirsh's hand and shook.

Hirsh made solid eye contact. "We've met before, a compliance seminar in Philadelphia."

Frank gave him a half-hearted "oh, yeah," and Hirsh turned to Kat.

"Ms. Wells, I've heard great things about you." Ben Hirsh couldn't help but stare at the scar running down the side of Kat's face, like every person who met her for the first time. The scar was less visible at times, but the heat and sunlight made it obvious through her makeup.

It didn't bother Kat; she had become used to it these last ten years. She was more interested in why Mr. Hirsh was there, of all days. She was not in the mood to meet new people. She maintained her decorum but let him know she wasn't up for nonsense.

"To what do we owe the pleasure, Mr. Hirsh?"

Sol Landsman interjected. "Ben is helping me with a matter pertaining to Bill's estate. I'm sorry for the timing, but would either you or Frank know anything about an account that Bill had with E. F. Hutton years ago? It was a blind trust, and I'm afraid I have no idea where it came from."

Kat shook her head. "I don't know anything about his finances."

Sol turned to Frank. "Anything?"

Frank thought for a second. *Jesus,* he thought. They had done so many deals together. Although he had been drinking quite a bit lately, he never lost his memory or genius with numbers. If there was something he had come across in the last ten years, even briefly, he would remember. With this, he had nothing.

"Hutton? Didn't they go under a long time ago?"

"Yeah."

"No, nothing. I'm sure of it."

Sol knew that if Frank didn't know, Brogan never shared it with him. Sol didn't care much for Frank's personal habits but knew he had a remarkable mind. "Well, then I guess Ben here has some work to do." He turned to Hirsh. "Sorry, Ben." He changed the subject. "Frank, there is a matter of some urgency that I must discuss with you." Hirsh took his cue and started wandering out into the graveyard beside the church.

Frank noticed that Kat shifted uncomfortably, and he knew immediately that she knew what Landsman was going to say. He knew it was coming eventually. Sol and Kat shared a look, and Sol went on.

"I've seen the will. Bill has left most of his money to his charities, family, and some to Kat and her husband. He has left you with something more substantial, the mansion on the corner of Sixty-Seventh and Fifth. It has been valued by the estate at over thirty-five million. It's yours to do with as you please, but Bill left a request. He would like you to take over his charitable pursuits. The mansion can be the headquarters as well as your residence."

He turned to Kat as if to ask for help. She lowered her head, left him hanging.

"There is a stipend set aside for the maintenance of the property. It was his wish for you to continue the work you and Kat have been doing together but, more importantly, to keep the residence and to devote most of your energies to his charitable interests. He felt that Kat is fitter right now to run the business, which leads me to his requirement for the transfer of the property to you. You have to fulfill one of his last wishes before this can take effect. You have to complete three months in a rehab facility before any of this can take place. He chose a place for you. It's a relatively short distance from here."

Frank had known this was coming eventually. He was a drunk, and he had people who depended on him but, more importantly, cared for him. He had let people down the last couple of months. His condition was rapidly deteriorating. Shit, he was half drunk now. He was offended for a second then relieved. Like with his first trip to rehab many years before. He was ready. He was tired. Lying and drinking had worn him down.

He wanted to say thank you, but instead he turned and said, "Kat." She walked over and put her arms around him. Frank thought that they had known each other for over ten years, and this was the first time she had ever hugged him, neither of them being much for that type of thing. Instantly, he was overwhelmed with everything. The emotions came in a rush, and Frank couldn't hold back. Tears started flowing, and he silently cried, trying to stifle himself to keep it from Kat. Brogan was gone but still picking him up. He closed his eyes and said, "Fuckin' Brogan" into Kat's shoulder.

The phrase broke the tension, and Kat laughed. Sol didn't get it, but if you worked with Brogan as Frank and Kat had for years, "fuckin' Brogan" were words that were muttered daily, to the point of becoming an inside joke for them. Kat put her hand on his shoulder.

"Go now, Frank. It's all set up. Willy and I will come see you in a week or so."

"Now?"

"Yes, now. No thinking about it. Agent Howell is waiting at the car in front of the church. Just go. Everything you may need will be shipped to you."

"What about you, the firm? What's going to happen?"

"I'll be fine. I have Willy. Everything has been arranged. Clients will think you are on an assignment out of the country. The case log is thin anyway, nothing I can't close up in a week or two. I could use some time off also. Besides, you look like shit."

Frank laughed. Kat was a tough broad, no doubt. Willy, her husband, was a lucky man as was Frank to have her as a friend. He hugged her, and she wept a little. Frank turned to Sol and shook his hand. He walked away toward the front of the church. Agent Howell held the door of the SUV. Frank got in, and the car drove off.

The moment the door of the SUV closed, Kat spun toward Sol. "Why the hell are you bringing this guy here for this? To see this?" She pointed over at Hirsh with her thumb over her shoulder. "You should have some fucking respect for Frank. He saved your ass plenty over the years."

Sol was taken aback. Kat was one hell of an investigator and not one to mince words with anyone. He realized instantly what a mistake he had made. He could see the pain on her face. Losing Brogan and Frank on the same day was a lot—even for someone as tough as her. Sol was embarrassed by his clumsiness. He attempted to put a hand on her shoulder, but she flicked it away with her left arm.

"I'm so sorry, Kat. It was a stupid thing to do, but I knew this would be the only chance I would have to ask Frank about this account in front of Ben. I thought maybe Ben could pick up on something. It was indelicate, I admit."

Kat turned and started marching toward Ben. Sol followed along the narrow footpath between the revolutionary-era gravestones. He didn't want to alienate Kat at this point. Sol knew that the two of them together would make a great team, and it would be good for him and his firm, but realized now that he had overstepped. Kat was going to rip poor Ben to shreds.

Kat picked up her pace. As she approached Ben, he turned toward her, right into her wrath.

"What the hell are you doing here? Who the fuck are you?"

Ben smiled at her as though she had offered him a glass of lemonade on this very hot afternoon. He looked up to her and squinted from the sun.

"I asked to see you. Please don't take this out on Sol. I do apologize, but as you will see, this was a matter of great importance to Mr. Brogan. I, of course, didn't know him as well as you, but what I do know of him leads me to believe that he would not have wanted to wait on this. I was hoping to meet you as soon as I could. Sol was gracious enough to invite me."

Kat crossed her arms and leaned on her hip, giving him a clear go-ahead but not much time to explain. She looked down on him. At over six foot, she had him by four inches.

"I wanted to meet the best. Your tenacity, Frank's intellect, his tactics—you're both feared but respected." He started to get comfortable. "I was in college at the time, so I didn't remember it until just yesterday, looking you guys up. He killed a serial killer. Your face, the scar, you were there. There are other stories, some mob guy in an alley; a trader disappears. Shit, you guys are my role models. I just didn't know who you were until yesterday."

There was a lot more than Hirsh knew, but it was their policy as a firm to never comment on such matters. The rumors and innuendo were good for business. Kat liked Ben's enthusiasm but was losing patience. He was bordering on kissing ass, and Kat had no time for it.

"I asked who you were."

Ben started walking back toward Sol, who had stopped on the path ten yards behind Kat. She stood firm, so he stepped into the grass to go around her. She turned and looked down at him as he passed. Ben started to speak as he walked, making her follow.

"I worked for the SEC for seven years. I started right out of college. I ran down some big names. I got more convictions than anyone else in my group." He stopped walking and turned back to Kat. "You know what? Of all the guys I busted—seventeen, to be exact—not one of them went to jail. Not only that, most walked away with more money than when they started. The crime paid. The penalty for the stealing was far less than the amount they stole. So I got out and started my own investigative firm. Figured I might as well get paid a decent wage. I've done a few jobs for Sol, and here I am."

Sol walked over to the two of them. He put a hand on Ben's shoulder and spoke to Kat.

"He's very good. I thought you two would work well together. This account, the one in question, it was a great burden to William. The way it was presented to me is troubling. I know this isn't the time, but I was hoping that you would work with Ben on this."

Kat took a breath and closed her eyes with her head up to the sky. She reached into her bag, pulled out her sunglasses, and put them on, signaling her imminent departure. "Convince me."

Sol paused to allow Ben to respond. "Mr. Brogan left the brokerage statement with Sol. Well, actually he slipped the statement into his files without telling anyone. The reason it's vital that we find out is that Mr. Brogan wrote a name across the bottom: Carter Handley. We're assuming that Brogan was referring to the chairman of Axis Financial; at least that's the best guess right now. It could be nothing, but you know Sol here. It has to be cleared up, and he asked me to help. It's that simple."

Kat knew that there would be nothing simple about this. If William Brogan's and Carter Handley's names were on the same piece of paper, it would be complicated. She immediately thought to ask Frank a question. She caught herself. He was gone. She would have to run this herself. The fact that Sol would bring this up today was enough to make her think that beyond complicated, it was urgent and quite possibly very messy. It would be like Sol to get ahead of any kind of scandal. She turned to Sol and back to Ben then gave an order.

"Tomorrow, eight a.m., at our office." She turned to leave and realized that there was no "our" for now. Brogan was gone, and Frank was lost, and her heart ached.

CHAPTER 6

Leandro walked the abandoned twelfth floor of the building on Maiden Lane that morning. It was the closest he could get to Trinity Church. He had known before he got there that it would be difficult to get a decent sightline for a good shot. It was a waste of time and money. He called his NYPD connection, told him his information was a fucking joke, and threatened to take the money he'd wired him out of his ass. The guy stepped up and gave him Landsman's address.

He was strolling West Ninety-Second Street for the fourth time. Each time he took a different angle, a different approach, no set time or pattern, but it would start getting suspicious soon.

After getting Landsman's address, Leandro spent the afternoon in his hotel room, going over the logistics of the neighborhood. There was easy access to Central Park, and Simmons planned to use it. His NYPD source had informed him that Landsman had been under protection from Homeland Security for a few months the previous year because of a threat to one of his firm's clients. He upped his fee to let Leandro know Landsman's nightly routine. Simmons had to go to the hip again to get it. He was told that he would walk his dog at 10:00 p.m. every night he was in the city. After leaving his building and walking over to the park, he would walk south along the wall separating the park form Central Park West. Leandro figured that to be the best place to hit him.

He was dressed in running gear. He parked his car on East Seventy-Eighth, across the park. The plan was to pop him and go over the wall then through the park. He had run in three triathlons that year alone. Leandro was confident in his ability to get away.

He straightened as he saw the doorman swing open the front door of Landsman's building. The doorman had his hand to his cap and bent down a bit and said something to Landsman as he exited the building. Landsman turned left and headed for the park just as Leandro had hoped. He waited to see if anyone followed Landsman, although he knew that the secret service had been sent back to Washington at five today, a fact he got from another source that had hit him up for twenty grand. He started adding his expenses in his head and thought that this job would hardly be worth the risk at the rate he was paying out. He stretched as he watched Landsman head toward Central Park West. From watching him walk, Leandro could see that Landsman was old and weak. He would go down easy. What came after the shot would be the challenge. He would have a long run after pulling the trigger.

As Landsman turned the corner, Leandro turned and headed after him. He took the safety off the SIG P938 in the pocket of his black hoody. It was a popgun but the right choice for this job. Leandro planned on taking the shot with the gun pressed against Landsman's head, knowing that he would get only one chance with such a high-profile hit. As Landsman turned the corner, heading south and out of sight, Leandro broke into a light jog in his direction.

There was a smattering of people walking on Central Park West. Of course, there were plenty of cars and cabs on the avenue. As he jogged, Leandro looked for any cop cars or a foot patrolman. All was clear. This was his best opportunity. Landsman was walking head down with his little white terrier ten yards ahead of him on the expandable leash. Leandro picked up his pace and pulled the SIG from his pocket. He didn't break stride as he held the gun up and pressed it to the back of Landsman's head right under the back brim of his brown fedora. He pulled the trigger simultaneously with the contact. There was a sharp pop, and from the corner of his eye, Leandro saw Landsman thrust to the right, toward the avenue. Leandro turned sharply to the left and jumped the brick wall into the park.

The drop was higher than he expected, but he made the adjustment and rolled on contact with the ground. He bent his knees on impact and leaned his body weight forward. He turned over his right shoulder and allowed his weight to follow his legs to get his left leg under him. He then got up in stride to a dead run. He heard a woman scream behind him, up over the wall. Leandro sprinted east toward the reservoir. He didn't hear any commotion, nor did he sense that anyone was following him. He was too experienced to think of relenting for even a moment; he kept the sprint at the running track and turned south. From the hours going over the map of the park paths that day, he knew to turn onto a quiet path headed southeast, weaving its way through the park. As he approached the east-side exit just south of Eighty-Sixth, he looked both ways for any police activity.

Simmons saw a patrol car with flashing lights a few blocks south and heard a siren in the distance. He reasoned that this was New York, and the siren could be for a number of things. He put the gun back in his pocket, no longer anticipating a confrontation. He jogged straight across Fifth Avenue to the car. He turned south on Park and east on Seventy-Eighth.

When he got to his car on Seventy-Eighth between Second and Third, it was boxed in by a van with two men unloading furniture. He didn't want to attract any suspicion, so he walked past. If the car was still blocked after a lap around the block, he would have to eliminate the men and move the van himself. He walked slowly and turned right on Second Avenue. It would be easy, he reasoned, to shoot the men and move the van to get his car out. He thought better of it. As easy as that would be, he didn't want another complication, so he stepped into a diner on Second. Leandro sat in a booth and ordered coffee.

CHAPTER 7

B en couldn't sit shiva for a second day. His wife, Randi, went to represent him and sit with Sol's widow. She left early with bagels and whitefish from Barney Greengrass. Kat Wells had been there yesterday with her husband, Willy. The Landsman penthouse was unlike anything Ben had ever seen—an old New York palace or a castle on a building top. Kat sat with him in the penthouse, and they agreed to meet that day to get to work on this. Both Kat and Ben were more pissed off than saddened. "This shit won't stand," was all Kat had said. He had looked at her face as she said it, and Ben got the message. She would go hard on this.

He got off the seven train at Roosevelt Avenue and Seventy-Fourth in Jackson Heights, Queens. There was a message on his phone from Kat. The voicemail said, "Call." He hustled down the stairs to the avenue, cut across Roosevelt to a bodega, and dialed. Kat picked up on the first ring.

"Homeland Security raided Sol's office. I was just escorted out of the townhouse. They're going to go over everything we have. They'll seize all the files. Where is the statement that Sol talked about?"

"In my pocket."

If she was impressed, she didn't say. She was all business.

"Good work. This is going to be heavy. Are you prepared for this?"

"Yeah, I'm good."

"Bring the statement back here. I'll be at the townhouse. They should be leaving soon. Where are you?"

"I'm in Queens. I'm going to see someone. I'll be back with something to go on."

Ben could hear her take a deep breath over the line. Then she blew.

"This is not acceptable. Let's get this straight right now. I run the operation. 'See someone,' 'in Queens' are not the responses I expect. What are you doing, and who are you seeing?"

Ben held the phone back away from his ear. The guy wearing a turban behind the bodega counter smiled at him, hearing her volume over the phone. It was a "we are all in this together as men" smile that crossed all ethnic boundaries. Ben put the phone back to his ear and walked away from the man's listening range.

"I'm seeing my friend Pap Martinez. I'm going to ask him to run down information on Carter Handley. I'm also going to have him get all he can on Sol and Brogan. There may be some things we don't know about them."

Suddenly Kat didn't seem so bent out of shape. In fact she finally did sound impressed.

"You know Pap Martinez?"

"Yeah, we go back."

"Queens? I never would have thought."

"Hey, he would be pissed if he knew that I let you know that much. I'm not supposed to tell anyone I'm seeing him."

"Yeah, I know how he works. I just never met him." She paused. "All right. Get all you can. This is going to cost, huh?"

"I don't know. We never talked money before. I would imagine that he isn't cheap."

"I'm sure, but he is the best. We'll figure it out. Don't worry about cost. Come over here tomorrow. I start work at eight."

"I'll see you then."

"Good work, Ben."

He hung up the phone, turned, and walked back to the turban man. "Give me a pack of Marlboro Lights."

Having made contact with the turban man and a cell phone call, Ben walked down Roosevelt to the next stop, Eighty-Second Street. He smoked one cigarette on the way, threw out the pack then took the seven train back into the city. Having completed Pap's protocol of leaving traces of contacts in outlying areas, he took a cab from Times Square and paid in cash, grateful that he didn't have to take the Long Island Rail Road out to Syosset and circle back like last time. *What a pain in the ass that was*, he thought. He got out at the Flatiron Building, the headquarters of Pap's tech firm.

Ben and Pap went all the way back to high school. Back then Ben was an athlete but was too small to fit in with the jocks. He could have made the teams but would have ridden the bench. Pap was a genius but not a nerd. Each of them didn't fit neatly into any one slot. Ben didn't remember how they met, maybe the school bus. They spent many afternoons hanging at Pap's house. His old man was an IBMer. Ben never met Pap's mom. The old man was out a lot, and Ben and Pap would hang out, smoke pot, and listen to his father's old jazz records. Bill Evans, Stan Getz, Cal Tjader. Ben still remembered the *Several Shades of Jade* album cover and using it to roll joints on.

Even then Pap was scary smart. No slouch himself, Ben couldn't keep up with him once he got rolling. Pap was building computers by hand and writing code in ninth grade. They went their separate ways after high school, Pap to MIT then Columbia. Ben stayed local, went to Hofstra on the island, drank too much beer, and faced few prospects at graduation. He signed up to join the Securities and Exchange Commission, thinking that most of the good students were going to Wall Street, and he would have a better shot at getting accepted. He was right and started not two months after graduation. Pap stayed on the fast track and was a big hitter at Goldman Sachs when they got back in touch.

It was Pap who called Ben. He was starting his own firm after leaving Goldman. At first Ben couldn't believe it. Why was the smartest guy he knew leaving the hottest firm on the street? It didn't make sense to him. They met downtown for a drink, and after ten minutes it was like they were back in high school again. They must have been twenty-four, maybe twenty-five at the time, and Ben still felt like a goofy kid, but Pap had blossomed. In fact he was fucking beautiful. Not five minutes into their time in the bar, two girls sent over a round. It was clear that the round was for Pap. Ben might as well have been invisible next to him, and it didn't feel that good when he realized that Pap, who was always smaller and frailer, had shot past him. He was tall, dark, and handsome, a regular Latin heartthrob. Even now Ben's wife didn't like when he went out with Pap, knowing that wherever Pap went, there would be women.

Ben had been with the SEC for about four years at that time and was still basically pushing paper around, trying to stay out of trouble and work his way up the ladder, when Pap called. He told him he'd started a new firm and was looking for clients, and the SEC would be a good fit. The first question Ben asked him was how he got his number. Ben would never forget Pap's answer: "I can find anyone." Hearing that, and believing it since this was Pap, Ben had a reason to meet him.

At that first meeting Pap gave Ben his business plan. He had developed a new program that could find anyone anywhere. Of course Ben asked the obvious.

"Like Google Search?"

Pap smiled; he must have anticipated the question. "No, this is much more comprehensive than that. If I have a name, I can find that person within three days at a ninety-three-point-eight-percent rate of accuracy."

Ben laughed and sipped his beer. "C'mon, Pap. You must be bullshitting me."

"This is no bullshit. This is research."

"How?"

Pap turned to Ben, and it was clear that this was no longer the dreamer he had known back then. This was a man who was putting the dream into action. This was serious business, and Pap was a serious man.

"Everyone in this bar, everyone on this island leaves a trail behind them. Bank transactions, credit card purchases, cell phone calls—it's all traceable. There are reams of documents compiled on every person in this country and around the world every day. Every day! I found a way to access these documents, a legal way."

Ben wasn't sold. "Shit, we do the same thing every day. Point out someone in this bar, and I can tell you everything you want to know about him tomorrow."

Pap smiled. "I don't know if you are aware, but there is software now that allows me, or anyone with the knowhow, to track a person by their cell phone. You give me a guy's cell number, and I can follow him around the city from a satellite, like watching a rat in a maze. The NSA has it as do a few others. I'm the only citizen with the capacity to run it, but everyone will have this soon. I'm talking about tracking people who are aware of such things, the type of person that will use multiple cell phones or buy one for a single call. These are the types I can track, and no one else can. I can tell you what they're going to have for lunch tomorrow, or if they're likely to buy insurance, where they're going to retire, among other things. You see, Ben, everyone has a pattern. I've found a way to predict future actions based on people's past behavior. I can gather as much or more information as any agency or research group, public or private. I can then establish a pattern and plug that information into my proprietary algorithm and predict behavior to ninety-three-point-eight-percent accuracy."

This was starting to sound like a magic trick to Ben. "Where did you come up with this?"

Pap raised his hand then turned toward the bartender. "Another round for us and please send a round to the ladies at the table and extend our apologies since our wives will be meeting us shortly."

Ben chuckled. "You're used to this, aren't you?"

Pap blushed. "Ah, I don't know. Oh, how did I start this? Yeah, how did I start?"

Ben slapped him on the shoulder, and they both laughed, Pap exposed as still being a bit of a nerd and clearly flustered. Ben wondered how he would be acting if he wasn't around. It was an interesting dynamic, both of them slipping back into their old personas, Pap the analytic and Ben the backslapping jock. When their drinks arrived, Pap got back on track.

"I know some poker players. You know, professionals. I started kicking around this idea a few years ago. Gaming is a bit boring to me. It was the players' patterns that I found interesting. I spent a week in Vegas with a few of these guys. You would know them if you watch any of the poker channels or shows that they go on. By the third day I was up over three hundred thousand dollars. Three hundred and six, I recall. After sitting across from the same guy for a while, it was pretty clear to me how he was going to bet and what level hand he had. I could see the pattern. As you might expect, one of the casino managers asked to speak to me in private. They thought I was cheating in some way. There was a bit of drama, but by the end of a very long evening, I had a contract with one of the big casinos."

"Doing what? I don't see you as a poker player."

"Oh, God, no. They hired me to look at the tapes they took of players. I would give them my recommendations on how players would bet. Mostly high rollers. Remember, before, I said legal. I checked with a lawyer before I started this. The players know they're being taped by the house, so it was all legit. If I gave this information to another player, it would be a problem but not the house."

"All this while you were working at Goldman?"

"To be honest, Ben, this whole Wall Street thing is a bit boring. There are so many smarter ways to make money."

Ben hoped to hear more about this someday, but that day he had an agenda. When Pap said he could find anyone, Ben immediately had a person in mind that needed finding. He wanted to hear more before putting Pap to the test.

"So how do you go from playing cards to finding people?"

Pap didn't seem offended; it was as if he expected cynicism. Ben couldn't have known that Pap was surprised at first at how accurate his program had become. "I became more and more fascinated by this idea of patterns. The things people do and why they do them. For me, it became a social experiment using technology. So in my free time, for three and a half years, I worked on a program that could tell me what people will do. Not what they have done or what they are likely to buy from past behavior—plenty of programs can do that—but how they will act. Well, you know how I can get. This has been an obsession of mine, and now I'm ready to put it to use."

Ben did know how he could get. Pap would pull all-nighters in high school, researching something that Ben found trivial and that Pap himself claimed to have forgotten about days later. Ben knew better, though. Back then Pap was somewhat embarrassed by his intellect, the "trying to fit in during high school" syndrome. But Pap didn't forget. He never forgot a fucking thing.

"How's it work?"

Pap smiled at the question. "The breakthrough came when I started tapping into the information that was for sale. Snooping is easier than you may think. Shit, I could delve into anyone's life if I was so inclined. To make this a business, I knew I had to stay within legal boundaries. So I started gathering all the information that is in the public domain. As you know, all the companies that you deal with daily—the bank, the cell phone carrier, all of them—they sell your data. Marketing firms buy it to sell you things you don't need. What makes what I do different is that I focus on the individual. Data research firms look at demographic groups. It's not profitable to focus on one person, but I think there is value in what I can provide to the government. Hey, I can find terrorists, criminals. I'm telling you, man, this is high-level stuff. I gather everything that a person has done for years. I know where his bank is. From credit cards, I know what he buys and where. I funnel all the information down and layer my algorithms over it. The common tendencies people have—from their ethnic backgrounds, religious beliefs—it's all there. A person's family structure is a surprisingly accurate indicator. After I throw that all into the pot and add the way they were raised, their schools and jobs, I can tell you what they will do and where they will be next. After I run someone through my program, I can tell you where they're going to have lunch the following day, their route to work, where they'll be on a weekend. I ran tons of beta tests on this. I would take a name out of the paper or somewhere online and run them through the program, and I would wait at the train station two or three days later, and there they were. Or the deli or restaurant, ballgame, whatever. I'm telling you it works up to ninety-three-point-eight-percent accuracy. I don't think it will get any better than that. There are some variables in the world, after all."

Ben was entranced. He noticed that he hadn't taken a sip of his beer since Pap ordered it. He took a long slug. "It's fascinating, but can you tell me how it works? Like, exactly."

"Sure I can, but to be honest, Ben, it's very high-level programming. There are four other people in the world that would understand what I'm doing at this point. Two of them are researchers at universities, chasing their tails. One just started at Google, and the other works for the Chinese government. They call him Sheng; I met him once. You should be concerned about him."

As Ben stopped at a Starbucks on Twenty-Third for an iced coffee since he was early, he thought about that day and why it had stuck in his mind. It came down to one name. Ben challenged Pap with the name, and three days later both of their lives had changed.

"Find Mark Pinto."

Pap had smiled and said, "I'll call you in three days."

They wrestled over the tab, finally agreeing to split it, and said their good-byes with a hearty man hug. Pap was the only man Ben had ever hugged or planned to. He was hopeful but not confident that Pap could find Pinto. The file had been lying on Ben's desk for over a month. It had been kicked around the department for over two years. The case seemed unbreakable.

Close to three years before their drinks that day, Mark Pinto had booked a flight to LAX. On the stopover at Denver Airport, he walked out the front door of the terminal and disappeared off the face of the earth. Two days later, $70 million disappeared from the New York bank where Pinto worked. The flight to LAX never left Denver since all the passengers weren't accounted for. That meant that Pinto had no more than a three-hour jump on the authorities, yet they never found a trace of him. Pinto became a legend within the department. No one knew a thing. There was no trace, nothing. Even now Ben didn't know how he had remained on the run for so long. He imagined that Pinto had some kind of inside help. He remembered now. It must have been that since after his arrest he didn't hear another word about it. The case kicked around awhile since jurisdiction was a problem. After six months it ended up at the SEC because the bank had a brokerage division. The fact was no one wanted it since there was nothing to go on, along with the sad fact that $70 million wasn't a very big case in the modern world of bank fraud. At the agency the file kicked around for a couple of years. No one wanted to touch it, until it landed on the desk of Ben Hirsh. Looking back now, Ben hadn't remembered much about asking Pap, never thinking he would hear about it again, until Pap gave him a call on his private agency line.

"Mark Pinto will be at the SunTrust Bank in Tampa, Florida, between two and four p.m. tomorrow. Six oh one Platt Street."

"Wait, Pap. How did you—"

"We'll talk after you pick him up."

"You're confident with this? I send out the cops and he isn't there, I'm going to look like an asshole."

"You'll be a hero. You have my word. I got to go. We'll talk after the arrest."

After that phone call everything changed. Pinto was there; Ben became a star overnight. Pap was on the way to becoming a legend. Pap helped him with a few more cases. After a while people started talking, wondering if Ben had some contacts on the wrong side of the law. Ben asked Pap to back off. He convinced Pap that there would be some business out of this, but he had to back off for a while.

That was a few years back. Since then Pap had been hiding in plain sight. He was Richard Sanchez now, tech entrepreneur and software developer. His firm, Nube, was one of the fastest-rising Latin American companies in America. Pap's entire life history had been wiped clean and reborn as only someone with his talents could do. The only links with his past were his past associations, which was why Ben had to take such precautions.

Ben arrived at the front desk of the office at the precise time, only to be met by a smartly dressed young woman.

"Mr. Hirsh?"

"Yes."

"I have a note from Mr. Sanchez for you."

She handed him a folded piece of paper. It appeared to be from a yellow legal pad, torn from the corner. The note read:

> The NYPD is outside.
> Call me at 212 715 3482 tomorrow at noon.
> Hand the paper back to Isabela.

Ben refolded it, committed the number to memory, and handed it back to the woman.

"Thank you, Isabela." She tore it up in front of him, and then he turned and walked out the door.

Before he could get to Twenty-Third Street, a man approached him, wearing a sharp suit and a face that looked like it had been punched in recently. Ben took him for a cop and was right. He held out a badge.

"Mr. Hirsh, I'm Detective James Boyle. Would you mind coming with me?" His hand was already on Ben's arm, and he didn't like it. Ben shrugged the cop's grip away.

"What is this about?"

"Commissioner Marshall would like to meet with you. Follow me, please."

Ben had a second to mutter, "Jesus Christ" to himself before the cop turned and headed toward Twenty-Third. He caught up to the cop, and they stood side by side in an awkward silence, waiting for the light to change. As Ben stood there, he wondered for the first time whether he was getting paid for this or not. Everything had been rolling so quickly, he hadn't had time to put his thoughts together. He was just going with it, doing the legwork. Suddenly he thought of the statement tucked in his breast pocket. The light changed, and the cop trotted across Twenty-Third, trying to make the expanse of the block in one shot. Ben jogged behind and thought that Kat was right when she said that this would be high level. He was in the big leagues now.

Ben walked a few paces behind the cop through Madison Park. He removed his jacket and felt for the statement then folded the jacket over his arm. Ahead he saw Police Commissioner Marshall sitting at a metal table with a Shake Shack meal spread out before him. It looked like a meal for two, and suddenly Ben was very hungry. It must have been one by then, and all he'd had was coffee that morning.

The cop whose name Ben had already forgotten took a stance about twenty yards shy of the table. He turned out from where the commissioner was sitting and nodded for Ben to walk past. He noticed four other wide-shouldered cops in plain clothes standing around, forming a perimeter. As Ben approached, the commissioner stood. He wiped his hands with a paper napkin and walked toward Ben for the last few steps. Ben thought of the mantra he had learned years before when he had just started at the SEC: deny, deny, deny.

Marshall put out his hand to shake, and Ben took it. Marshall looked different than he did on television. Standing behind the mayor or at one of his own press conferences, he looked supremely polished. He had always reminded Ben of an actor in an insurance ad—running down the beach and throwing a piece of driftwood to a Lab, that kind of guy: white teeth, perfect hair, fit for an older man. Up close he seemed a lot less than perfect. The hair and teeth were the same, but he just seemed a little goofier. His features were too big up close. It made Ben more comfortable. Marshall pantomimed putting a hand on Ben's shoulder and had the other open, pointing toward the table.

"I hope you're hungry. The best burger in town."

Ben nodded his response and walked to the table. He draped his jacket over the seat and sat down with his back pressed against it. As he pulled his chair in, it scraped along the cement. Marshall sat. Ben picked up his burger with both hands and spoke.

"Ever been to the Burger Joint in the Parker Meridien?"

"Yeah, they make a nice burger, too, but Danny Meyer is a friend of mine, so I don't have to wait on line."

"I wouldn't think you would have to wait on line anywhere."

"You'd be surprised. New Yorkers are pretty serious about their food. Besides, no one likes a line jumper."

Ben chuckled and felt at ease. He was aware that Marshall was trying to work him; he also knew that he didn't have to say shit. He asked the first question.

"Why am I here?"

Marshall raised a hand and nodded his head since he was chewing on his last bite. Ben took the opportunity to take his first. It was pretty fucking good. Marshall took his time, swallowed, and wiped his face then picked up his shake and took a long pull on the straw.

"Jesus Christ, that's good. Not too often but once in a while, huh?" He put down the cup and leaned forward. Ben held his burger in both hands. "First off, I'm not here about our friend across Twenty-Third Street."

Ben stoically took another bite. Marshall smiled.

"It's okay. The department has worked with him in the past. He approached us, in fact. He's helping out antiterrorist efforts. Pro bono. He's a hell of a guy, your friend." He looked at his shake cup again but thought better of it. "You're not here about that. We're good. I would like to ask you about William Brogan's funeral."

"What about it?"

"Well, Ben, I personally supervised the security for the event. You're the only one that didn't seem to belong there. I ran a background check. I must say I was impressed, but I can't figure why you were there. Landsman insisted, of course, or you wouldn't have been there, but still you're the odd man at the party. No offense, but that's some pretty heady company."

Ben was eating his burger. When Marshall paused for him to respond, he took another bite and reached for his fries. Marshall smirked, realizing that

Hirsh was no sap. He would have to press more.

"That night Landsman gets popped by a pro. There's no doubt it was a hit, by the way. You were observed talking with Frank McGinley and Kat Wells after the service. What were you talking about?"

Ben had finished the burger and didn't have it to hide behind any longer. He took his time, dipped a fry in the ketchup, and then put it back down.

"I was there to support Sol in a time of need. I just expressed my condolences to the others."

Marshall sighed, wiped his hands a last time, leaned in, and dropped the politician demeanor and became a cop. "I don't have time for bullshit. I'm personally running the investigation into Landsman's death. There must have been a compelling reason for you to be there. Believe me, Sol pulled some strings to get you inside that churchyard. What the hell is so important that you had to be at William Brogan's funeral?"

Ben didn't respond. It was obvious to Marshall that he was trying to come up with something, likely a lie.

"Who the fuck do you think you're sitting here with? This is the New York City Police Department. We've had a guy on you since the funeral. You've been in touch with Kat Wells at least once since. I don't know where the hell McGinley is, that scumbag, but I'll be on him soon." He paused for a second, and Ben was silent, adjusting to the sudden turn in the conversation. "What were you doing at the funeral, and what are you doing with Wells and McGinley?"

Ben was about to reply when he realized that Marshall had never formally introduced himself. Ben didn't know whether to respond with "Mr. Marshall" or "Commissioner," so he did neither and blurted out what was on his mind.

"Scumbag?"

"Yeah, Ben, I would have thought that you knew that, having dealt with a number of them over the years. McGinley's a scumbag, all right. We have him as the chief suspect in at least two murders. The kind of prick that thinks he can do whatever the hell he wants. He has high-level contacts, no doubt, very high up, but he'll screw up eventually. He's a drunk also, a sloppy drunk. He'll screw up, all right, and if you spend any time around him, you'll end up getting screwed as well. Now do you want to lose your private practice over a drunk like McGinley?"

Since Ben had heard all of the rumors about Frank, and Sol had implied he had a substance problem, none of this was news to him except that the commissioner had a bug up his ass about him. This was a personal thing between them. Ben didn't know what it was, and he didn't give a shit. He just wanted to get the hell out of there. He stood and noticed movement behind and around him. The bodyguard cops were moving in closer, reacting to the rise in volume of Marshall's voice. Marshall raised his hand, and the cops froze. Ben thought of a game he'd played as a kid. Red light, green light, one, two, three. He wondered if Marshall flipped his hand, would the cops roll over? Marshall leaned back, more relaxed now that Ben knew he wasn't going anywhere yet. Ben was wondering whose side he should be on, the drunk's or the pompous ass's? He tried to remain calm outwardly but made an attempt to speed things up.

"I don't know how I can help you."

"I told you. I want you to tell me what you were doing at the funeral, and I want to know what Wells and McGinley are up to."

Ben thought of the most viable lie he could. "Sol wanted to get us together. He thought I would be a good fit for their group. He was helping me out. He knew I wanted to move ahead, get involved with bigger cases. Brogan was dead, obviously making an opening. I don't know if Sol talked to them beforehand to set it up. He was killed before I could ask him. I got in touch with our friend across the street to do a little research about Wells and McGinley. I met Frank once a few years ago. He seemed pretty straight to me at the time, so you can imagine that all this is something of a shock to me. It's only been a couple of days since I met them. This is all going very fast now with Sol dead." He shook his head. "I don't know what's going on."

Marshall didn't seem convinced. He reached into a front pocket of his jacket, pulled out a card, and handed it across to Ben. It had a maroon trim and embossed letters and numbers.

"I want to hear from you once a day. What they're doing, where McGinley is. I want all of it. I don't have to tell you how badly I can fuck up your private investigative practice. Your wife works on Wall Street, right? Maybe we'll take a look at her firm. You can never be too careful." He sighed as though the whole threatening thing was beneath him as it should have been. He stood. "You got a gun?"

Ben was surprised by the question. "Huh?"

"I know you received a permit to carry with your license. I was just wondering if you had one."

"No, I don't."

"Get yourself one and learn how to use it. Here's what is going to happen next. Either you cooperate with me, or I get the word to McGinley that you are. When he finds out, he's going to send someone for you. Might as well give yourself a fighting chance. I don't expect it to help much. I'll say one thing for him: he's good at what he does. Someone from my team will be in touch." He walked south toward Twenty-Third. His men fell in behind him.

Ben let out a long breath, and a chill that started at the top of his head washed down over his body. The police commissioner, Jesus Christ. He tried to figure out what his next move was, when it hit him. He didn't want to make a move. He wanted away from this crew, Frank and Kat Wells. He didn't know enough about them to stick his neck out, and what he did know, he wasn't too cool with. To hell with the police and whomever else might be interested in Sol's murder. He had enough contacts to run this down himself. Besides, he had Pap. That is, if he would be willing to help after this afternoon. He couldn't know until he called the next day, but for now he was going to go up to Kat's office and politely back out.

It looked like a thundershower was rolling in, so Ben trotted across the park to Madison Avenue. He was lucky enough to get a cab uptown. He knew the location of Wells' and McGinley's office, having Google Mapped it the previous day. He planned on popping in unannounced, hoping to get some unrehearsed answers from Kat Wells.

The opulence of the townhouse didn't intimidate him. Ben had been in many others, one on that street in fact, although he usually had a subpoena in hand and two cops in tow. This time was different; he had been invited in. He was buzzed in without a word as he approached the front door. As he finished one spin around the grand lobby, a woman entered through a heavy black door. She was short, fat, and walking fast, wearing a business suit and an attitude that wasn't from Fifth Avenue, likely Brooklyn or Queens. She spoke; it was Brooklyn.

"You Hirsh?"

"Yes."

"Don't have you for an appointment. You're gonna have to wait."

"I'm here to see Kat Wells."

She rolled her eyes. "No shit. You're gonna have to wait." With that she turned and went back through the door, slamming it shut.

Ben had waited a little over ten minutes when the door reopened. He heard Kat from inside.

"Come on in, Ben."

He strolled across the marble floor and entered. The room was an office, modern and sleek in deep contrast to the old New York surroundings. Kat sat at a glass desk, an iMac opened in front of her. The room was about twenty-five feet long and just as wide, a living room in most houses, a studio apartment in Manhattan. The walls were some kind of off-white, probably eggshell, or linen, or some other paint marketer's idea of the color off-white. There were a number of paintings scattered on the walls, none at the same level. It all came together nicely. Someone with a trained eye had decorated the room.

Kat closed the lid of the notebook hurriedly as if she didn't want anyone to see what she was viewing.

"I see you met Hilda."

"Yeah, she's charming."

"Oh, she's in a good mood today. You should have been here yesterday; she just about threw me out of the house over a broken vase."

Kat let her Colorado accent slip. Ben didn't know whether it was legit or part of an act. Either way he didn't care much. He was convinced now, more than earlier, that he was going to back out of whatever deal he had unknowingly entered. Kat stood and walked from behind the desk. She led Ben over to the area of the room with a couch, a chair, and a coffee table.

"Do you want anything to eat or drink?"

Ben didn't sit. "I don't plan on staying long." He sighed and relaxed his stance. "I don't know what is happening here. Is this some kind of job interview? Are you testing me or something?"

"What are you talking about?"

Ben didn't answer Kat's question. He continued on. "I'm not looking for a job. I have a pretty good thing on my own. Believe me, I want to nail the guy who's behind Sol's death, and I will, but I don't need these problems. There's nothing—"

Kat stood to interrupt him. She raised her arms as if to brace him from ten feet away. "What's going on, Ben? You seem pretty riled up."

"The police commissioner just interrogated me downtown. One of his bent noses put an arm on me and led me over to him. He's got a bug up his ass about McGinley, I can tell you that."

Kat interrupted him again. This time she walked over to him slowly. She spoke calmly in a soothing tone. "I need you to tell me everything he said to you. Don't leave anything out." She turned around and went back to her desk.

Ben had the impression that she was going to take notes. He had a decision to make. A minute after the commissioner threatened him, he knew there was no way he would be on his side of this little turf war. Now he had to decide if he wanted to be on Kat's side—or any side. Kat opened the Mac and punched a few keys. She looked up with a "well?" look in her eyes. He didn't respond, thinking that it might be better to stay silent and turn and walk out of the room, just walk away.

Like the experienced cop she was, and still was in some ways, she read Ben's eyes immediately. She leaned back in her chair. "All right, Ben, here's the deal. If you're going to be around us, Frank and me, you're going to get some heat. It's just the way it is." She said this in a matter-of-fact fashion. "I can't tell you how many times I've been pulled in front of some investigator or commissioner or something—the FBI, secret service, Homeland Security, and that's just in the last year. Everyone wants to know what we know and how we learn it. With your relationship with Pap Martinez, I'm shocked you haven't been pulled in till now. There are times when we are dealing with high-level stuff, big-name people. We had a good relationship with the last commissioner. I guess now with Brogan gone, the new guy is trying to undermine us a little. It's to be expected, but it does get tiresome."

She reached over to an old-fashioned call box and pressed a button. "Hilda, would you mind bringing in some coffee?" She rolled her eyes at Ben and released the button. "I can't guarantee she'll bring coffee for you. I don't think she likes you just yet. And before you ask, yes, we are all afraid of her. She took good care of Brogan, so she gets away with murder." She chuckled to herself. "I know this is a lot right now. Damn, Sol and Brogan are only gone a few days." She paused and looked up at the ceiling, thinking ahead and reminiscing at the same time. "I think Sol was right about you; you have good instincts. I like that you came to me right away. We don't like bullshit around here. You can tell me what the commissioner wants from you or not. That's your call. I can handle him. I do want you to stay around long enough to help us get a line on this. To be perfectly honest, your relationship with Pap is what I'm interested in now. If you can get to him and ask for his assistance, it would be very helpful. I have no doubt that with Frank's connections and my efforts, we'll find the guy who killed Sol eventually, but you can save us a lot of time."

"And the account Sol asked about?"

"I haven't forgotten. It's not the number-one priority right now, but that little mystery will be solved also."

Ben liked the honesty. He picked his side. He pulled the commissioner's card out of his pocket and flipped it onto the desk. "He wants me to call daily with updates on what you are doing. He said that if I don't rat to him, the word will get to Frank that I am, and Frank will come for me. He told me to get a gun."

Kat cackled and spun in her chair. After a full rotation, she held the desk to stop her raucous spin. She picked up the card. "Can I keep this?"

"Sure."

She examined the card and smirked as she flipped it in her fingers. "I'll take care of this, believe me."

A side door that seemed to be a part of the wall opened, and Hilda came in with a cart. There was a coffeepot, milk, and one cup.

Kat walked around the desk. She spoke openly in front of Hilda. "When are you going to speak to your friend?"

"I'll call him tomorrow at noon."

Hilda turned and headed to the door. She stopped and turned. "You wanna cup?"

"Yes, that would be nice."

Hilda paused at the door for a moment then walked out, and Kat smiled. "Oh, my, I think she likes you."

They spent the next couple of hours chatting, getting to know each other. Ben asked a lot of questions about Frank and got a lot of partial answers. McGinley was still a mystery to unfold. Hilda never returned with the cup.

CHAPTER 8

K at walked up Central Park West. Sol's wife, Esther, called the night before and invited her to tea. Although she hardly had time, Kat couldn't say no. It was nine-thirty and already as hot as hell. They said ninety-six for the day. Kat stopped at the wall the assassin had jumped after shooting Sol. There was no trace of anything, of course, but she wanted to touch the wall, the same wall he had touched. It helped. It kept the anger at the surface, where it belonged.

The simple act of standing still, hands pressed against the cool, thick wall, allowed her to compartmentalize her thoughts. Kat leaned over the wall and looked at the route the assassin had taken to escape. It was a far drop. The man must have been in good shape.

She was allowed to speak to Frank on the phone the previous night. The rehab facility only allowed it since the call was about Sol's death. She pressed the doctor after the call, and they agreed to a daily. It would be good to have Frank's input. Although she knew she was capable of doing this particular job, it was her first assignment on her own. It was good to speak to him even though it had been only a few days. Kat was reassured when Frank responded to the news like his old self. After digesting her words, he gave her a list of specific things he needed done. He was back to work.

She also wanted to get back to speak to Ben about the Pap Martinez call. That would take place at noon. After the previous afternoon, Ben knew what to ask to get what Kat needed to know. There was also paperwork to do. She had the monthly billing statements on her desk. Frank would always handle them. She recalled watching in amazement as he would calculate the payments, even on the deferred, interest-bearing accounts, in his head. She had to get him back online. They would need Frank soon, in person, to get things done. His connections, the relationships he had built, would be essential to bring this to a conclusion.

Kat looked at her watch and noticed that five minutes had gone by. She had taken a little mental vacation. She pushed off the wall with both hands and turned with urgency to get to the tea with Esther Landsman.

Ben was down to the lobby of his building a little before ten. He had slept in. He and his wife, Randi, had been trying to start a family for over a year. It had gotten to the point where their bathroom looked like a laboratory, with all the test kits and vials strewn about. Last night the test showed she was ovulating. They got to business then and again that morning for good measure. Ben didn't know how she did it, but Randi hopped into the shower after they finished and headed to work. As he headed for the door, he thought about what a lucky man he was. He was married to a woman who could kick his ass in the sack then go out and take on the rest of the world. They had met shortly after they both graduated college. She was from Long Island, like him, although she was from one of the wealthier areas. They shared the same view of the world. After three weeks he knew he wanted to spend the rest of his life with her. It just happened. Randi had told him that she felt it after a few days. He was on his way now to pick up some flowers for Randi and maybe grab a quick smoke before the day got away from him. There would be another session of lovemaking that night. The second night required more romance, a little extra something. It was easy to fall into routine, having sex on a schedule like that. They had figured it out after a couple of months. More accurately, he figured it out. He'd make reservations for a nice dinner. He had to make sure to clean the apartment and get all of the testing equipment put away. Nothing turned Randi on more than when he did unexpected household chores. He had his call with Pap that day, so he figured he would get as much done as he could before noon.

As Ben walked past the doorman's podium, he called out to him. "Mr. Hirsh, there is a note here for you." The doorman reached out with a white business envelope in his hand. Ben took it and turned it over. The envelope was written by hand.

BEN

He tore it by the corner. There was a handwritten note and a card. He took out the card and saw that it was a Shake Shack lifetime pass card. It was the same type of card that Commissioner Marshall had the day before. He opened the note and read.

> Ben, Sorry for the way I spoke yesterday. Bad day, I'm afraid. I hope my unfortunate behavior doesn't come between us having a healthy working relationship moving forward. Enjoy the burgers, and be sure to send Ms. Wells my warmest regards.
> Brendan Marshall

Ben stood stunned. Jesus Christ, he thought, Kat Wells had him pissing in his pants. The police commissioner of New York City was apologizing to him. Un-fucking-believable. He chuckled out loud. He desperately wanted to save the note and show it to Randi. That would get the juices flowing. He thought better of it. As he walked out the door, he tore the note up into little pieces and tossed them into the air. As one of the pieces landed on his shoulder and stuck, he thought that working with Kat and Frank might be pretty interesting.

CHAPTER 9

Kat made a left onto Ninety-Second from Central Park West. Esther's building was the second one in on the north side of the street. The ten-foot wrought-iron doors were open as she walked past, into the lobby. There was a concierge at a desk in the marbled and cooled lobby.

"I'm here to see Esther Landsman. Kat Wells."

The concierge smiled and looked down at a thick ledger. He used a silver pen to track the list from top to bottom.

"Ah, yes. Ms. Wells. Very good." He stood, short and neat, and walked over to the elevator. He pressed the up-arrowed button, and the door immediately opened. He leaned in with one arm holding back the elevator door then pulled a key from his pocket. It was on a retractable cord attached to his waist. The little man pulled the key to its capacity to reach the PH on the panel. He turned the key, and the PH button lit up. He slid the key out of the slot, and it slipped from his fingers and recoiled with a snap against his waist. He didn't show any signs of embarrassment but turned to Kat and again said, "Very good."

Kat stepped in as the neat little man went back to his desk. The elevator opened to the penthouse lobby. To Kat's surprise, Esther's assistant, Gracie, was waiting. As always Gracie was well dressed and professional. Kat had met her a few times and liked her, although she was a bit too deferential for Kat's tastes. She chalked that up to her own ignorance of the ways of the wealthy.

"Good morning, Ms. Wells. She'll see you in the reading room." Gracie walked, and Kat followed, both of their shoes clacking on the marble floor. Gracie looked straight ahead and walked with purpose as she turned left onto a hardwood-floored hallway. The walls were dark-stained oak.

Kat had been in the penthouse twice now. She corrected herself; this time made three. The first visit was for a cocktail party and then, of course, the shiva. The penthouse was much different from just the other day. All the doors were closed, making the space seem smaller, older. The doors she passed now she remembered as the entrance to the ballroom. They looked like barn doors, twelve feet high and four feet wide apiece. Kat remembered gasping the first time she walked through them. It was autumn, and the view of Central Park and the color of the leaves was one she would never forget. This day it seemed that they were walking through the center of the penthouse. When Kat was there for the shiva, the doors were open, and the space was filled with light from the rooms, most of which seemed to go on forever. All of them had high ceilings and classic art. It was the type of apartment one would see in a movie but that a New Yorker knew was scarcely affordable to even the wealthiest—a rarefied space. With the doors closed, it was cold and dark, despondent. A different residence altogether from the glorious penthouse she had sat in just days before.

Gracie stopped halfway through the hallway and turned outward at one of the doors. She shouted politely, "Esther, Kat Wells is here to see you."

Kat heard Esther from inside. "Oh, my, oh, yes, yes, send her in."

As Kat was about to enter, she caught a look from Gracie. Her face had sunk at the sound of Esther's voice. Kat noticed then that Esther did sound different, weaker, smaller, than when Kat saw her last only a few days before. The look from Gracie was heartbreak.

Kat was surprised when she walked through the door and saw Esther, who was wearing a bathrobe and slippers. Kat had sat with her many evenings at social occasions over the years, but she never imagined her without hair. She knew that Esther had quite a collection of wigs. She thought now that they must have been very good since it was a shock to see Esther like this. There she sat, bald, save for a few wispy white hairs hanging limply from the back of her head. She looked ten years older than just the past week. Kat had never seen her not dressed impeccably. Esther was one of the leading social figures in New York. She was chairwoman on various charity boards and museums. Esther Landsman had been a lioness only a week before. Now Kat saw before her a broken old lady. She tried not to show her shock, and Esther didn't seem to notice. She seemed lost in thought. She started speaking before Kat could sit.

Kat was walking toward an Eames chair in the sparsely decorated room when Esther started speaking. She stared at the wall as she spoke. There was a large window overlooking Central Park, but Esther sat facing a dark corner, her head facing down, shoulders slumped.

"We spoke of the end, Sol and I. Quite a bit actually. I've been sick. We've been keeping it from people, but we both assumed it would be me to go first. Sol, well, he was still strong as a bull. We met at college so many years ago. He was on the crew team. I remember his arms. He had big, strong arms. Always walking around with his sleeves rolled up. We laughed a lot. That's the key right there; you have to laugh. Do things, go places." She lifted her hand as if pointing at something that wasn't here. Perhaps there was something there, Kat thought, but only Esther could see it. She pointed, and her hand soon began to shake. Esther seemed to notice and let it drop. She continued.

"Sol would always say that someone has to have a thing. You know, a hobby, a calling of some kind. It can't be all work and family; you have to have something just for you. He sang, you know. Took lessons for years. He wasn't very good but good enough to sing at weddings or family gatherings. Yeah, he liked to sing." She smiled, and then her lips quivered a bit. "And the kids, he loved them so. They're out in California now. Matt and Jesse. Lawyers. I have four grandchildren, smart little things. So precious. I have to go. Get out there. They left, went home. I said I would be along, right along."

She stopped as Gracie came in with a tray loaded with a silver tea service. She placed the tray on the table between Kat's Eames and Esther's thick old chair.

"Esther, honey, do you need anything else?"

"No, no, Gracie, we're just fine."

"Well, let me pour your tea for you. Nice and hot, just how you like it." Gracie poured for Esther. "Yes, here it is now, nice and hot."

Esther put her wrinkled hand on Gracie's arm, and Gracie turned to Kat. There were fresh tears in her eyes. Kat knew they were tears for this broken woman. Gracie cried for the widow, not the dead husband.

She spoke to Kat. "You go easy now with my girl here."

"Just a nice tea is all," Kat replied.

Gracie stroked Esther across the head, turned, and left the room. Esther continued speaking as soon as Gracie left. She jumped to another random subject.

"We had a house a long time ago, out on the island. Not now, no. Too fussy now. Jesse was sick. Burning up. Oh, my baby. Burning up. Thrashing from a fever. Sol ran with her in his arms, ran across the hospital parking lot. I remember; I remember him running. Holding my girl." The story ended, and there was silence.

Kat gently urged her along. "Are you going out West to see them? Your children?"

Esther didn't answer. She stared silently at the spot she pointed to. Kat was heartbroken herself now. The transformation in Esther was too striking to believe without some shock. In the silence Kat thought about her husband, dear Willy. What would become of her without him? It was a thought she could hardly stand. He was her everything. She worried about her survival without him. Esther spoke as if reading Kat's mind.

"I've seen you with him. Your husband. I can see it in your eyes. You are a lot like me. The bond you have, it's more than a marriage. Yes, I can see it. Like me, yes. You are. You're the one in this."

Kat wasn't sure what was happening. This woman seemed to be looking into her soul, saying aloud the things Kat had begun to think lately, her feelings of an imbalance in her marriage.

"I don't understand what you mean, Esther."

"You're the one who gives. I know this. It comes from you. Every gesture or simple act of kindness—politeness, actually—he made. I saw it, saw your eyes. You grant this esteem on him. It's not bad. You see, I'm the same. You're the giver; you bestow this higher level of love on him. It's your perception of him, and your life together, that makes it special. I see it in him. He knows what he has in you. You're like us, you see, like us. You know, you would know what I'm asking. You'll help me."

"What are you asking, Esther?"

She responded in the same soft voice. "I want you to kill the man who took away my Sol." She reached over and picked up the teacup, her hands now steady as a surgeon's.

"We're looking for him now. We'll find him soon, I can assure you."

Esther finally turned to look at Kat. Her eyes were red and glossy like she had been crying for days, the eyes that she had been hiding by staring straight ahead at the point in her mind. She sat up, the lioness of New York rising from a slumber.

"I know you will find him. That is why you are here. When you find him, I want you to kill him. Before I'm gone from this earth, I want this piece of shit that took my Sol to die. You can do it. Think how it would be if he took your husband, your Willy. Kill him for me."

"It's a lot to ask."

"Is it? A great man like Sol—and he was a great man, as you know—taken away by some thug? No, it's not a lot to ask at all. It's the right thing to do, and I believe you know this. You know what should be done. Kill him. I would do it myself if I could."

Kat sipped her tea and thought a moment. It was the likely outcome of all this anyway. She thought how she had gotten soft in the big city. After all, she originally had come to New York to kill someone. A mass murderer, yes, but Kat had the conviction to kill her. She had her Western sense of justice then. She thought about Sol and how Esther's life, what was left of it, would be without him. She placed her cup down.

"I'll do it." Then she asked the first question that popped into her mind. "What is your thing? You said that Sol thought everyone should have a thing. Sol sang. What was it for you?"

"It was Sol, don't you see? It still is. He's my thing, like your husband is for you. I took care of him. I loved him."

Kat smiled, but her lips almost quivered and went to a weep. She held strong and smiled as she looked into Esther's eyes. "I have to leave now. I can't be seen with you, or over here, until it is done." She stood. "Good-bye, Esther. I'll be in touch."

Esther tried to stand but couldn't. Kat walked around the table and took both of Esther's outstretched hands in hers. She looked up, and her eyes seemed clearer, sharper.

"Thank you, my dear. Thank you."

Kat waited until she got to the lobby before she let her tears flow.

CHAPTER 10

Her voice came through his phone on its dock. "Mr. Handley, Walter Peterson is here to see you."

"Okay, Paige, send him in."

Peterson entered Handley's office. He would have liked to stick his head in and whisper the message, but the expanse of the room required a twenty-yard stroll. Handley had his head in some paperwork as he approached. New York Harbor spread out through the large window behind him. Peterson took note how small the Statue of Liberty looked from there.

"The Leandro Simmons thing should be happening about now."

Handley didn't look up. "Let me know first thing."

"Yeah." Peterson turned and got out of there.

Miami

Leandro finished his run on Meridian and Eighth Street, around the corner from his place. He checked his Polar band. Five miles in just under twenty-eight minutes. He needed to get better before the triathlon in San Diego. It had been his thirty-ninth birthday the week before. He had one year to win one of those things before he entered the masters division. His back and hamstrings were tight, throbbing. He sat and spread his legs to stretch out his back, lowered his head and allowed the brief thought to enter that maybe he was past it. Maybe he couldn't get there at this age.

"Hey, you."

Leandro looked up to see Mrs. Gainsborough on her bike. As always her dog was in the basket. She was turning circles in the intersection like he had watched her do every day for the past two weeks since he had changed his route to finish up there. She was a local character, one among many in that area of Miami. He knew her name since every time he walked past, she would holler at him.

"Get over here, you. I'm Mrs. Gainsborough."

That day she was wearing a long green silky-looking thing. It flowed behind her as she rode. There was nothing underneath, and despite his attempt to keep his eyes averted, Leandro saw her saggy breasts hanging around her midgut. She had long white woolen socks, sandals, and didn't seem to have pants. He hoped that there was something underneath down below. What was most striking in this mideighties heat was her hat. She had on a woolen ski cap, the kind with the flaps over the ears, with long braids that could be tied up against a piercing wind. It looked like it had been yellow thirty or forty neglected washes ago. The dog was an ugly thing. It looked to be half boxer and the rest mutt. It didn't seem to be enjoying the ride. The dog was so fat that its fur was popping out through the squares of the metal basket.

"Hey, you," she yelled again. "I need some help here. At my house, over to my house."

Leandro kept his head down, hoping the old bag would move on. It only encouraged her. She pulled up next to him. He noticed from this angle that she was wearing green stretch shorts under the shirt. The dog seemed to be asleep.

"Are you stupid? Dontcha hear me? I need help. Something heavy, you can lift it. C'mon. My house is over here." The dog woofed on cue.

Leandro lifted his head. "You got water over there?"

"Yeah, I *got* water." The crazy old bag was mocking his grammar. "C'mon, already. It's getting hot. It'll only take a minute."

She got off the bike and started walking it toward a cement wall surrounding what he figured was her house. The dog was so heavy that the bike almost tipped. She put her hand on the mutt, preventing it from jumping out in panic. Turning left, she arrived at a metal gate and turned to him.

"Are you stupid? C'mon." She waved her arm, and her saggy breasts jiggled like clam chowder in a Ziploc.

Leandro sighed and stood. He walked over to help her and, more importantly, shut her up. Checking his Polar, he saw that he had about eight more minutes of downtime before he had to get on his bike. He could help her out and get back to his place and onto the bike in time, but there wasn't much of it to waste. He trotted over to the gate.

"Okay, okay, let's go."

She swung open the gate, which protested with a harsh squeal. The grass in the yard was up to his waist. She walked ahead on the slate walkway. The yard smelled of dog shit. There was a small porch up two steps. She gently laid the bike down, and a foot before it hit the ground, the dog tumbled out. It rolled but stayed on its back for a second. Leandro figured that it wouldn't be too long until it stayed that way, like a turtle abandoned on its shell, with its stubby legs in the air. The dog then made a surprisingly agile maneuver to get itself upright.

Mrs. Gainsborough got to the door and yelled into the house, "He's here."

A black kid leaped out at him. Leandro was about three yards away from the steps, and the kid reached toward him like a pitcher pushing off the mound. A hand was raised with a black device in it. Leandro made flash observations. His sniper training kicked in. He had a half a second.

The kid smelled of weed. He was high, wearing a Dwyane Wade Miami Heat jersey, a red do rag on his head. The device was a handgun. It looked like a Ruger SR40, a shitty piece, scratched at the muzzle. He held it at an angle. The kid's aim would be off to his right. Leandro leaned slightly to his left and heard what sounded like a large, brittle stick being snapped. He felt a flame on his head and went down. He was blinded but could hear out of his left ear. He heard another snap and felt the old lady's body fall next to him. Then he was out.

He felt as if he were on a beach, close to the water's edge. Waves were lapping up against his face. The waves got stronger, rougher. He took a breath, expecting to swallow water, but instead felt smothered like there was a pillow over his face. His head was being rocked from side to side. Then he felt it, a searing heat turning to pain. The pain on the side of his head woke him. There was dark then light. Something was passing over his eyes. It scratched him. He tried to rise up, but the pain pinned him down. He opened one eye and could see the stems of blades of long grass. Something was standing in the way, blocking his view.

It took a moment then Leandro realized it was the dog. He made out what was in front of him—the dog's two back legs and balls. The dog, the fucking dog, was half on top of his head, licking at him. He tried to shake the dog off of him, but when he moved his head, pain shot through it. It felt like someone were sticking a hot crotchet needle through his ear. He screamed in agony, and it made the dog jump, woof, and turn and waddle away.

Leandro was on his side, and he could open only his left eye. The old lady's head was a foot or so away. He smelled the dog shit, and it reminded him of what had happened. Unable to move his head, he swiveled his body around to try to get a sightline on the front gate of the yard to see if he was alone. There was no one there. He waited a minute or two to make sure his movement hadn't aroused someone lying in wait. A pro would have put another in his head. His first observation had been correct. The hitter was a stoner, probably in a gang, did the job for a couple hundred bucks or some drugs. It was this observation that enabled him to move. No little stoned prick was going to kill him.

He turned to the old lady. He was facing the top of her hat. He reached out with his right arm, and the hot needle went through the side of his head again. He pulled the hat off the old lady and lay on his back. He thought of reaching up to touch the side of his head but thought better of it. It would be too much of a distraction. He had to get himself up and out, to his safe house, a storage shed he kept about four blocks from there. He had a charged phone, some cash, and the number on speed dial of a man who would pick him up. He'd been paying the guy a grand a month for years to have someone on call for such an emergency. Leandro knew that if he could get up and out of the yard, he would make it.

He reached over, took the hat in both hands, and lifted it up over his head. It was harder than the 285 he'd benched that morning. *Was it this morning?* he thought. He wasn't sure. Fighting the distraction and the pain, he pulled the hat over his head. As his right arm brushed past the wound, it felt wet and mushy. The weight of the hat felt like a lead helmet. He rolled onto his side and pushed himself up to all fours. A rush of air made him lightheaded. He concentrated on the grass beneath him. When the grass stopped moving, he continued. Leandro tried to lift his head, but it wasn't moving. It wasn't the pain this time. The muscles in his neck weren't functioning. For the first time in his life, he was suddenly scared. He never allowed fear to enter into his planning, but now he couldn't keep it out, and it was debilitating.

He said, "Fuck, fuck, fuck" to himself, took a deep breath, and started crawling over to the front gate. He didn't look at the old lady or the dog; his sole focus was on that gate. Get to it and pull himself up to his feet; that was the only thought he allowed in. It seemed to take forever; he fell to his belly once, but he got there. He pulled himself up to his feet and tried again to raise his head, but it wasn't happening. He was lightheaded again, so he wrapped an arm around the gatepost and let his body slump. He dug in his right foot to gain purchase and straightened. He was going to make it—walk over to his shed, call the guy, make it.

He turned, taking a look at the old lady and the dog. He couldn't see her through the grass, but the dog was on the slate walkway. It was chewing on what Leandro thought was a piece of rubber or maybe a dog toy or something. He looked closer, not to see what it was but to focus his eyes and clear his head for the walk. As soon as his vision cleared, he regretted turning back. Leandro's head shot back like he had taken a whiff of smelling salts. The dog was chewing on his right ear.

CHAPTER 11

"Hey, Pap, sorry about the hassle yesterday." Ben was on his house phone, knowing that Pap's would be scrambled since he was given that number.

"What are you into, Ben?"

Ben didn't hesitate to tell Pap all he knew. "Have you heard about the killing of Sol Landsman?"

"Nothing more than what was in the papers."

"Well, we were pretty close."

"Jeez, I'm sorry, man. You need anything?"

"Not personally, but, yes, I need information. I'm working, I guess, with Kat Wells and Frank McGinley on this."

"Them I've heard of."

"I figured. This started a few days ago. A man named William Brogan passed away. He left behind an account statement. I'd like to fax it to you, or I can scan it and email if you prefer. On the statement Brogan wrote a name: Carter Handley. Sol thought Brogan was referring to the CEO of Axis Financial. The same day that he told me, Frank, and Kat this, he gets killed. There's something very big going on."

"Okay, Ben. Fax the statement to this number after I hang up. Redial then erase it. I don't want your email on this. This line is only alive for five minutes then it goes away. Tell me what you need, and I'll do my best."

"Thanks, man. I need all you can find on Carter Handley, William Brogan, and Sol Landsman. I need to know if they are connected in any way."

"Okay. I'm sure there are many firewalls here. Shit, Carter Handley, huh? I'm guessing he has a good security system. I need two days. I'll get the information to you or Kat Wells somehow after I'm done. How much longer will McGinley be in rehab?"

"But how?"

"What? McGinley? Ben, I have to know what everyone that matters in this town is up to."

"Shit, man, what color shirt am I wearing?"

"Oh, shut up. I'm doing my thing here. You want my help or not?"

"Don't get pissy with me, Pap. You just never cease to surprise me."

"Speaking of surprises, I've met someone."

"That's a surprise? Shit, man, you meet someone every night."

"No, no, this is different. We've been together for a few months now. Listen. I want to get together with you and Randi."

"Great, a night out would be fun. Wow, Pap. What the fuck is going on here? It's too hot for hell to freeze over."

"Fuck you. Make sure you have access to all of your lines for the next few days. I don't know yet how I will contact you. Then I'll call your cell later this week about setting up a dinner. Got to go."

"Sure."

CHAPTER 12

The bench was at the water's edge in an inlet as large as a pond on the Hudson River. The water lapped up on the rocks gently as if it were a lake. It was cool down there. Clean.

Frank McGinley put one leg up on the armrest of the bench, stretched his head as low as he could toward his thigh, and reached his hands out toward his toes. He didn't go far. There was a pinch in his hamstring. He lowered his leg and sat back down on the bench. The sun had just come up, so he had a few more minutes to think about the dream before he got started.

This was his fourth or fifth morning at the facility. He didn't know which. He had slept so little since he had been there that he had lost track of time. It was the same the last time he rehabbed. He had gone to bed drunk for so long that he didn't remember how to sleep naturally. The last time was twelve years ago, but he remembered the lack of sleep—the rest of it, not so much. Most of it was bullshit to him then. It was AA that kept him in line for a long time, but he knew all along he would drink again. He had planned going back to it years before he took that first drink. He had bought a nice glass two years before he bought the bottle. It was a memory that triggered the relapse, but Frank knew that was his own bullshit. The memory wasn't the trigger; it was the excuse.

When he went into his first rehab, he was a falling-down drunk. He drank away his job and his fiancée. This time, he knew, was worse. He had become a sneaky drunk, drinking alone, at home, or at a distant bar where no one would know him. He had a whole elaborate process: hiring a driver to get him back and forth, lying about his name and profession in a bar in Astoria, Queens, or Long Island City, or some other place that none of his friends or colleagues was likely to frequent. It was pathetic, and he knew it. What scared him was his inability to handle it. With all the power and money he had acquired these past sober years, he still couldn't stop drinking until he fell on his face. This time was different because of the shame. That a man of his stature could stoop to acting like a teenager sneaking a cigarette was so pathetic to him that he was humiliated about himself. He had to get past this, he knew. He had to find the strong Frank, the guy that had overcome all the odds to become as successful as he was now. The kid who shoveled snow off the basketball courts in the winter to work on his game. The guy who killed Carla Pugliese, stared down the Goldman executives, stood up to Brogan. He had lost that guy for the last few months. A pussy had taken over. A fucking pussy.

He sat and stretched his arms wide across the top of the bench back and crossed his legs at the ankles. He closed his eyes and concentrated on what he had dreamt early that morning. He had been awake only an hour or so. The dream had woken him in a sweat. It got his ass out of bed in a hurry, made him throw on shorts, a T-shirt, and running shoes. He had come down here without thinking.

The dream disturbed Frank—not the substance of it or anything that had happened. What disturbed him was that it wasn't just a dream. It was clearer than anything he could remember. He didn't feel like he was in a dream. He lived it; he was there. He had given up on religion long ago, thinking that it was all mystical bullshit. Heaven, hell, feeding thousands of people with a couple of loaves of bread, or whatever else they came up with, was all a load of crap to Frank. This was something different. His first thought was that it was the alcohol leaving his system, but he knew better. He was there, in that world. He felt the ground beneath him when he walked, the air and the warmth of it on his skin.

A realization suddenly came to him. It raised shivers on his back, and he leaned forward, elbows on knees. He looked out at the Hudson, toward the middle, where it flowed over a rock and the water churned white but remained gentle. He died last night. He died then came back. He was suddenly cold. He crossed his arms across his chest.

He closed his eyes and tried to recall everything about it. He wanted to examine every detail. He needed to remember everything.

In the dream he was walking in a processional inside Saint Patrick's Cathedral. The air smelled of incense, and the pews were set up differently. They made up four squares on the main floor. The cathedral was mapped out with aisles in an X formation.

It could have been a cross, he now thought to himself.

The four aisles met in the middle of the floor, and Frank was walking among the priests and altar boys with their flowing robes. They were carrying flags, and Frank felt, even there in the church, that the spectacle of it was ridiculous. He turned behind him and saw that Kat and her husband, Willy, his dear friends, were sitting down around the corner of the aisle that Frank had just turned onto. He was panicked for a moment, realizing they were approaching the altar in the very center of Saint Patrick's. He needed to avoid that altar, knowing that it would take him to a place he wouldn't be able to get out of. He looked to his left and saw a few empty seats two rows back. He quickly ducked out of the procession and sat down.

Even on this bench on the shore of the Hudson River, he could feel the side of the wooden pew brushing against his left thigh as he maneuvered his way in.

When he sat, he turned to his right and saw Kat and Willy sitting together. Kat was wearing a green dress and one of those crazy hats you see at a royal wedding, and Willy was wearing a suit, a garment Frank had never seen him in all the time he'd known him. He waved over to them and made a hand gesture that he would go out the side door after the ceremony and meet up with them. Kat nodded and looked down at her hymnal. Willy stared straight ahead.

Suddenly he was out of the church and on the side. It was a lot like the side of Trinity Church after Brogan's funeral, only it was still Saint Patrick's. He walked over to Fifth Avenue.

There was no Rock Center, no traffic, cabs, or tourists. He crossed the avenue to grounds of a wealthy estate or perhaps an Ivy League campus. He walked away from the church along a path. It was completely silent and serene. Off in the distance there were two men playing tennis on a clay court with ivy growing on and through the fencing surrounding it. Beyond the court were long rolling hills washed in green grass. The air was perfect. It left a clean blue film on him. The film clung then dissipated suddenly in a mist. He felt as if he were walking through the air, parting it with each step, creating a dry splash of freshness on his body. Suddenly the serenity ended. It ended with an acrid foul smell. It was cigarette smoke, pluming up the left side of his body to his face and nose. He looked to his left, and there, walking beside him, was his dead father, the old drunk bastard Frank had reviled for years. He was far older than the last time he had seen him. Back then he was a child, and he vividly remembered now that the old man was sitting at a table, smoking Lucky Strikes, with a bottle of Canadian Club and a glass on the kitchen table. For a second Frank relived that day. He didn't know if it was remembrance of the dream or his current thoughts on the bench.

Frank's thoughts went from the dream to that day. His mother, with her face swollen and purple, stomping out the door, Frank, a boy, lingering, not sure what to do, so he wandered over to the old man.

"What the fuck are you lookin' at?" His father's last words to him.

Another chilling thought came to Frank now, a new thought jumping at him since the process of figuring out the dream had just begun. Maybe it wasn't his father; maybe it was who he would become if he stayed on this path. It was heaven, after all; he knew that as fact. Why would his father be in heaven, or why would Frank think him there? He focused again back to the dream.

His old man was ranting about something. It seemed as if Frank caught him midsentence. "These fucking people think that I'm going to…" He couldn't figure what the man was saying beyond that. The words sounded like one of Charlie Brown's teachers were speaking, only harsh, mean, and angry. Suddenly the old man stopped walking and took Frank's arm with his non-smoking hand. He turned to him and said, "You can go back now."

Frank turned toward the church and came to an elevator bank on a wall of an old brick building that appeared from nowhere. The elevator panel was art deco, like the lobby of the Empire State Building. There were three buttons on the panel; they read 222, 99, and 1. Frank pressed one, and the door opened. He got in, and before he felt any movement, the door reopened. He looked up, and the light above read 99, but when he looked out, it was Fifth Avenue again. He quickly jumped out like you do when you realize the elevator is at your floor after not paying attention. On the quiet avenue he thought to himself that it was a good thing he'd jumped out since he didn't want to go lower. He had saved himself.

On the bench by the Hudson, Frank realized the importance of this. He had saved himself. It was a conscious act. He had come back.

He crossed the dream avenue, and in front of Saint Patrick's was Danielle Wieters, the woman he loved and had last seen dead in front of him, tied to a chair, covered in blood.

The memory of it had put the bottle in his hands. He corrected himself on the bench. It was the excuse, dammit, the excuse he used when he drank down that first vodka, the first of many.

Goddamn, she looked beautiful. She was wearing a formfitting white dress, a softer version of the New York City little black dress. She cocked her head to the side and smiled like she always did when he would approach her. His eyes welled up, knowing even in the dream that she was dead. He had failed her, let her die. He was so nervous; it was heaven. He was there, with her. As he got close, she put out both of her hands. He didn't hug her; he took both of her hands in his. His heart exploded in grief and love at the same time. The emotion was too much for a living person to grasp. He knew then that he would never feel this deeply ever again in the living world. She didn't speak, so he did.

"I was just on an elevator; it had three buttons: 222, 99, and 1. I wanted to go to the bottom, so I pressed 1. But the door opened at 99, and I was here. That means that—"

She interrupted him with a smile and said, "Next time take the stairs."

He woke up.

He jumped on the bench, realizing that he had nodded off, back into the dream. Sitting straight on the bench, he felt his heart racing, flop sweat on his back and neck. He took a second to decipher if he was really there on the shore of the Hudson River. He stood and walked closer to the water's edge. The sound of the water gently lapping up on the shore assured him that he was there, alive, in New York, but that was no dream. It was a vision, a voice, a call; it was something he couldn't understand, but it wasn't a simple dream. He couldn't have been more out of sorts than if the Loch Ness Monster strolled ashore or Bigfoot sat down on the bench next to him. He didn't believe any of this shit, this coming-to-Jesus nonsense, the hand of the Lord. No, it was him, his mind. He needed to figure out what was in his head. Take the stairs, she said. What the fuck? Maybe he didn't die and come back last night. She came to him; that is what mattered. The rest was his baggage that he had to figure out over time. He thought that at least he had something to add to the next group session circle jerk that afternoon. *Take the stairs. Yeah, get to work.* She came to him. His Danny, his love. She took him by the hand. Take the stairs.

He turned toward the path and started jogging.

CHAPTER 13

Mush had a hard time answering because of the noose around his neck, but Guzman asked again.

"What happened to the man?"

Guzman shook his head in frustration and turned to House and waved his hand. House eased up on the rope, and Guzman asked a third time.

"Where is the motherfuckin' man?"

Mush coughed violently. "I told you. I shot that motherfucker right in the fuckin' head."

"Then where the fuck is he? Huh? You shoot him in the fuckin' head, and he disappears? What, he rose up to heaven? Like some kinda saint or sumptin'? Shit." Guzman waved his arm at House again.

"Wait, wait. I'm tellin' you. I saw his fuckin' ear fly off his head right onto the grass. There was blood all over."

Guzman strolled back over to his table in the empty factory floor. As he took a seat, House let the rope loosen. "What you think, House?"

Guzman didn't often ask what he thought of anything, and House certainly wasn't one to volunteer an opinion. He paused for a second. "I think this motherfucker is high."

Guzman took him literally and smirked. "I can see he's high, House."

House didn't give much of a shit what Guzman thought of him. The money was good. Guzman knew that House was stronger than he looked, but he didn't realize that he was smarter. At six-foot-seven and 340, House was used to people underestimating his mind. In this case he meant that Mush must be out-of-his-mind crazy to think that anything he said was going to save his ass.

House figured fuck it. He knew where Guzman kept his money, and he had figured a way to get to it. He needed a couple of days, but after that Guzman's neck would be in the noose. Fucking Guzman, the little shit. He'd go up easy on the rope. House could hardly wait to snatch the cash and head to LA for some of that West Coast pussy, like in the Kid Rock song.

House didn't respond. Instead he looked up to admire his work. It was his idea to put up the pulley on the rafter. It came to him when he stopped once to watch a tow truck pulling a truck cab up onto the flatbed. House was impressed with the strength of it, the way the pulley turned slowly and deliberately. At the time they were having trouble with Lilly Shanks. She was a fat fuck. He knew the pulley would be a good way to hang the bitch. He got a big-ass pulley, mounted it on the beam, ran the rope through, and tied a noose. Easy as that. It was also his idea to let the second guy go after having him dangle a little. Shanks had to die, of course, but with the second, he wanted to spread the word about the noose. Soon enough the street started calling Guzman "The Hangman." He was still House, but people knew who pulled the rope.

Guzman leaned on the table and crossed his legs and arms. He grabbed a pack of smokes off the table. As he lit one, Mush struggled with the tape around his wrists behind his back. Guzman took his time with the smoke, dragging slow and deep.

"You shot his ear off. His fucking ear. Do you think maybe that means you shot him in the side of the head? What about the woman?"

"Yeah, she dead. I got her in the chest then put one in her head just like you said. But the dog, man, the dog went fucking crazy on me. It was making so much noise. I thought I should get out of there. I must have forgot to shoot the guy in the head."

"You forgot? You know how much this is going to cost? Me running guys all over town, looking for this white boy's ass? Motherfucker." He stood and stomped his foot in anger, and Mush winced. "You forgot."

Guzman waved his arm down in a slicing motion. House jerked the rope hard with his right arm. Mush went up quick, and his neck snapped immediately.

CHAPTER 14

Walter Peterson cleared his throat. He didn't have time to answer before Carter Handley asked again.

"Where is Leandro? How can you come in here without knowing this?"

"I thought it best to keep you informed. We don't know where he is. When the police arrived as planned, he wasn't there. A woman was dead, which I was not aware of myself, but Simmons is gone."

"Gone? How the hell can he be gone? What the hell are you saying? There's a dead woman but no Simmons. What the fuck is going on?"

It was unusual for Handley to use harsh language, and Peterson knew that if he didn't give a hard answer, there would be hell to pay. Handley would hang this on him.

"I hired a reputable man out of Miami. The hit went wrong. I was assured that his top gun was on the job. Simmons was lured to an out-of-the-way location. The police reported that a man's ear was found on the scene. Apparently the woman's dog was chewing on it. My guy made the anonymous call to the police. They moved in a few minutes after the shots were fired. All they found was the woman, the dog, and the ear." He braced for another browbeating, but it never came. Handley stood from his desk, walked around the front, and leaned against it, legs crossed.

"His ear was shot off. He can't have gotten far. How many men do you have on this?"

Peterson knew that what he was about to say wouldn't be received well, but he had to be honest.

"The number of men won't mean anything. A guy like Leandro, he's underground if he's not dead. The police have searched the surrounding area. My bet is that he has a go bag and a safe place to keep it. He contacted someone, and they got him to a location. It can't be too far away since he'll need medical help. I'll check medical supply dealers, local MDs, that type of thing. He definitely won't show his head. There must be dozens of people who want him dead. He would be prepared for this. We'll have to wait him out, keep the pressure on the local docs. My man in Miami is scouring the streets to see if there is any word. We'll find him."

"I can't tell you how disappointed I am with this news. Walt, this shit can't happen. It must be dealt with and put to bed as quickly as possible."

"I know, Carter. We'll get him soon, I promise you. A couple of days at the most."

Handley turned, walked back behind his desk, and looked out the window, signaling the end of the meeting. There was no doubt in Walt's mind that this would be pinned on him if he didn't get Simmons and get him soon, and when he left this office, Handley's mind would get to work on a plan to cover his own ass. He stood and practically ran out of the room.

Handley listened to Peterson go. He looked down at New York Harbor and watched a ferry pull away from Liberty Island. It was clear that he had to accelerate Peterson's departure. He'd make the call to the reporter from the *Journal* who had been after him for an interview, start a whisper campaign about dissention in the ranks of the company, imply that Peterson's weak leadership was holding the stock price down. The press would eat it up since Axis had built a reputation as a very discreet company about internal matters. Peterson would hang himself in his office in a few days or maybe at home. He'd have to speak to his security officer, Mr. Castle, about that. *Yes,* he thought, *Mr. Castle should handle it.*

CHAPTER 15

B en placed his legal pad on the coffee table, signaling to Kat that he was finished. She glanced up at him over the screen of her laptop. Her hair was pulled back behind her, in full work mode. Ben noted that she was starting to feel comfortable around him, letting her guard down. She looked back down and continued her furious typing. Ben picked up his coffee cup and sipped. He was surprised that the coffee was ice cold. Hilda had brought it to him on the second pass, after lunch. The coffee made him realize that they must have been at it for hours. The time had flown by. Ben was as juiced as when he was a young agent with the SEC. It felt good to be collaborating after years of relying on his own counsel.

The pad had ten pages of notes from his phone call with Pap earlier that day. As he read the notes, Kat would interject with questions and ideas. They bounced some theories off each other. When neither would come up with anything new, he would go back to the notes. He was very particular about his note taking. Each interview or interrogation had the same routine: new pad, new pen, each page dated and numbered, with the name of the interviewee on the top—although he knew better than to write "Pap" on paper.

He waited for her to finish and swallowed the coffee, which was fine despite the temperature. Kat stopped typing abruptly and looked up from the screen. She put her elbows on the table, pressed her fingers to her forehead, and closed her eyes. She didn't open them when she spoke.

"There's enough here to put Handley away for a long time."

"We going to use it?"

"We'll sit on it until we need it. The shooter, Leandro. Tell me again why he's the one."

Ben leaned forward to pick up his legal pad; Kat interjected. "No, no, no, I have the notes. Give me your take on it."

"Okay. I figured that there are only a handful of people who would be trusted with such a high-profile target as Sol. Pap agreed. He checked the NSA, CIA, and Interpol databases."

"He can get in there?"

"Oh, yeah. He looked for the highest-profile unsolved assassinations in the last five years. From there he got a list of the six top suspects by cross-referencing information from each of the agencies. Pap could track the movements of five of them. Credit card purchases, tollbooths, movie tickets— it's amazing what he can find. Anyway, only one of the six was untraceable during the two-day window around Sol's death. That was Leandro. Since they're all such pros, the one that's off the radar is the killer."

"The address I have here is still accurate?"

"It should be. Pap would have told me otherwise."

"Okay." She scrolled down her pages with the sleek mouse to look at the address. Ben could see the determination in her eyes. She spoke without looking up. "What's your take on all this? I mean your gut. What do we have here?"

"I'm convinced that Leandro killed Sol. There's no doubt in my mind. The rest, the connection between Mr. Brogan and Carter Handley, is pretty speculative. I mean why would a guy with that much power and money go to all this trouble? It all seems kind of trivial for the chairman of Axis Financial. The connection is too subtle."

"No. I disagree. If what Pap found gets out, that an account was set up for Brogan shortly before the assassination of Handley's biggest rival, there's plenty of documentation here to show how much this CFO, Feldman, resisted the takeover overtures. Handley couldn't have known that Brogan would go on to be the man he was. He probably assumed he had duped a young justice department kid. Yeah, there's enough here to ruin Handley. You're talking about a guy whose career started by having a rival killed. What I can't believe is that Brogan could have been duped into killing the wrong man. There must have been someone inside the CIA who was paid off. Pap traced the order back to the CIA, correct?"

Ben turned back to his notes. He couldn't find his place for a moment, and Kat took the opportunity to sip her cold coffee.

"Yeah, here it is. CIA, that's right."

Kat put her cup down gently. "Handley was quite wealthy even then. The connection with Senator Marche convinces me that Handley is the one pulling the strings here. Everyone in Washington knows that Marche is the financial industry's man. Bought and paid for. A guy like Handley says jump, and he asks how high. How did Pap determine that it was Marche that ordered the seizure of our files?"

"Through the texts and emails of his staff. They all chatter too much."

"Yeah. No, Senator Marche convinces me that Handley was behind the seizure of the files. He was looking for the statement. It has to be. Did you run down the broker ID on it?"

Ben flipped through his pad again, turning the pages and folding them over. "Oh, yeah. I have it here. Hutton broker. He's long dead, but Hutton was the brokerage firm for Axis at the time. So the account was set up in Brogan's name with Axis Financial. I have no idea why, though. Wasn't Brogan rich? Would two hundred grand be worth much to him?"

Kat ignored his question. She was thinking fast, her pace accelerating. "Is there any clear link between Handley and Leandro? A phone call, something?"

"No. There's nothing. I could have Pap take another run at it, but if he doesn't get anything on the first try, there's nothing there."

Kat stared into her screen, not reading, thinking. She skipped ahead again. "You know what? It doesn't matter what the brokerage statement means; Handley's actions after Brogan's death prove that he is behind this whole mess." She waved her hand as if dismissing her own doubts. "Brogan dies, so Handley had Sol killed because he was the logical person to have this statement, which could come back to haunt him. He hired Leandro to kill Sol, no doubt. We're going to have to move on this. He could send this Leandro after Frank or me soon enough. Yeah, we're going to have to move."

Ben leaned forward, shocked by the abruptness of the turn in the meeting and more than a little pissed that Kat had come to this decision without further discussion. "Move? What are you talking about? We have nothing here. It's all speculation. We can't go to the police with this. Nothing Pap gave us is permissible in court."

Kat didn't respond. She ignored him while reading her notes—more accurately, his notes, his research based on his friendship with Pap. There was an element to this that he had thought of on the way over. He thought it was better left unsaid at the time but not at this time, not now that Kat had decided to treat him like some kind of pisher research analyst.

"You're putting a lot of blind trust in Mr. Brogan."

Kat looked up from her screen at the mention of the name. "What do you mean, Ben?"

"You're completely ignoring the most obvious connection here. Any objective investigator would think that Handley paid Brogan to kill that guy. They were in on it together. C'mon. It's pretty clear that Brogan was an assassin outsourced to the CIA. How many kills? I stopped counting. So he pops another and takes two hundred grand. He never cashed in, that's true, but maybe he had second thoughts. I don't know; maybe he wanted the money to get away from his rich wife and then had a reconciliation. Who knows? You have to admit. No matter what comes of this, Brogan is going to look like an accomplice. You go to anyone with this, and his reputation is going to be tarnished."

Kat closed her laptop slowly and deliberately. She leaned back in her chair and burned holes in Ben's forehead with her glare. "'Blind trust' is one phrase you can use. 'Faith in a man's character' is another." She looked away, to Ben's relief, closed the laptop, and leaned back and swiveled a bit in her chair. "You didn't know Brogan, so I understand your question. Let me ask you this. You knew Sol Landsman. Do you think he would take a bribe? Do you think he'd kill an innocent man for two hundred grand?" She stood and started pacing the room. "This can be a messy business at times. People get hurt; mistakes are made. Sometimes the bad guys win mainly because there isn't enough evidence to take them to court. Shit, some of them are just very smart and good at what they do. Handley is one of the smart ones. Besides, we're not going to anyone with this information. This is between me, you, and Frank. Got it?" She stopped, planted her front foot, and turned to him like a pivot in the low post. "Do you want a job?"

The question seemed to come from left field. Ben stumbled over his answer. "I don't know. I haven't thought about it."

"I spoke to Frank yesterday, our daily call; I brought up the idea."

"How is he? I mean I don't really know the guy except for what I have heard."

"Yeah, well, don't believe everything you hear. Do you want to go up there? Meet him?"

"Up where?"

"He's at a facility near Beacon, New York, on the Hudson. I can set it up."

Ben started to think a little more strategically. "Kind of unusual going on a job interview at a rehab center."

Kat smiled. "If you wanted the usual, you would have stayed with the SEC. I'll talk to Frank this afternoon. Can I say you'll go up there? We'll get you a car."

"Sure. What the hell. I could use a day in the country."

"Good." Kat went back to her desk and sat. "No need to involve Pap any longer. We'll work this out from here. I'll let you know when you can meet with Frank. Should be tomorrow or the day after."

"Great, I'll wait for your call. Take care."

He walked out without saying another word. He wanted to get outside to gather his thoughts. As he walked out the front door and down the steps, the heat hit him like a wet mop. He turned left toward Fifth Avenue. He figured he'd walk across the park to the West Side. Before he crossed the avenue, he allowed himself to think that someone was going to kill Handley and Leandro. He hoped that he wasn't going to be asked to do it himself as some type of interview.

As he got to the shaded side of Fifth, he sat on a bench. What was this? What was he getting involved in? If he moved forward with them, did he become a gangster of sorts? Kat was a good person; he could see that clearly. She wouldn't be involved in anything underhanded. It was too confusing and layered for him to figure out on this bench. He knew that he had to meet with Frank McGinley to feel him out. If this was some kind of vigilante group, taking big bucks from corporate interests to make problems go away, he couldn't be involved. *Mr. McGinley better be pretty impressive.*

A bum that smelled like sour milk sat next to him. Ben rose and started down Fifth. He thought he'd pick up flowers again for Randi. She liked it when he brought home flowers.

CHAPTER 16

Vinny Castlenni sat on a bench across from Riverside Drive. He was in a little park just north of where the drive forked into a quiet tree-lined street, sitting hunched on a bench, waiting for Walter Peterson to finish fucking the black chick in the apartment across the street.

He'd normally bitch to himself about sitting out there in the dark, but in truth this was the best job he had ever had. He picked up the job when his buddy Lefty went to jail. He snorted to himself now, thinking that it was always the stupid shit that got you busted. Lefty was pinched for a job he did three years earlier. Back then Lefty ran a job with a couple of his regular guys. They robbed a jewelry store in Jersey somewhere, a smash and grab. One of the assholes decided to pop an old lady across the head. This put a stick up the ass of some local cop who knew the lady somehow. Three years later they nabbed the guy who popped the old lady, and he ratted the whole crew out. Lefty went up for ten years. Before Lefty went he passed this job to him. As agreed, Vinny had been holding out 10 percent from every envelope for Lefty when he got out. He should have a nice stash after a few more years. Vinny didn't know when he was going to get out, but there was no way he'd do the whole ten. It would be a shame since he didn't want to give up this job.

It was Lefty who started calling him Castle. The name fit since he was six-foot-six, 280. Vinny slouched down low as a man walking his dog walked by. *Fucking dopes with these pets,* he thought. *Two o'clock in the morning, and this guy is out walking so he can pick up dog shit in a bag. Stupid.*

He didn't mind waiting. He's gotten used to it over the years. It had been a long run. He started young, seventeen years old. He dropped out of school, or he was thrown out; he had forgotten which. He grew up in Elmont, New York, in a shitty little house in the shadow of Belmont racetrack. Even as a teen he knew his father was connected in some way. The old man would stroll across Hempstead Turnpike to the track in the afternoon and come home nine, ten o'clock at night half in the bag. He always had cash on him, folded over and held together with a metal Knights of Columbus clip.

After moping around and drinking beer and getting high that first summer, Vinny went to his father and asked if he could work for him. Two days later he was beating the shit out of a jockey behind one of the paddocks.

Vinny mostly did grunt work for the old man, roughing guys up, collecting. One night his father was stumbling across Hempstead Turnpike blind drunk, and he was hit by a Vette. It flipped him a hundred feet in the air, and he landed headfirst. It squashed his skull like a pumpkin. It wasn't the driver's fault, but Vinny found him anyway. Some little Jew from Great Neck. When he found him, Vinny laid the schmuck's arm flat on the kitchen table, put his knee on his upper arm, and pulled his forearm up to this head. It nearly snapped his arm off at the elbow.

After that he took his mom down to Florida, set her up with the money from selling the house. He hung around there for a while. There wasn't much work for him, so he headed back North, caught on with Lefty and his crew. He stole some cars, some jewelry, but mostly he was muscle. He was good at it, beating the shit out of guys. They always came up with the information or the money or whatever else they had done to deserve a beating, after he was done with them. Lately he'd done a couple of hits. It didn't matter to him, and it paid better. He thought he might have a problem after, when he would think about the fact that he had killed someone, but it didn't bother him. It was all the same shit to him. He reasoned that with the way he left some of the guys he beat up, they would have been better off dead. Some of them asked for it before he was through.

He'd never met the guy running him on this job. When Lefty gave it to him, he said the guy would contact him through a text message. That was how it went from there. He did a few jobs for the man, mostly intimidation. They were all businessmen, not too hard to put a stain in their pants. He got the text for this job the previous day, to follow this Peterson guy around, find out what he was doing and where he was going. Vinny figured it for blackmail since Peterson was obviously pretty fucking rich. He reported back that afternoon about this little hideaway that Peterson had. He didn't mention the black chick. He got a good look at her that afternoon and thought maybe he could hook up with her after this was over. It wasn't clear she was a hooker, but she was young and beautiful, and Peterson was old and rich, so Vinny did the math.

Three hours earlier he got a text: "Eliminate him."

Vinny wrote back: "20K."

The return was: "Ok."

He got there a half hour after the text and had been waiting since. He heard a door swing open. It sounded like a metal gate. He sat up straight and looked across the street to the building entrance. Nothing. Then out of the corner of his eye, he spotted someone walking briskly south on Riverside. It was Peterson. He must have come out the back or the side of the building. Vinny hopped up and cut through the small park area and picked up the pace on Riverside. He wanted to get to Peterson before the fork in the road, where it widened under streetlights. He was ten feet behind him when he pulled out the gun. He wanted Peterson to turn around. It didn't seem right to shoot him in the back of the head like a pussy. The first two he'd popped were facing him, and he liked the panicked looks on their faces. He shouted something to get him to turn.

"Hey, asshole."

Peterson turned, and Vinny raised the gun. He got the look he wanted and pulled the trigger.

CHAPTER 17

K at couldn't sleep. She tossed and turned for hours thinking about that afternoon's phone call with Frank. She worried about the logistics but not the consequences of their mutual decision. Things had already been set in motion. The delivery was on its way, and Ben would be up there that morning.

Despite all that was happening now and what lay ahead, the thoughts of work and revenge and retribution had passed. It was Esther Landsman that kept her awake. Kat thought about those two long strands of gray hair and the touch of Esther's weak hand on her wrist. She got out of bed and went to the kitchen. Willy would be getting home from the restaurant soon. It was quarter to two. She figured she'd wait for him and join him in his nightly ritual: glass of Jim Beam on the rocks with a twist, and a shower. She thought that it had been too long since they played. They were still romantic, made love, but they hadn't played in a while. As she reached up for two glasses, she smiled as she remembered their theme nights in their little house on the San Juan River. They still owned the place but hadn't been back there in years. They would dress up, dance, or act out any number of roles. Kat loved the nights when they would go back to another era, the '40s or the '50s. She loved the outfits, A-line skirts, bobby socks, or elegant hats. She was a long way from Placerville, Colorado, but her heart would always be there. It had been over twelve years now. She had heard from a friend back home that the Telluride police chief would be retiring soon. Maybe then she could go back, at least for a visit.

She was unnerved by her conversation with Esther. Work and the things that had to be done were the weight she carried throughout the day, but on this night, alone in her bed, the burden had shifted. That graceful woman had changed

Kat's entire mindset over a cup of tea. She thought now how amazing it was that one afternoon could change the path of the rest of her life. She stood in the dimly lit kitchen, held her robe closed, and put her hand on the table, and she admitted to herself that she had thought this way for quite a while. It was Esther who had given her the permission to act on it. For years now Willy was enough. They were enough. As a gangly, awkward child growing up, she could have never imagined anyone loving her like Willy. Esther was right; she saw how it was between them. Kat was grateful that he loved her—adored her, in fact.

She poured two Jim Beams, forgot the lemon, and took them to the table and sipped hers. As the bourbon settled and warmed her, she made a decision. She would finally say he alone wasn't enough for her. They weren't enough. She deserved more.

The front door swung open gently. Willy stuck his head in seeing that the lights were on. As he entered, Kat felt an excitement upon his arrival that she hadn't felt in years. Her mind went back to the old days in their house. He would come home from a three-week shift at the ranch, smelling of horseshit, and she would rush across the room, jump up, and wrap her legs around his waist. He would lift her, and she would feel his rough hands against her pale skin. Willy would take her to the shower, and they would make up for the three weeks in one night. Tonight she walked over to him as he took off his jacket and hung it on the hook by the door. She came up from behind and wrapped her arms around him. The smell of horses had been replaced by the smoky scent of steaks and seafood.

She kissed him from behind. When he started to speak, she said, "Shhh."

He turned to her and looked up at her eyes. He placed his still-rough hands on her cheeks and kissed her slowly. Kat disrobed him while she kissed his neck, and they made love on the floor.

Kat stood to refill their glasses. She had thrown on a nightshirt, and Willy sat in his boxers, chatting like a schoolboy. The menu change had been a big success. There was a rumor that the *Times* food critic was there, and they hit it out of the park. He was delighted with the way the evening turned out. She remembered the lemon and made a show of bending into the refrigerator, and Willy whistled. She loved him so. He was her dream; to the world, he was not that tall, not that handsome, but she could see how beautiful he was. He was the nicest person she'd ever known. Her perfect man. As she sat back down, she crossed her legs underneath her, Indian style, and took a sip. Willy raised his glass in a toast.

"To my beautiful wife."

"I want a child." She said it so fast that it took her by surprise. They had been through this, of course. Years ago the doctors told them that it would never happen. It was Willy's sperm. They didn't swim very well. To spare his feelings, she rarely mentioned it.

Willy nearly spit up his drink. "Honey."

"I know, I know, but I've been thinking about it a lot, and I need more."

"What do you mean more? What happened? I thought we had a plan, a way of life."

Kat reached out her hands, and Willy took them. "We do; we did. I don't know, Willy. It's just…"

"Just what?"

Kat looked away from him and peered down at her drink, wanting another sip but knowing not to let go of Willy's hands now.

"We deserve more, you and I. We have so much to give. It almost seems selfish to have all we have and not share it." As she said this, Kat knew she wasn't being honest and wouldn't be on this issue for the rest of their lives together. He was so sweet and kind. She could never say that he wasn't enough for her. Kat knew he loved her so deeply that he truly believed that it was enough, but it wasn't. She could never say those words. She smiled with her mouth, but her eyes were sad.

Willy smiled back in the same resigned fashion. He let go of her hands and took a long sip of his drink. He quoted their favorite movie, "As you wish," saying the words as the grandpa in *The Princess Bride*, not the prince. Kat genuinely smiled back with a small giggle. He reached over and put his hand on top of hers.

"Don't be sad, Kat."

"Who's sad?"

"It's okay, baby. You're right. We have been lucky for so long. We should share our lives, and I know you deserve more. I've known since we met. I'm the lucky one. You're just starting to figure it out."

"Willy, I—"

"C'mon now, Kat. This is right. You're right about this. I mean I've been selfish all these years. Yeah, you're right. Think about it. Things can be so much better. We'll have someone else to love."

They sat in silence for a while and let the weight of the subject settle. Kat put her fingertips on the rim of her glass and twirled it. *This is love,* she thought. It wasn't clear to her whether Willy wanted this or he just wanted her to be happy, but he had agreed to change his life for her. Kat knew that this was a defining moment in her life. They weren't walking on a beach hand in hand as the violins swelled. They were at the kitchen table at three in the morning, and Willy smelled like tonight's special. It was perfect.

Kat stood to make him some eggs, and they talked through the remainder of the night. Although it was the happiest night of her life, after Willy fell off to sleep, she looked up at the ceiling above their bed and cried.

CHAPTER 18

Billy "Mac" McGinley sat in the Jeep parked in the pitch-black parking lot of the Beacon, New York, wastewater treatment facility. He had been told he had the clearance to park there, but he couldn't help glancing in his rearview mirror, worried that some nosy cop would try to clear him out. It was his first job for Uncle Frank, and he didn't want to blow it.

His instructions were to leave the car at 4:00 a.m. and get back to it by 5:00 a.m. It was ten to four, and Mac was getting anxious. He had never been one for waiting around. It gave him too much time to think. Despite himself, he glanced down at his gloved left hand and the smooth curve the custom-fit glove made over the missing fingers. He stuck the hand out the window and relived how he had lost them. He had been told many times to stop dwelling on that day, but for some reason thinking back to it calmed him in a way nothing else could.

Jesus Christ, he thought. *It's been three years now.* They had been heading back to base camp in that shithole country. The Humvee in front of him slowed to get past a rutty part of the road. He watched the front-left side of it dip and thought to turn right to avoid the crevasse himself, thinking the guys in the back might be dozing after a long night on patrol. It was the turn that saved his life. Without knowing, he had turned his Humvee away from the impact. He had the window open, and his hand was outside it when the Humvee in front of him blew. Connor, Hawk, Jimmy, gone in a flash. The front end of his Humvee lifted, and he looked at his hand. He instinctively put it up to protect his face with his fingers spread, and he watched his pinkie and ring finger separate from the rest. Something moving too fast for his eye cut through them. They stood there, frozen in midair for a second, then dropped down out of sight. In the days after losing them, he'd thought of a magician he once watched on TV. The guy threw cards. He flipped them at candles, and nothing happened. The magician said, "Wait" and in a second the top of two candles plopped to the stage floor.

He was lucky, getting out with just two fingers gone. Rather than being relieved and happy to get home—he had certainly done his service—he felt guilt ridden about it. There were many before him, and since, that went home much worse or went home in a bag. It took a couple of months to get over losing the fingers, but he still hadn't gotten past the urge to go back. There were nights, long nights, that he lay awake feeling the heat of the desert, tasting the sand and dust in his mouth. The feeling was like when he was a kid, coming home from the amusement park and still feeling the roller coaster in his gut. His old man helped. He was a navy man and knew how it could be. He'd seen action and shared some of his own stories with Mac. Uncle Frank was there also. Since returning, Mac had been doing odd jobs for his old man's corporate security company, but at age twenty-five he was adrift. Without that action, the adrenaline rush, the fear of death, he was a man without a purpose.

Mac looked at his watch to see that it was five to. He lifted the passenger seat off the rails and took out his pack, laid it across his lap, and reached over to the panel under the seat to do final inventory. He pulled out the gear: rod and reel inside a Plano rod tube, Anglers backpack, a small shovel, and a boonie hat. The hat was the lone tribute to his former life as an army ranger. The package and the adhesive strips were in the backpack, in a waterproof pouch. He took the small shovel and shoved it into an inside pocket of his chest-high fishing pants.

He would be a fisherman starting out early and lost if anyone came across him.

Mac closed the panel and slid the seat on its rails back into place. He opened the driver door, swung the boots around, and stepped into them as he stood out of the Jeep. He stomped his feet silently to get the blood flowing. It had been a long day. He'd taken Amtrak up from his home in Annapolis that morning. The Jeep was parked in a garage on Fifty-Sixth and Eighth, as he'd been told. All the gear and the package were inside. He had been given very specific instructions from Kat Wells the previous night. Having memorized the instructions on the train up, Mac tore up and threw away the two sheets he'd written them on, in a toilet at Penn Station. On the walk up to Fifty-Sixth, he rehearsed everything in his mind. This wasn't much different than nightly patrols in Afghanistan, he thought to himself. It paid better, that was sure. Ten grand for the night. Mac still wasn't sure what his Uncle Frank did for a living. Every time he raised the subject with his dad, he got a vague answer. It was getting to the point now that his dad didn't remember which line of bullshit he had answered with last—"Consultant, Wall Street investigator, I don't know." Mac figured that the truth was probably a little of all those things and more. It was fine with him. Uncle Frank was a cool guy, and it seemed that he paid well also. Mac was happy to do the job. It was good to be out doing another patrol.

After securing the backpack, his vest, and the rod tube around his back, Mac checked his watch as he did a final mental inventory. As always he started with the bottom of his feet and worked his way up. All was set, and his watch read three seconds to four. He paused then pressed the stopwatch function and set off. He walked south on Denning's Avenue toward the small bridge. The target area was the Denning's Point Nature Preserve. At least that was what Google Maps called it. Mac figured it for a corporate retreat or a private estate. The point was actually a small island in the Hudson attached to land by the bridge up ahead. Mac got to the bridge, sidestepped down the slope, and entered the water. He started west toward the body of the Hudson. The route called for him to hug the shoreline and wait until he got out to the Hudson proper then wade across to the western shore of Denning's Point. When he arrived at the mouth of the Hudson and the narrow creek he was wading through, the current picked up substantially. For a moment he lost balance but recovered and leaned into the river. The most important part of the mission was delivering the package uncompromised. Although he was sure that the waterproof seal would hold, Mac decided to try his best to keep the backpack above the waterline. He could make out the shoreline of the point thirty yards in front of him. Having done hundreds of night patrols in his service, he found that darkness didn't bother him. He did his best work at night.

He figured that Kat Wells must have run his service record when he didn't see night vision goggles with his gear. It was good to work with people that had their shit together, something he had found sorely lacking thus far in his civilian work life.

Mac used the current to his advantage. He hopped up and let it bring him southward toward the shoreline of the point. He paddled with his right arm to keep himself in line and treaded the water with his legs, not making contact with the floor of the river to be sure he didn't slip on any rocks beneath the surface. The last thing he needed right then was a turned ankle. It had been a while since he had to use his full strength for a task, and it felt good to know that, despite having limited use of one hand, his legs were still strong as steel. Mac was having the most fun he'd had since he'd been home. With three more hops and paddles, he came close enough to the shoreline that he couldn't help hitting bottom. The water level was up to his midthigh. Mac landed softly on the river bottom to find that it was all sand. He walked the last ten yards to the shore.

Mac glanced at his Luminox watch to see that only nine minutes had gone by. He immediately went up the riverbank to the cover of the shoreline. The foliage was dense, and it was a step up from the sandy shore to the roots of the trees that formed a small platform to stand on. He looked down to see how wet the roots were to be sure there was good footing. He reached up with his left hand, wrapped the three fingers around a thin tree, and pulled himself up as he stepped onto a dry section of roots. He was under cover and took a moment to catch his breath and think ahead to the next step of the mission.

The island was encircled by a walking path that he had been told to assume was monitored, which was why he had to enter the water before the footbridge. The path should be no more than ten feet in front of him, surrounded by fencing that was likely on a silent alarm system. Atop the fencing was barbed wire. Mac shimmied through the dense quilt of heavy branches. A thin branch scratched his face, and he had to turn sideways to get himself and the backpack through at one point. He could see the fence up ahead, but the branches were so thick he was forced to stop to try to find a route through them. It was important not to leave any sign of his presence after the mission was completed, so he couldn't break away any branches. He thought about moving to another location but knew that this spot was ideal since the growth was so thick there wouldn't be a trace of him after a few minutes. Mac decided to take off the backpack and lift one branch to form a hole. Then he pushed the backpack through to a foot or so from the base of the fence.

With the backpack secured, Mac raised the upper branch again and pressed down on the lower, thicker one. He stepped through with his right leg and slowly put it on the ground. When his foot was firmly planted, he sat down on the lower branch to test his weight. The branch held, and he put all his weight on his ass on the branch, pulled his left leg up to his chest, and crossed it over until it was down and his back was facing the water. There was still foliage in Mac's face. He was leaning back now, with his feet inside the branch growth and his upper body out. He limboed to his left and swooped his head low and around. The recoil of the lower branch shoved his ass forward, and he found himself standing with his nose six inches from the fence. Mac chuckled to himself since he felt he had just performed a circus trick.

He checked his watch. Fifteen minutes gone by. Time to dig. Mac took the hand shovel out of the pocket in his pants. He held it knuckles up for maximum leverage, with his left hand forward and right hand on the handle. He would start a foot outside the fence. Before starting, he looked up at the top of the fence. The barbed wire was high and angled inward toward the walking path. It was clear that the fence was to keep people in rather than out. He wondered if this was some kind of minimum-security prison and what Uncle Frank had gotten him into. Mac smiled to himself. It was good to be out in the dark with a shovel. The barbed wire didn't give him pause; it gave him purpose.

He slammed into the dirt hard, and it started to crumble immediately. His instructions were to dig deep enough into the opposite side of the fence to leave the package and the adhesive strips in the sealed pouch buried. It didn't have to be groomed perfectly; in fact Kat Wells said to make it clear where the hole had been dug from the inside. Mac assumed the inside person would pick it up soon after he left. He never gave a thought as to what was in the package. That didn't impact his mission, so it wasn't his concern. The dig went quickly. Once forming a hole on his side of the fence, Mac was able to spear the dirt wall under the fence. The ground broke away easily and fell in upon itself. Within a couple of minutes, the digging was done. He scraped the loose dirt from the hole and made a pile on his side. Mac removed the pouch from the backpack and shoved it into the hole on the other side. It fit perfectly, far enough from the fence inside that they could be dug up easily without touching it. He shoved the dirt from the pile over the bags and got down on his belly. Mac reached under the fence and up to pat down the dirt over the bags smoothly. Once that was done, he filled in his side of the hole. With this side he was more careful, taking some time to smooth the dirt out and tamp it down with his feet. He pulled an oversize leaf off a branch and brushed the ground with it. He then took the leaf, crumpled it up, and tossed it out into the river.

Time check again. Thirty-eight minutes gone. Filling and grooming the hole had taken longer than he had thought. He had to hurry. He turned back to the tree line and followed the same route out. He lowered the same top branch again and stepped over. His foot hit nothing.

He mumbled, "Shit, shit, shit" and quickly put his weight on his left back leg. He stood for a moment with his right leg in space, and his left rising onto his tiptoes and losing balance. He took a chance and put his weight on his ass on the bottom branch. It held, and he sat, both legs in the air. Mac grabbed on to the branch with his arms between his legs, scooched his right butt cheek lower on the branch, and extended his right leg. The foot hit ground. After a sigh of relief, he cursed himself for not considering the difference in ground levels.

He lowered his head and swung down and over the lower branch to the sandy shoreline. He went into the water up to his knees and turned right toward the creek and the mainland. As he approached the mouth of the convergence of the Hudson and the creek, he continued on the island side, knowing that it would be too risky to fight the current. He waded along the island side until the water was smooth and the footbridge was in sight then crossed. Once he arrived at the shoreline of the mainland, he checked his time. Six minutes to five. He had timed the walk on the way in from the Jeep to the bridge, and it was two minutes. He had some time.

Sitting knees up with his forearms resting across them, Mac took in the scene. He closed his eyes, tilted his head up, and listened to the sound of the Hudson River. The gentle rush of the river seeped into his bones. For the first time since he had been home, his body felt right. The mild muscle ache from hard work comforted him. He thought if only he could do this, work like this, out here, using his body. Use the skills he had been taught until they became instinct. Preparation, execution, discipline. If he could do this, he thought. The first morning bird started to chirp, and he looked down at his left hand and made a fist with his three fingers and punched the muddy bank. As he sat covered in mud and water to the waist, Mac was glad to be home for the first time.

He crawled up the creek bank to go back to the Jeep.

CHAPTER 19

The car pulled up at six, right on schedule. Ben tamped out his cigarette and got in. The car took him up the Henry Hudson to the Saw Mill then the Taconic. They got off at a remote exit and wound down the road west toward the Hudson River. There was one sign as he entered the quaint little town: "Welcome to Beacon." What struck Ben was the lack of traffic on the way up. Having grown up on Long Island, he'd expected bumper-to-bumper since this was a summer Friday.

It was a nice drive, peaceful. It gave him time to refine his questions for Frank McGinley. Ben was up most of the night, debating with himself about how far to go with his inquiries, how hard to hit. Kat had tossed out the job offer so casually that it hardly seemed realistic. Ben had a lot of questions, but he didn't want to come off as an interrogator. On the ride up he funneled down his thoughts to the few things he needed to know to make an informed choice. He wasn't sure how Frank would take to it, but Ben wasn't going to tiptoe around.

The financial reality of Sol's death wasn't lost on him. There was a chance that he might be looking for work before too long. Sol had been his biggest account.

The car passed the Beacon wastewater plant and continued on a dirt road. Fifty yards short of a footbridge, the car stopped.

"We're here, sir." They were the driver's first words of the morning.

"Here?"

"Yes, sir. A representative will meet you at the other end of the bridge. They'll call me when you are ready to return."

"Okay."

Ben opened the door, got out, and headed to the bridge. It was a beautiful morning. It would be hot again that day. He could feel the humidity starting at this early hour. It was only ten to seven, but the air was already hot and sticky. The bridge was a vintage covered bridge without the cover. It was perfectly maintained and wide enough for one car. Ben figured this for the delivery entrance. The boards were firm and sturdy under his now dusty shoes. He had dressed for an interview—best suit, polished shoes, and tie. Ben was already regretting his clothing choice since he was sweating and the back of his shirt was starting to stick. He loosened his tie as he came to the other side. No one was there, so he continued forward. Around a bend, out of view of the bridge, he came to a fork in the dirt roadway. To the right were a woman and a man. She was tall and an attractive sixty or so. The man was dressed casually but crisp. Ben had seen this before. He had walked into many meetings with hedge fund guys who were a little bent. There was always the sideman, a tough guy for personal security. Ben took him for an ex-cop or football player, maybe a boxer. It didn't bother him in the least except to make him more cautious about the upcoming meeting. He hoped it wasn't going to be bullshit. He was long past the days of a muscle head intimidating him. The woman looked down at a clipboard slung under her left arm and resting on her hip. She didn't raise it or look at him.

"Ben Hirsh?"

"Yes."

"Could I see some ID, please?"

Ben took out his wallet and flipped it open to show her his license.

"Please remove it and hand it to Mr. Conrad."

Ben rolled his eyes and pulled it out of its sleeve. The goon snapped it out of his hand and held it up to the light. He nodded to her but held the license.

The woman looked up from her clipboard and stepped forward to extend her hand. "Hello, Mr. Hirsh. I'm Dr. Nancy Delphi."

Ben shook. The pleasantries ended abruptly.

"With your permission, I will now take you through the visitors' protocol." She looked back to the clipboard. "Please empty the contents of your pockets and place them in the bag that Mr. Conrad is holding for you. Like at the airport." She managed a weak smile.

Conrad snapped a large clear plastic bag open and held it out at Ben's left hip. Ben emptied and waited.

"Your shoes, please, also any belts or jewelry. Thank you."

Conrad plopped down a pair of Adidas walking slippers on the dirt in front of Ben. He stepped out of his loafers and into them, took off his watch and wedding ring, pulled out his belt, rolled it up, and dropped them into the bag then raised both his arms, anticipating the next step. On cue, Conrad started patting him down.

Conrad was experienced. He was forceful but not aggressive, subtle enough to respect Ben's privacy but firm enough to let him know how strong he was. Ben knew then that Conrad was FBI. He wondered if he was on the job or not. He didn't know which he would prefer. The doctor read from her clipboard after the pat down.

"Please remove your jacket and tie, and then you may proceed down the path to your right to meet your host. Thank you for your patience. Mr. Conrad will be here in one hour with your possessions." She turned and walked purposefully up the path. Conrad spread his legs and put out his left arm for Ben to drape his jacket and tie over. Ben did. Conrad turned without a word and strode up the path and out of sight.

"So this is rehab," Ben said aloud as he looked around him. The path was peaceful and cool. The frisk routine didn't upset him, having escorted a few miscreants to Rikers. Shit, this was nothing compared to seeing a guy's eyes when the officer asked him to pull down his pants and bend over. That was when Ben would leave his white-collar felon, the circle of justice closed in his mind. There was nothing like a fist up the ass at Rikers to make a former Ivy Leaguer see the errors of his ways.

The introduction to the facility, while not unsettling, was another strike against his taking the job. *Who needs this shit?* he figured. Ben started down the path and thought of other contacts he could speak to about picking up some business. As he walked, it became cooler, and the branches overhanging the path closed and met, making a green tunnel. The path became a portal to a peaceful world. Like the curl of a surfer's wave, Ben was in it, surrounded by it. Green was ahead of him, to the side, and behind. He couldn't help but let his cynicism slip away. A part of him knew that it was hypnosis through landscaping, the clinic's purposeful use of the grounds to calm its drunks and drug addicts, but Ben enjoyed the walk and wished it wouldn't come to an end. He turned a slight bend, and the Hudson River came into view to his right. It was wide and slow. He could feel a cool breeze coming off the river. Directly across were the Catskills rolling hills. A moving shadow from a puffy cloud turned the tree leaves from light to dark green as it passed above. Ahead was a bench where Frank McGinley sat.

Frank rose as Ben approached. He didn't move from the bench, and Ben walked the final twenty yards to him. He looked good, much better than when Ben saw him at the funeral only a few days before. He wore matching gray shorts and a T-shirt, running shoes, and white socks. There was a small black electronic device clipped to his shorts at the hip. It felt strange to Ben to see Frank like this, so casual. He thought of when he was a kid and saw his high school principal in a bowling alley. The principal looked like a dork, but Frank looked like he belonged in a T-shirt and not a suit. Frank put out his hand to shake. Ben took it.

"Sorry for the hassle getting out here."

"Ah, I've been through worse. Nice place, although the shakedown out front was a little surprising."

Frank ignored the comment. He turned to the bench and handed Ben one of the two water bottles leaning against the back of it.

"Want one? No coffee, I'm afraid. No caffeine or prescriptions, nothing. I'll tell ya I think I miss coffee more than the booze. Sorry you're wearing a suit. Kat should have told you."

He didn't seem embarrassed by the circumstances. He tapped the electronic device on his hip.

"This is their version of the ankle bracelet. They know everywhere I am at all times. This is what keeps me from swimming downstream." He opened his bottle and sat back down. "I guess it's better than video or audio surveillance. Don't worry; Kat checked that out before she sent me up the river—literally, I guess." He chuckled. "She knew there may be a time when I might need some private conversation." He leaned back on the bench and took a swig of the bottle. "Take a seat."

"Nah, I'm good." Ben turned toward the river. "Nice up here."

"Yeah, I come down here every morning. Thinking about buying a place up here. How about you? You get out of the city much?"

Ben responded without turning. "I'm assuming that I'm here because of Kat's job offer. Since we seem to be on the clock, I have a few questions for you. What exactly do you guys do?"

Frank laughed. "All right, we're getting right to it."

Ben turned toward him. "I think that would be best since I schlepped all the way up here."

Frank placed his bottle to the side and leaned forward with his elbows on his knees. He was happy that Ben was being aggressive but didn't want it to show. Frank looked square at him.

"I'll start by telling you what we don't do. We don't fuck around, and we don't bullshit." He leaned back again on the bench, spread his arms, relaxed, and looked out at the river. "If you want to interrogate me, you can head back to the car now. This isn't the SEC or even Sol Landsman. You don't run this meeting. Got it? Do you want to sit, or are you going to try the 'stand over me to intimidate me' routine? C'mon, Ben. Let's just talk awhile."

The rebuke put Ben at ease. He relaxed and walked over to the bench, sat, and opened his water bottle. After a long gulp, he looked at the water himself and replied, "Fine, let's talk. No bullshit. So what do you guys do?"

Frank laughed again. He liked this guy. "For the most part we do the same type of thing you did for Sol. Except that we're researching potential investments for large firms and not Sol's private equity firm. We do background checks, all that. We dig a little deeper than you would be able. I have extensive contacts throughout the government and Wall Street. The government contacts I picked up from Mr. Brogan. You saw who was at the funeral. I have access to the head of any agency you can think of. Some of our larger cases are between private US firms and foreign governments. We're the people that firms come to for international investing research. There are so many regulatory hurdles in that business. I can cut through the bullshit and save our clients a lot of time and a lot more money. If a hedge fund wants to take an interest in a firm in France, for example, I can get the secretary of commerce on the phone or run down to DC for lunch. We charge a lot of money and work very hard. We always get results, always. If we can't answer our client's inquiries with our contacts then we advise the client to walk away because something is wrong. On the Wall Street side, we do a lot of consulting on risk aversion and compliance. That's mostly me. This is the part of the job I would want your help with. The international stuff takes a couple of years, at least, to learn."

He turned toward Ben. "It really is a hard question to answer in one meeting, although most people who tell you that are full of shit. You know that, though, but our official title is that we are a registered investment advisory firm. We don't even have a name, just a number. We're going to give the firm a name this year: Brogan, McGinley, and Wells. Both Kat and I have our RIA, CFA, Series Seven, Sixty-Six, Sixty-Three, Four, and Fifty-Four licenses. There's a couple more; I'm not that sure anymore. Kat keeps track of that. She lets me know what test is coming up, and I take it."

"I guess I would have to license up a bit?"

"Sure, but you can handle it. You aced your Seven. Perfect score, right?"

"Yeah. You guys know a lot about me?"

"Everything. As you can imagine, our background process is pretty extensive. You got a ticket for walking with an open bottle of liquor at Hofstra University. You should be ashamed, Mr. Hirsh."

It was Ben's turn to laugh. "So you want me to deal with the Wall Street crowd? You know most of them hate my guts."

"No, not most of them. The shit bags hate your guts. We're getting you away from that. We work with the heads of the firms, the guys who want to get rid of all that shit. Not because they are any nobler than the crooked hedges or the inside traders but because they make far more money playing by the rules than they could make stealing. Simple capitalism. You're used to dealing with guys who have done the risk-reward equation and came up with the correct answer for them that stealing is the better return. The guys you spent years investigating make more money stealing; ours make more staying straight. You must get frustrated seeing these guys walk away from most of this shit."

"Oh, yeah. That's why I started my own shop. It's hard to watch when you have spent months, maybe over a year, on a case. I mean I nailed some of these guys solid. We'd have a press conference, my boss stands in front of some cameras, and a few weeks later it's all over. Nothing happens. Everybody walks. You know all this, though."

"No, it's interesting coming from a man on the inside. Hopefully your days of frustration are over. What's your next question?"

Ben wasn't going to ask, but since the pat down, he couldn't let it pass. It was harsh but no bullshit, he thought. "What about this, the drinking? How do I know you're reliable?"

"You don't, I guess. Hey, I'm a drunk. I can't say otherwise. I can assure you, though, that you will be almost exclusively working with Kat." Frank waited for a response, but none came. "I spoke to Kat about this. Hey, we want you, or you wouldn't be here. We know everything there is to know about you, and we like what we see. Kat likes you, and that is really what matters. We've spent hours on the phone the last few days on this. You'll be working with her side by side after I get you up and running. I think she wants to move a desk into the office for you. As for compensation, once we come to an agreement, we'll set up an escrow account for your salary. This was my idea. I figured that if I were you and sitting with a guy who was on his second stint in rehab, I would want some guarantee. There will be a two-year contract. We'll put the entire amount in the escrow account, and you can draw out the funds as you wish. I expect to train you for six months or so. You'll start with sitting in on meetings with my contacts. Then I'm going to run Brogan's charities and the international business. I'll leave the day to day to you and Kat."

Ben was starting to get comfortable with Frank. He couldn't put his finger on it, this feeling; he felt the same with Kat. It might have been that they were both obviously smart and well connected, but they seemed like regular people. Informal yet brilliant, not unlike Pap.

"I have more questions."

"Sure, go ahead." Frank drank some more water, as did Ben.

"I've heard a lot of rumors about you two but very little about Brogan."

"You won't hear shit about him. He was too high level. They wiped him off the grid before the funeral. I'll tell you what, though. He was a hell of a guy. Really, he saved my ass. A great, great man." Frank paused, and Ben let him have his moment until a random thought popped into his head.

"What's with the 'fucking Brogan' stuff?"

"What?"

"At the funeral you both said it. Fucking Brogan. It seemed so out of place, cursing a man who you both clearly love and respect."

Frank lit up. "Fucking Brogan. Shit, it's been days since I said it. Kat and I would say it every day, many times a day. It was the only way you could describe the man. He was complicated, let's say that. One day he would be browbeating you; the next he slips you tickets to the opera or a ballgame. He was a cheap motherfucker, but he would slip extra money in your check. I'm talking a hundred grand or ten grand. However, there were times when you had to ask for your monthly check because he was holding on to it because he was pissed about some stupid slight that only he would notice. Fucking Brogan. See, you got me saying it now. He was a hard man, that's for sure. Kat mentioned that you know a little about his past. He was a trained killer. I know about a lot of it, but there was more. I don't know if anyone really knows all there was to know about the man. Sol knew him well. I tried squeezing him for some information, but you knew Sol; he wasn't one to give out anything. Yeah, he was complicated, that's for sure. Twelve years ago I would have shot him on sight; two weeks ago I would have laid down my life for him. That was fucking Brogan." Frank's eyes welled up. "Shit, Ben, what are you doing to me here?" He stood. "I was drunk at his funeral. Shit. It's something about Sol, huh? Jesus, this is a pile of shit we have here." Frank walked across the path to the shore of the river. He stood at the edge of the little inlet, and the water lapped up gently at Frank's feet. He took a deep breath and exhaled loudly. He turned back to Ben. "What else do you want to know?"

"You sure you want to finish this now?"

"Yes, I'm sure. Go ahead."

"I want to know about the rumors. How were you involved with killing a mass murderer? Why was it all over the papers then vanished almost overnight? I've heard about Brogan's wealth; the rumor is he killed someone to get it. I heard that you assaulted a hedge fund manager in Greenwich, Connecticut. There're a lot of things people say about you. Of course, the Wall Street legend is the missing broker. There are multiple stories about that. I researched it. I still know people over at the SEC. They looked some of this up for me. I know you were with him on numerous occasions. He was a Libyan. Was it some sort of international scandal? You should hear some of the theories."

Frank, composed by then, came back to the bench. He sat with an old-man groan. For the first time Ben took note of the gray on his temples and the damage to his face. There were many stories about that. Ben wanted to ask but thought that it might be too personal. He did get a chance to take a good look while Frank stared straight ahead. Frank had had a lot of work done. Some scarring was evident under his ear. His whole face seemed off kilter. It leaned slightly to the left, and his nose was out of line with his eyes, not squarely in the middle of them. He looked like a very bad boxer, a guy who had taken too many to the face.

"Jesus Christ," Frank said. "You are full of questions, aren't you? All right, let's see. I'll take them from simplest to most complicated. Brogan's wealth, that one is easy. His wife was very wealthy, 'came over on the Mayflower' kind of money. She died; he got it. That simple. The hedge fund guy—shit, what was that guy's name again?"

"Litchfield."

"Yeah, very good. I clubbed him over the head with a basketball trophy. Believe me, he deserved it." He smiled and rubbed his hands down his face. "The murderer. God, it's been a while. Her name was Carla Pugliese, the sickest bitch you could imagine. She was responsible for at least eleven murders. She worked for her uncle, an old mob guy. I got caught up in a Wall Street scam; that's how I met Brogan. The scam was run by another mob guy, and he sent this Carla to kill me. I got away; it doesn't matter how, but she eventually came after me." Frank paused and took a drink. "She killed my fiancée and waited for me in her apartment. She jumped me there. Threw a knife in my side and gave me this face. I saw you looking. She was beating me to death until I was lucky enough to knock her off of me, and I crushed her fucking head with the same trophy I hit the Litchfield guy with. I smashed her fucking head flat."

He'd run through the story without taking a breath. He let go and breathed out. His chest trembled a bit. Ben wanted to ask how the story got buried but knew it didn't matter now. He thought of the phrase "smashed her fucking head flat" and how calmly Frank had said it. Who was this guy, Ben wondered. What was he getting into? His mind told him to shut it down, get out of Dodge while he could. Go back home. Meet Randi for lunch. He didn't leave. Ben was pinned to that bench, compelled to sit there and learn as much as he could about Frank McGinley. A thought came to him, and he knew it would break the tension.

"What's with the math thing? Everyone says you're like Rain Man or something."

Frank was still in a daze, somewhere far away from there. Finally he snapped out of it and smirked like the question was beneath the level of the conversation. It clearly was, and Ben felt a fool for asking it.

"Ask me."

"What?"

"Ask me some numbers. It will clear my head."

"Two hundred eighty-seven times fifty-three."

"Fifteen thousand, two hundred, and eleven."

"Times eighty-eight."

"One million, three hundred thirty-eight thousand, five hundred and sixty-eight."

"Wait a second. How do I know these answers are right?"

"They're right. I'm getting slower. I have to think about it now; the numbers used to just pop into my head. I use it when I'm giving a presentation. I'll ask how many employees a company has and multiply it by whatever cost saving or expense we're talking about. Or divide or use a percentage. That type of thing. It works every time."

"That's something."

"Yeah, well."

The tension was subdued a bit. Frank stood to stretch. Ben tried to read a cue. He stood also.

"Do you want to walk?"

Frank suddenly had a look like he had forgotten something, and he went back to the bench and sat. "No, let's stay here. I don't want to run into anyone on the path. I have the bench for an hour."

"Who might we run into?"

"Best I can tell there are four of us. I'm the only one you haven't seen on TV or in the movies in the last couple of years. What was the other thing?"

"The broker."

"Yeah, the broker. What do you want to know?"

"What happened to the guy? What's the story?"

Frank stared straight out at the river. "You sure you want to hear this?" Ben was about to speak, but Frank held up his hand to silence him. "I tell you this, and you and I are tied together. You can't unhear what I'm about to say. Think about that."

Ben turned toward the river himself, his back to Frank. He was telling him that something bad had happened with the broker, most likely something classified or possibly illegal. Either way Frank was right. He would be tied to the hip to Frank and Kat for a long time, depending on what went down. *Shit*, he thought. He hadn't even been offered a job, and he already had a make-or-break moment. He wondered if this was a test of his loyalty. If he backed off now, there would be no job; if he pressed for an answer, he was with them. He thought about what Police Commissioner Marshall had said about Frank. "Do you have a gun?" he'd asked. Suddenly one of the other questions he had in mind popped into his head. He blurted it out to give himself more time to think.

"What's the story with you and the police commissioner?"

Frank laughed. "Oh, man, Marshall. What a putz. I slept with his mistress. I didn't know it at the time. Just one of those things. He hates my fucking guts, I'll tell you that. Besides, he's been married for over thirty years, so fuck him. He may become a problem in the future, though. My sources say he's next in line for mayor. He's got a lot of money behind him, real estate guys. I heard from Kat he came at you. Nothing to worry about. I'll probably end up going to him, hat in hand, if he does become mayor. Part of the game, I'm afraid."

Ben smiled toward the river, his mind made up. He knew he had to know. He was an investigator. He couldn't walk away not knowing. He turned around, walked back to the bench, and sat.

"So tell me. What happened? The broker, how did he disappear?"

Frank stared ahead. "Once I start, you're going to have to let me tell it. Don't interrupt and don't ask questions. You'll be the only other person alive who knows this now that Brogan is dead. Not even Kat. I'll give you another chance here. This has nothing to do with the job offer. You're going down a path without any turns. We can move on to your next question if you like."

Ben didn't answer.

"You sure?"

Ben nodded, unseen by Frank, who waited for verbal confirmation. He took a deep breath. "Yeah, tell me."

"He didn't disappear; I killed him."

Frank took a deep breath like he was getting ready to go down a steep ski slope, knowing that there would be no turning back or stopping once he started. "He wasn't a broker. He was what they call a fixer, a go-between for countries that American businesses are not supposed to work with. I think he was of Saudi descent, but he was a Brit through and through. Hakim Marcos, went by the name Hank or Henry Marsh. London School of Economics, Harvard Business School. His background was solid. His back story was that he had ties to Prince Alwaleed, you know the guy who had that big stake in Citibank for years."

He took a sip of his water.

"Brogan got the case from one of his Justice connections. They were investigating New York brokerage firms doing business with banned countries on the State Department's list. This particular case was with Libya. That's probably where that part of the rumor came from. I'd tell you the brokerage firms, but it was just about all of them. There was so much fucking money involved, crazy money. I'm trying to remember; I know there was a truckload of cash confiscated out in Long Island City. I kid you not. A truckload. I saw the picture. I'm telling you it's like drug cartel money. Somehow this connected back to Marsh. A truckload of cash attracts the fed's attention. Brogan came to me with the idea."

Frank breathed deep then continued.

"The setup was in place before he brought me in on it, which was his normal way of doing things. Fucking Brogan. There, I said it again. You'll get used to it. There was a hedge fund that was going to go down for massive insider trading, front running, all the typical shit. The feds busted them, and to avoid going to jail the principals in the fund agreed to be the front for the sting. I was brought in to act as the portfolio manager for the fund. Brogan got me a meeting with Marsh. I had to put together a strategy to pitch him. It wasn't hard; I remember it being some kind of covered call strategy. That was the thing. It's an unspoken arrangement with these fixers; the portfolio or trading strategy wasn't the point. It was all money laundering, creating layers to filter the massive amounts of cash these corrupt leaders amassed. As long as money was placed in a legitimate account, trades were made then closed, the money was washed. What better way to have your money turn squeaky clean than withdrawing from a major brokerage clearing company? Of course, it's great for the brokerage firm also. Open an account, make a few trades for hefty commissions, and slowly watch the account get drained out, charging fees all the way.

"I met Marsh for lunch at the National, a restaurant on Fiftieth and Lex, I believe. Maybe it was Fifty-First. Anyway, he was an impressive guy. Well bred. Nice clothes. He was well put together, but I could tell he didn't know shit about the markets. It only took a couple of minutes for me to see he was an empty suit. He knew how to play it, though. The wine list, all that shit. He was what they call a schnorrer. You know what that is, right? You Jewish? It doesn't matter. Marsh was a major schnorrer. I had to take him out a half dozen times. Only the best, the top places. He loved going to Scores, the strip joint. I don't know if you have ever been. I'm a little too old for that scene now, but I'm telling you, man, there were some crazy-hot women in that place. I'm talking about former Miss USA contestants, models. Really topflight. I must have put down at least ten grand a couple of times with him and some of his hangers on. It was in these places that I started to see something I didn't like. Marsh was a pig. I don't mean a typical strip joint bozo. I could see there was a deep hatred inside him. The way he treated the girls was downright abusive. He would wave a girl over for a private dance. When she was done, instead of handing her a twenty or even trying to stuff it in her G-string or something, he would drop the money on the floor, tell her to get down on all fours to pick it up. Most of them walked away or called security. He would apologize and slip the bouncer some of my money, and it would pass. But once in a while a chick would pause and look down at the cash. Then he could tell she wanted it or, more accurately, needed it. He would drop more money down there, maybe drop a hundred or a handful of twenties. Get this; this is really fucked up. If a girl got down there on all fours, he would tell her to shake her ass, and drop more money. Then as she was about to grab the cash, he would push her in the ass with his foot and knock her to the floor. One time he really kicked one of them. I tell you it was great when she got up and popped him in the mouth. He wiped the blood off and smiled. That smile, man, it was creepy."

Frank took a long breath, and for a moment Ben thought he was going to stop or ask him something, but he didn't. He put the water bottle to his mouth but didn't sip. He hurried back to the story as if he didn't want to break his momentum.

"This went on for weeks. It was clear that Marsh didn't give a shit about the fund or how the money was invested. We figured he was checking my back story while getting wined and dined all around New York. That's why the hedge fund thing was the perfect setup. The fund had a track record and a reputation for cutting ethical corners. All Brogan had to do was put me in the mix, set up a history, and we were clean. I'm telling you Brogan was the master.

"I was starting to get sick of hanging around with this guy. The longer I was around him, the more condescending he became. Like everyone in his life was a servant, and I was becoming one. Finally he took the bait. He pulls me aside and tells me to bring his management fee, three hundred grand, in cash to his hotel suite. He gave me a day's notice. It was a test to see if I was really a player. I had to remind him that I still hadn't made my formal proposal. He said I should bring that along with me. It was a fucking afterthought to him.

"I should have brought more water out here with me. Shit, this is the tough part.

"The next day I go up there. A big suite in the Pierre. He had a few rooms attached. I have my papers, a flash drive of the proposal, laptop, folders, brochures, the whole bit, along with a briefcase of cash. He comes to the door in a silk robe. The main room of the suite was a shithole, trays of food laying around, cigars burning in ashtrays. It was clear that men had been trolling around the room for days. They were probably all sent out for my meeting."

Frank turned to Ben for the first time. "By the way, I can smell the cigarette on you. That has to stop; the smell makes me sick." He turned back again toward the river and continued.

"The first thing Marsh does is grab the briefcase. I was sure that the other guys didn't know about the cash deal. It was clear the way he grabbed that briefcase that he wasn't going to be sharing with his crew. He leads me to another room, but as we pass a door, I look in. Phew, fuck, man. I look in, and I see two little girls. I'm talking maybe nine or ten. They're on a chair together. One of them is naked and the other, the bigger one, wearing a hotel robe. She had her arms around the little one. Jesus, to think about it now. I mean I feel embarrassed just to have seen them. I was looking at a naked little girl. And the look, the look on the face of the little one sleeping, God, I can't describe it, just sad as anything I ever saw. I'm telling you, man, to this day it sends a shiver through me. I knew. I knew what he was doing to them. It was like being in a horror movie. Little girls, Jesus."

Frank didn't stop. His face was determined, and his cadence sped up like he was at the steepest part of that ski slope, out of control, careening down the hill.

"Marsh saw my face. That fucking animal, he saw me. I didn't know what to do. We went into the other room, and I fumbled through part of the proposal. I don't even remember. It felt disgusting just being there. Fuck, man. I should have run out and grabbed the girls or called the cops or hotel security or something. Shit, where was I? Damn. I got out of there as soon as I could and called Brogan from the lobby. I remember saying to shut it down, get someone over here; he's fucking little girls. That was it. Not too subtle, I guess, but I didn't know what else to say. Shit, I'm forgetting the order now.

"After I left I think I walked up Fifth to the townhouse. Brogan was there. He told me they all got out of there within minutes, and they took the girls. I think I just sat in one of the back rooms in the dark. It must have been a couple of hours later that Brogan walks in. He tells me there is something I should come see downstairs. There's a shooting range in the basement of the townhouse. You can see it if you want. Let me see. Yeah, he tells me to come with him downstairs.

"Marsh is sitting in a chair. He was trying to get on a private plane at Teterboro Airport. Brogan called the airport and had his private jet grounded. I was so mad that I couldn't even look at the guy. There was something else, though. The guy was so abhorrent that it made my skin crawl just to be close to him. Even now it's a creepy feeling. Also, you gotta understand, Brogan was so heavily involved with children's charities. Kids of nine-eleven victims, cops' kids, firemen, he ran a whole charity for these kids. He was fucking pissed, man. He didn't see it, so he wasn't as creeped out as I was. I guess this is why people like Marsh get away with this stuff. The subject is so disgusting that people don't want to think about it. Not Brogan, though. He didn't fuck around with this guy. He asked where the kids were, and when Marsh didn't respond, he picked up his hand and popped one of his fingers back; I heard it crack. Marsh squealed like a pussy. He started yelling about diplomatic immunity. We can't take away his items; we had no right. His items. His fucking items. I don't remember how long this went on. Two or three more fingers, I guess. He gave up the other guys, where they were.

"It was clear, though, that he didn't have any change of heart. A shit like him wasn't going to change. After he gave them up, he copped an attitude. He had the balls to tell Brogan to his face that he would have him arrested, 'you don't know who I am,' all that shit.

"I remember standing there not caring one bit about all the dramatics. I knew that this motherfucker was going to abuse more kids. There was no doubt in my mind. He had this entitled air about him. He truly felt that these young girls were his possessions; he could do whatever he wanted with them. I turned around and picked up one of the pistols on the deck behind me. I took two sets of earphones and handed one to Brogan and put on my own. Brogan just looked at me. He knew. Marsh is trying to bully me. Daring me, the stupid fuck. Saying I don't have the nerve. I wasn't even listening. It was decided. I loaded the piece, turned around, stood over him, and put two shots in his chest. I put the gun back and went home.

"The only thing Brogan ever said about it was two weeks later. He told me he'd found a home for the girls. That was it."

Ben let out his breath. "Jesus, man, I didn't know."

"Yeah, you didn't know, but you know now, don't you?"

"Yes, I do. When did—"

Frank raised his hand. "No more questions, all right? You asked; I told. That's the end of it. I will say, though, that I've lost a lot of sleep over things I have done in the past or things that have happened but not over that fuck. Let's move on now. You got the time?"

"No, they took my watch."

"I don't know how much time we have. Here it is. We want you to join us. This isn't like a regular job. You're married; you have to keep that in mind. You may be out of town in Europe or on a case without any contact for weeks at a time. I know we are going through a delicate situation now, and with the story I just told. I mean this type of thing comes up very rarely. The Marsh thing was over five years ago. Most of the time we are going over company books, doing research on job candidates, advising about risk management, basic business."

"I don't know, Frank."

"Yeah, I know. You're sitting on a bench at a rehab facility, and I just told you that I killed a guy. I can't change that. What I can say is that after the first six months or so, you'll be working almost exclusively with Kat. I'm going to run the charities and manage our assets. There's a trust fund for the charity work, and I handle Kat and Willy's money and my own portfolio. Have you met Willy?"

"No, I haven't. What is the offer?" Ben took his last gulp of his water.

"Five hundred grand a year, two-year contract. The first five goes into an escrow account as I mentioned."

"Wow. That's a lot of money."

"Like I said, we want you. It is a lot, but this isn't a job; you will be joining us, becoming part of our team. You have to be in one hundred percent."

Ben stood up and stretched. "This isn't easy, man. The offer is great, maybe too good. Are you offering me this much money because of what is happening now? Let's face it. Kat told me that Leandro and Handley had to go. Those were her words. Or it had to be dealt with, I don't remember, but we both know what that means. This is a pretty heavy job you're offering me here."

Frank stood also and walked past Ben to the water's edge. He faced forward as he spoke. "Ben, you're a smart guy. You've spent enough time around some of the more unethical people in the financial industry, so you have a healthy dose of skepticism. That's a good thing for this job. I see that, but you don't have to be involved with this particular case if you don't want. I'd understand. Like I said, we don't bullshit around. I'm not going to pitch you the job. I'm not." He turned toward Ben. "Under the bench is a package. I want you to open it."

"A package?"

"Yes, under the bench."

Ben walked over and squatted down. He reached under the seat of the bench and felt around. He came to an overstuffed envelope attached by Velcro to the seat bottom. He pulled it out with a loud rip.

"What the hell?"

"I had it delivered last night. I put it under the seat this morning before you got here."

"But how?"

"Oh, you would be amazed at what I can get done. Open it."

Ben instinctively looked both ways before opening the package. Frank stood with his arms crossed like Ben was opening a present.

CHAPTER 20

"More coffee, Pap?"

"No, thanks. When are they calling?"

"Should be any minute. I know this was an unusual request, but it is our first hire. Who knows him better than you?" Kat placed the pot back on the table.

"When Mr. Brogan said he may need a favor from me someday, I laughed it off like it was some kind of *Godfather* reference. If I had known the favor was to have coffee with you and Willy, I would have stopped by long ago. By the way, that lobster omelet was amazing."

Willy answered from the kitchen. "Thanks, Pap. I'm trying it out for our brunch menu. You liked, huh?"

"God, yes. How do you do that? Make the eggs so fluffy without the lobster getting dried out? I could try that a hundred times and not get it right, and I like to cook."

Willy walked back in, kissed Kat on the head, and turned to Pap. "You two aren't the only ones with secrets around here. Let me get out of here before the phone rings. I'll see you in a few, babe. Nice meeting you, Pap. I'm assuming we won't meet again." He pulled the dishtowel off his shoulder, wiped his hands, and put out his hand to shake.

Pap took it and smiled. "Not likely. Take care." He waited for the door to close then turned back to Kat. "I can't stay much longer. I've been getting some static lately from the police. I may have to drop off the grid for a while."

Kat was concerned. "Not because of us I hope."

"No, no. I'm involved in other things. Nothing to be concerned about."

"Well, thanks again for coming. I know how hard it can be for you, and I must say that you are nothing like the legend."

"Ha, the legend."

"You see, you're much sweeter than they say. Thanks for all the research on Leandro and Handley."

Pap raised his hand. "No, not a word. Listen, I don't know how I feel about this. I agreed to get this for you based on my respect and gratitude for Mr. Brogan and Frank, but there is no reason for me to know what you're going to do with the information."

"Fine. Not a word."

They sat in silence, waiting for the phone to ring.

CHAPTER 21

B en was surprised when he pulled the item out of the package. "A phone?"

"Yes. Not any phone. It's a satellite phone. I'm not a technical guy. My security team arranged it. One call, that's it. I don't want any chance of the staff here knowing what I'm doing. Dial three-two-eight-two. It is programmed. It will speed dial."

Ben stared down at the device. It was larger than a cell or a smartphone. It was the size of a house phone off the cradle. He looked up at Frank. "Security team?"

Frank smiled. "Just dial."

Ben dialed and listened to the phone chirp and beep its electronic language. It rang twice.

"Hello, Ben."

"Pap? What the hell?"

"Good to hear from you, too, buddy."

"I mean what…why am I calling you?"

"Frank and Kat asked me to take the call. I guess I'm their reference."

"How do you know them? Why didn't you tell me?"

"C'mon, Ben, you know I have to keep my business relationships private. I met Mr. Brogan and Frank about four years ago when I was trying to change my identity. They got it done for me."

"Does anyone else know this?"

"Well, I'm sitting in Kat Wells' kitchen. Her husband made me an omelet."

"Jesus, Pap. Do you work with them? Are you part of the operation?"

"No. I haven't spoken to Frank or Kat in years and probably won't for a long while. I know who they are, though. They're the real deal. You have my word."

Ben turned around and walked back to the bench, leaving Frank alone by the water. "What do you think? I mean you must know how they operate. This Leandro thing and Handley…what's your gut?"

"Ben, this is a much higher plane you're entering now. Decisions like this have to be made. I've wrestled with this myself years ago when I got to this level. I'm backing them on this. I think it's the right thing to do. Handley is too slick. He will get away with it; you know that. I didn't know Sol Landsman, but I know the Handley's of the world. It's the right thing. Ben, I'm timing this call. I gotta hop in a couple of minutes. Time for one more question."

Ben swiveled on the bench, turned his back to Frank, and held his hand over the mouthpiece. "How reliable is Frank?"

Pap paused. "I think he has a good heart, and he's very smart; I don't say that often. But he is an alcoholic. I would use caution around him, but Kat is one of the best you'll ever deal with. Overall it is a good deal as long as you stay close to Kat. Frank won't disappoint her. She's the boss, no matter what he might think. That's it. I have to go. Kat's in the other room. I'm going to call her in and hand the phone over. Take care, buddy."

Ben wanted to ask about his new girl and when they might all get together but thought better of it. Instead he said good-bye. Kat picked up after a couple of seconds.

"It's decision time, Ben. I can't go any further without your answer. Frank made the offer, I'm assuming."

"Yes, he did, but if I'm going to hand over my life to you, I need something more than just a salary. I want an equity stake. I'll need some type of ownership."

Kat grunted her displeasure. She had discussed this with Frank. Frank was for it, she against. They had worked very long and hard to build up the business. It made her uneasy to give away any part of it. Frank reasoned that they would have to expand eventually, and if Ben was as good as they thought, he would likely ask for a stake. He saw it as a sign of strength that Ben would ask.

"All right. This is what I can do. After the second year, when the contract is up, we'll talk about an equity stake. I'll have the contract drawn up that it will be part of the terms of renewal."

It made sense to Ben. If things worked out, he would renew with equity. If not, he wouldn't renew anyway. Either way he had a contract for a half a million a year for the next two years. It would be perfect since he and Randi wanted to start a family. Two years of security was a rare luxury in today's world. He turned and looked over at Frank. He was staring out at the river.

"I'm in, Kat. Let's do it."

"Good, great to have you. Throw the phone into the river, say good-bye to Frank, and get back here. We'll go to Willy's restaurant tonight for dinner. Bring your wife. He's been bragging about the new menu. I've been dying to try it, and I would like to meet your better half." She hung up.

Ben looked down at the phone. He turned it in his hand, end over end, walked over to the river's edge, and threw it into the Hudson. It landed about forty yards in.

"Nice toss," Frank said. He walked back over to the bench and sat. "You in?"

"Yeah."

Frank got up from the bench and walked over. To Ben's surprise, he gave him a hardy hug. Frank sensed the awkwardness of the gesture, released him, and stepped back to give Ben a handshake.

"Sorry about that. The touchy-feely shit in this place must be getting to me. Every day now I'm hugging someone." He chuckled and stepped back a pace. "All right, good. Here's the first rule you need to remember: Kat's the boss. Remember that, and you'll be fine. Go ahead; get out of here. I'll be in touch."

He slapped Ben on the right shoulder then tore up the package in his hand and held it tight in his fist. He turned and started jogging up a hill to the left of the bench, leaving Ben alone by the river. Ben started back to the car.

CHAPTER 22

*G*oddamn, *there's a lot of tail down here,* Vinny Castlenni thought to himself. Dark girls. Nice and thick. He was getting sick of those bitchy skinny girls in New York. *Yeah,* he thought, *this is nice. I could get along fine down here.* He was sitting at a table outside the Cardoza Hotel on Ocean Drive in South Beach.

He was waiting for a man named Guzman to join him for lunch. He got the text from his boss the day before. As promised, there was a flight in his name, a room at the hotel, and a hundred grand in cash in a bag in the room. The job was to spread around the cash and find a guy named Leandro and kill him. Seemed simple enough to Vinny. He knew that cash was the only method to get things done with the type of guys he ran with. A hundred grand should do and leave plenty left over for him. Another text that morning said a man named Guzman would be there around one. It was twenty after. Vinny didn't mind since the table next to him was full with four girls with big asses and small shirts. It must have been a girls' weekend or some shit. He sent over a round and was ready to send another, when some greaseball stood over his table.

"You Mr. Castle?"

"Who the fuck are you?"

"I'm Guzman. You Castle?"

"Yeah. Who's the house behind you?"

"That's funny, man, 'cause his name is House."

Vinny sized them up. Guzman was wearing a nice linen suit. He looked classy, nothing like he would have expected. He'd had some kind of *Scarface* image in his mind, but this guy looked like a Hamptons banker. His buddy,

House, was something else, though. Jesus, the dude was big. He was wearing baggy basketball shorts and shockingly white sneakers that matched his flat-brimmed ball cap. The shoes looked like the latest Jordans. Vinny knew that a lot of dudes stood on line for the latest versions of the shoe, but he didn't see this guy waiting on any line. His polo was painted on, but then Vinny couldn't imagine a shirt that would fit him. There was a layer of fat on the guy, but Vinny was under no false impression. This was a strong motherfucker. He would have to be careful with this one.

"I thought I was meeting just you."

"I don't go anywhere without my man House here." Guzman turned to introduce the man, but he just muttered a "what's up?" and moved toward the table.

"Come on, sit."

Guzman sat, and House moved gracefully around the table to face the street. He grabbed a chair from the table with the four girls and pulled it up and sat. Two of the girls whispered to each other and giggled. House ignored them. Vinny figured he wouldn't have a shot with the girls now that House was there. Guzman waved over a waiter.

"You guys eating? House, you up for a bite?"

House looked over at Vinny, and he could see the nature of their relationship with the one "this guy is a rude fucking asshole" look that House gave him. He asked, "We eating here?"

"Yeah, go ahead; order what you want."

They ordered, a steak for House and some kind of seafood salad for Guzman. Vinny had a beer.

They ate in silence and watched the girls walk by. They had all done this before. They each knew their roles. No need for small talk. Vinny ordered a second beer as they were finishing.

"I'm here to find a guy named Leandro. You know him?"

Guzman did the talking for them. House crossed his massive arms and looked straight ahead.

"Yeah, I know him, but he's a private guy."

Vinny was getting tired of sitting there. "How much?"

"How much what?"

"C'mon, man, I don't have time for bullshit. How much will it take to give him up? I want to get out of here and back to New York."

"You got cash?" Guzman leaned back and pulled out a cigarette. When he put it to his lips, Vinny reached out, yanked it out, and threw it onto the street. He didn't give a shit if the guy smoked. It was a test to see what House would do. He was getting an idea.

House put a hand on Vinny's arm but nothing more. "Hey, man. What the fuck?"

"I don't like smoke." Vinny pulled an envelope out of his pants pocket and put it on the table. It was crumpled and a little sweaty. It was also filled with hundreds, ten grand worth.

House picked it up and looked inside. He used his thumb to shuffle through the crisp bills. He nodded to Guzman and closed his hand around it. The envelope disappeared except for a small frame of white around his big black hand. Guzman took out another smoke. He didn't put it to his mouth; he twirled it around in his hand.

"I know the dude. Yeah, I can get him here for you. I'm gonna need another envelope, though."

"I see him, you get another."

"Let me make a call." Guzman got up and buttoned his jacket even though it was about ninety degrees. Vinny took it for what it was, a signal to House. House raised up in his chair to slide the envelope into his hip pocket. Guzman walked to the back of the hotel lobby and out of sight. Vinny knew he had to talk fast.

"You guys gonna jack me, right?"

House put his elbows on the table and leaned in. "Yup."

"You're a smart guy. You think I came down here from New York without anyone knowing where I am? I figure you got a choice here. You pop me for a few grand and spend the rest of the year running from New York guineas, or you let me pop the greaseball, and you keep the cash. You kill me, and you're getting yourself into some deep shit. My people won't stand for it. Guzman there is gonna get you in trouble."

House didn't respond. He was waiting for a better deal. Vinny looked over House's shoulder to the lobby. No sign of Guzman.

"I like it here. I like the girls. I can do some things here. You got a pipeline to New York? What are you running? Coke, reefer? I got some guys up there using a distributer from around these parts. Ripping them off. They would be open to a sit down. This asshole is beneath you. You see it."

House didn't answer. He looked at Vinny and smiled. Guzman came back to the table, hopping on his tiptoes. Vinny could tell he had snorted a couple of lines in the bathroom. The fuck was a street hood, no more.

"The man you want is being sent over to my office. It's a few blocks. Want to head over?"

"Sure, let's go." Vinny got up and looked over at House. House winked.

They turned left on Ocean and headed north. At the Betsy Hotel, Guzman said, "Over here. My place is around the back."

They walked alongside the hotel, Guzman in front and House in the back, boxing Vinny in. They came to a spot that was out of sight of the street and not yet around the back of the hotel. Guzman stopped and turned; he smiled over Vinny's shoulder.

It was a narrow walkway, and House came up behind Vinny. He said, "Excuse me," and Vinny pressed himself against the cool whitewashed wall to let him get by. House walked past Vinny and faced Guzman.

"What the fuck you doin', House?" Guzman said.

House smashed his head against the wall. He used such force that the side of Guzman's head stuck there. House let go, and Guzman slumped but didn't fall. His head held up his body, and his eyes were open. He was dead; Vinny could see that.

House turned to Vinny. "C'mon, my car is around the block." He squeezed past him and headed to the street.

As he hustled around the corner, Vinny pulled out his phone and took a picture of Guzman stuck in the wall.

CHAPTER 23

The day after sending Mr. Castle to Florida, Carter Handley received a text from him with a picture attached: a man with his head stuck in a wall. Handley could see that his head was crushed flat. The man was dead. The copy with the text read: "Leandro/Simmons/Guzman."

Handley wasn't aware that Leandro had a third alias, but it was reasonable to assume so, considering his line of work. He wished he had a picture of Leandro to confirm his identity, but this was all he had to go with. Mr. Castle, and Lefty before him, had been very reliable to this point. He didn't have any reason to doubt the claim. Handley decided that the best course of action would be to believe the claim but keep his contacts on the ground in Miami. It would be an ongoing expense but worth it. The shot clearly was taken shortly after the incident. There was very little blood, and the body hadn't dropped from the wall yet. Mr. Castle had killed him. He just wished he could be sure it was his man, although he couldn't figure an angle for Mr. Castle to lie. He had always been reliable and never took money without finishing the job. Handley couldn't imagine the man would be stupid enough to rip him off for a hundred grand.

He had a bigger problem to deal with at the moment. Someone had breached his security settings. As the CEO of the largest credit card and financial services company in America, Carter Handley had the most elaborate encrypted privacy settings on the planet. The encryptions were updated randomly throughout the day on a loop algorithm. His service had never gone down in twenty-five years until two days before. He received a call from the service provider that there was an interruption for less than a second at 4:23 in the afternoon. The provider explained that it was most likely a surge in one of the servers that his settings were randomly bounced to. Handley knew different. With the Leandro, Mr. Castle, and Landsman thing going on, this was no coincidence. He was well versed enough in the technology to assume that this was intentional.

Handley knew that there were only two people who would have the ability to breach him. One was Sheng, the hacker for the Chinese Red Army. The other was the mysterious Pap Martinez. It would be difficult and costly to speak to the Chinese on this. It could be done—anything could be done—but it would cost millions. Many millions. He'd push that button if he had to. There was too much at stake. The Libyan and Iraqi sovereign funds they managed—and the money they pulled out as the regimes collapsed—the offshore accounts, the many fixers he'd paid under the table over the years…no, this had to be stopped now. For the sake of expediency, he decided to go after Martinez first. He put his demographic research team on Martinez. It didn't take long for them to come back with their results. Nothing. The man no longer existed. Handley had figured as much. He called the outside investigative firm they used to research hedge funds or other companies that Axis might have an interest in; they had nothing for him. He tried private investigative teams, American hackers, one of which laughed at the name Martinez and the possibility of ever finding him. After an afternoon of pounding the phone and racking up fees, he had nothing on Pap Martinez.

Handley sat in his office and waited. He waited for the clock to read 8:00 p.m. He looked at the Picasso; he thought of the villa, the yacht, the young women, and the idea that he could lose all of it. At exactly 8:00 p.m., he dialed the phone. It was 8:00 a.m. in China, and Handley knew that Huang Jao would be in his office. The phone rang nine times before it was picked up.

"Carter?"

"Yes, Huang, thank God you're there."

The man spoke in stilted English. "Carter, my friend, what is the trouble? You sound distressed." Huang sat back in his chair behind his large desk. As the finance minister, he was one of the most powerful men in the country. He was also a degenerate gambler and drinker. Handley had been picking up his debts in Vegas for years, along with providing many other services that would be frowned upon among the communist elite.

"Huang, I need your help. I fear my company may go under any day now." Handley purposely started with the worst case since Huang had steered billions into Axis bonds and held a large equity stake. All told, the Chinese investment into Axis Financial came to around 5 percent of the company's value, all of it placed by Huang himself.

"Carter, Carter, how can this be? Surely, you are being a little dramatic."

"No, Huang, I'm afraid not. Someone hacked into my system. You know the contacts I have, the deals that have been made over the years."

Huang answered in a panic, "You are calling on your office number?"

"Don't worry; everything's rebooted. There hasn't been a breach since. We both know that there aren't many people who could have broken my code."

Huang anticipated the next sentence. "I don't know how I can help you."

"Yes, you do, Huang; I need to contact Sheng."

"I'm afraid that would be impossible. Sheng is not to speak to anyone outside of the country. You must know that."

"Yes, I know, but this must be an exception. I don't care if it was your group behind it. I will pay. I need to know who it was. You have placed a lot of your government's money into my company. The stock will get killed if any of this gets out, but once I know I can take care of it, the stock will be fine. Please, Huang, I need this."

"You said that not many people could have broken my code. Who else do you have in mind?

"Pap Martinez."

"I've never heard the name. Still, my friend, I don't think I can help."

Handley didn't have time go through the bribe song and dance. "Ten million. Your fee to speak to him."

"Carter, please, it is not necessary."

"Huang, I need this to happen today. I don't have time."

"I will see if I can make contact with him. You can send the funds to my account."

"I'm sending now. Please, Huang, I'm counting on you."

"I will call soon."

Handley spent the next hour pacing his office. He jumped when the phone rang.

"Yes, yes."

"Carter, my friend, you are in luck. First, let me assure you that it is not us that have broken into your system. Sheng has confirmed this, but he is very excited to take on this assignment. It seems Mr. Martinez is something of a rival. It is beyond me, of course, that anyone can rival Sheng, but he seemed quite anxious to take on the task. Of course, Sheng is a very valuable person in our country. His time is of great importance. He thinks he could get to it in a month or so."

Handley saw it for what it was. Huang was squeezing him after years of his bailing him out. After supplying him with cocaine, girls, anything he could ever need, along with the Axis stock doing better than the S&P for the time he had been invested in it. Huang had heard his desperation and seized on the opportunity. Handley wondered if he knew it was the opportunity of his lifetime. He quickly had his answer.

"The expense will, of course, far exceed our usual arrangement."

"I'll go fifty million."

"If you want your information in a week or so, that would suffice, but I believe you mentioned today as your timeframe."

"Can Sheng get me what I need?"

"Carter, you know Sheng can get you anything. Any piece of information in this world is at the touch of this remarkable man's fingertips."

Handley felt like saying that Sheng was a hacker, not a mystic, but he had always allowed his Chinese friends' cultural references to the sublime. "I need to know where Pap Martinez is right now. Tonight. I'll also need some men to pick him up and sit on him for me. Can you deliver?"

"Yes, I believe I can. One hundred million."

"Dear God, Huang, how can I come up with that?"

"My friend, I know the funds you have access to. I'm afraid it is not negotiable. Sheng is quite insistent on his fee. I will need my fee plus a premium for the risk I'm taking on. This is not something that my superiors will take kindly to should this be exposed. Yes, I think one hundred will be the price."

Handley took a deep breath. "Okay."

"Fantastic. Sheng will send you an account number to transfer the funds.

Once received, he will get to the task. I would expect you will hear something by your early morning."

"And some men. I need some good men for this."

"Yes, of course. I must go now. You will be contacted shortly with the information. I must say my good-byes to you, I'm afraid. Sheng was quite insistent. This will be the end of our relationship. Good-bye, my friend."

Huang hung up without waiting for a reply. The moment Handley hung up, he received a text with an account number. He opened his laptop and punched in the numbers.

It would be a long night. Handley had to make plans for Martinez and talk to his attorneys about damage control—should anything come out.

CHAPTER 24

"Three days this motherfucker has been partying," House grumbled to himself. He was with him the whole way up to previous day. Man, the dude loved to drink and fuck. He liked him some big ass also. What the hell? The dude was throwing down cash, so House rode with it. He knew lots of girls. They liked to smoke that rock and weren't shy about how to get it. They partied straight through the night after he killed Guzman. They started at the Ritz, where the dude was staying, then to a couple of clubs and on to one of his girls' pads. Lena. She brought her friends in. House had had his share of pussy, so he got out of there. Too much drama with them bitches. Vinny loved it. House ain't never seen a white boy party like that. He was sure now that he would never get into business with the man. He talked too much and too loud when he was drunk, and it looked like he drank a lot.

House was in his apartment over a spent bowl of weed. The shit was kicking in. He was tired and thought he might sleep a little before heading out. The place was packed up and wiped clean. That night he would go over to Guzman's stash house, clean it out then head West. He had called a guy out there he'd played ball with at the U. The dude said he could crash for a week or so. That was all House would need. Guzman had at least a million and a half in the safe. Stupid fuck blurted out one night that the combination was his prison number during his last stint. House figured Guzman had never heard of the Internet or more likely thought he was too stupid to look it up. Well, who was stupid now?

He lay back on the couch and let the weed mellow him. He did love getting high; it was the only time he could let his mind go, let the thoughts come in and out as they wished. At times it wasn't pleasant. His thoughts could be dark when he got into a funk. Despite having Coltrane on and the AC cranking, this high was one of the dark times.

House thought about the game. The fucking game. There were times after thinking about it that his knee hurt for weeks. It was a long time ago, but the old pain came back. He had been left tackle for the University of Miami. It was the last regular-season game before the Sugar Bowl. The draft people had him going late in the first round. Had an agent and everything. Two more games before the paycheck, the green for all the work he'd put in. He did work, harder than at anything before or since. He'd been playing ball his whole life. One fat fuck, that's all it took. They were trouncing Boston College forty-seven to three. Coach should have taken him out, but then who really cares about a lineman? House was in there. They called him Big House then, Carlton "Big House" Williams. The fat fuck was on the ground; his boy André, the center, had pancaked him like a bitch. He lay there like his daddy had slapped him down. Then he rolled. That fat fuck rolled up on House. His foot got stuck in the turf, and House couldn't pull it out. For a second he could feel the entire weight of the fat fuck on his kneecap. Then came the snap. The sound House would never forget. The memory of which made him jerk to attention through the fog of his high on the couch. The memory of that sound that would make his knee ache for the next week or so. The snap then the bend of his knee backward. Folded right up. The way it wasn't supposed to. He remembered lying there and looking down at his leg. It was bent in a forty-five-degree angle, like a broken leg of a G.I. Joe he'd played with as a kid. He knew then he was done.

House got up from the couch and walked over to his balcony. His knee made the clicking sound it did after he sat for too long. He looked at his watch. He had dozed for a half hour or so. His place was a few blocks from the beach. He couldn't see sand, but he had a nice view of the Atlantic. House watched a cruise ship slowly creep north, rubbed his face, and turned to go get his money.

Guzman's stash house was up in North Beach on Seventy-Eighth. House had the key. He went into the little bungalow, and it was like an oven. No window had been open for days. There was a dead rodent somewhere in the place. The place smelled of decay. House went directly to the kitchen and the fridge. Inside he found the safe. He hadn't thought to bring a bag, so he rummaged around under the sink a bit and came upon a plastic drugstore bag. He laid it out flat on the floor in front of the fridge.

After a quick few turns of the dial and one snap of the handle, the safe swung open. There was less cash then House would have liked. From the looks of the stacks, it was maybe a couple hundred grand. Instead of more cash there were two bricks of coke, packed tight and wrapped in plastic with gray tape around them. Guzman must have been in the middle of a transaction. House thought about packing them but decided against it. He didn't want the hassle of trying to sell the shit. He knew some guys, but it would set him back a few days. Fucking Guzman, still fucking him.

After packing the cash into the plastic bag, he wrapped the handles around the piles and held the package in one hand. House grabbed a sour dishtowel that was hanging over the edge of the sink and wiped down the safe inside and out.

He went to the front door and turned around to make sure he didn't leave anything behind. He turned the door handle with the dishtowel in his hand and started singing his favorite song. "I'm gonna rock that bitch up and down the coast…"

There were two unmarked cop cars out front, parked nose to nose. Four cops were leaning on the hoods and pointing their guns at the front door. It took a second for House to realize what was happening.

One of the cops yelled at him, "Put your hands in the air!"

House dropped the bag, put his hands up, and responded, "Motherfucker!"

CHAPTER 25

K at brought it up as they were going through the Prime Equities account. It was decided early in the discussions that Ben would be the lead on this account since he and Sol Landsman had had a good working relationship. Most of the people at Prime were familiar with Ben. She casually changed the subject.

"We still don't have anything on Sol's killer."

"Have you spoken to Pap?"

"No, not since his phone call with you. Can you contact him?"

"When we hung up, he said he was going to be out of touch for a while. That means he's changing all his contact information. He does it once every six months or so. I'm sure I'll hear from him soon."

"We can't wait. I don't want this guy to slip away. Frank has everything on Carter Handley."

"From Pap?"

"From Pap, yes, and some of his own sources. You weren't his only visitor in the last few days. He knows a few guys over at the NSA. We know where Handley will be. There's a plan for that. There was a text on Handley's phone. It shows a picture of a guy with his head smashed in. The copy says, "Leandro/Simmons/Guzman." We had the local police check it out. The victim was Pedro Guzman, a local dirt bag. Pot dealer, hustler. The text came from Vinny Castlenni, a known organized-crime hitter. With his tie to Handley, he's the probable killer of Walter Peterson, the president of Axis Financial. You read about that?"

"Yeah."

"Of course, we can't use any of this in court, but Handley is a bad guy. We had the police pick up Castlenni and Guzman's guy, named Carlton Williams, known as House. Big guy with a scary rep on the streets. We won't get anything from Castlenni about Leandro. He clearly didn't know him since he sent the deceptive text. Pap was right about his address and his daily routine, but he hasn't been seen in two days. There was a shooting reported in his neighborhood, along his workout route. I figure Handley tried to silence him, the hit failed, and Castlenni was sent down there to clean it up. This House guy, he may know. Guzman was a small timer, but from what I hear he knew the scene in South Beach better than most. House has been with him a few years. I'm betting House knows something. I want you to go down there and find out what he knows."

"Yeah, sure. When?"

"Fly out tonight. You can see him in the morning."

"Okay. Why me?"

"You're an interrogator, aren't you? This is going to be one of your roles with us from this day forward. We are counting on it."

"What are my parameters? How much control do I have? I mean are there Miranda rights to consider? I've never gone in without a consultation with an attorney."

Kat smiled. She sat back in her chair. "No attorneys on this one. You can do whatever you want. The governor has been contacted. Make up anything; threaten anything. Whatever. You have broad discretion."

"I have to ask. I guess you will show me eventually, but how do you have all these contacts?"

Kat took her laptop and tilted it as an invitation for Ben to come to her desk and view it. He stared over as she typed. He leaned in. Kat pointed the cursor at the top of the screen as if she was about to do a PowerPoint presentation. She clicked a file folder, and a list scrolled down the screen.

"I put this together a few years ago. I have all of Brogan's and Frank's and my contacts on one page. Everything is cross referenced. I want to plug in yours soon. I can plug in a piece of data, a name, a place, and see what the connection is. Here, let me show you. When I got Leandro's address from Pap, I plugged in 'South Beach, Miami.' This is what came up." She typed the word and hit enter.

"Here it is. Brogan trained the attorney general of Broward County at the Justice Department in 1981. He did that for a time, Brogan. Also we have that Frank bailed out the chief of Miami Police ten years ago. He wasn't the chief then, but he was married. He had a bit to drink and slapped a stripper. Frank was there on a consulting job about compliance with new federal regulations. We save all of this, and when we need something, we use it. I put in a call to the chief. He'll let you do whatever you feel is necessary."

Ben smiled. "Can I follow up on threats or promises?"

"I guess this is where I should give you some kind of warning or guidance, but I don't have any. It's not something I do for the group. I would think that you would have more discretion with the threats than the promises. There's only so much we can deliver."

Ben thought about Frank and the fixer. He also realized that this was the first time he had thought about it since meeting with Frank. He had already given himself permission to act as Frank did since he knew he would have done the same thing to that animal.

"I would like the police to put him, this House guy, in solitary until I arrive. Let's shake him up a bit. Do you have much information on him?"

"He has quite a file. Go home and pack. The flight is at eight-forty. A car will pick you up at six-thirty. I'll arrange a morning interview for you. The file will be in the car when they get you."

"Do I tell my wife where I'm going?"

"Your choice. I found that Willy stopped asking after a while. You have to have trust, right?"

"Yeah, I guess. How long do you think?"

"Shouldn't be more than a day or so."

Ben stood and started gathering his belongings.

Kat waved him over to the desk and leaned in. "We have to get the location of Leandro. Do whatever it takes. Are we clear? And be careful. I hear that this House character is supposed to be a tough guy."

"Get him into solitary. I'll call you with the information tomorrow."

CHAPTER 26

B en looked around the room and thought that nothing in his career had ever looked like it did in the movies except for right then. The interrogation room was right out of a Hollywood B movie—gray cement walls with a mirror on one of them and a green table bolted to the floor. There were two chairs, both of which had the yellow stuffing coming out of the seats.

Despite the décor, Ben was thrilled to be there. He was getting a little antsy sitting in the office of the townhouse with Kat. She was very particular about how she wanted things done. After the first day Ben decided to stop asking her questions and just wrote down her instructions. He figured there would be more important disagreements in the future. Why spend whatever goodwill he had as the new guy on office procedure?

He had spent the night reading up on Mr. Williams. Up until then Ben had interrogated only business types. He did have someone who was assumed to be a connected guy in a room once, but the guy ended up being a poseur. He wasn't even Italian. This would be his first sit down with a real criminal. Well, a violent criminal at least. He was looking forward to it.

Ben always had a plan going into an interrogation. Most of the time it was about money and how he could take it away from the suspect. This wouldn't be the case here. He had a theory about Williams. The research Kat provided was much more comprehensive than anything he had ever received working for the SEC. He had Williams's high school and college transcripts, football scouting report, and most of his standardized test scores. The one consistent piece of data about Williams was that he was a bully. There was a string of fights and suspensions during his school years, and after school he became muscle for various dirt bags in South Florida. Williams had acquired quite a rap sheet in the past ten years or so. Most of the charges were for assault. He was a head buster; he fucked guys up. Lately the cycle of violence had escalated. Williams was a hardcore killer at this point.

Ben had had his fill of bullies by the time he entered high school. He was short and had a wise mouth, which made him a natural target. He knew how to handle a guy like Williams. Ben had made sure to get the police chief's permission to run a scam on him. Before he went into the room, he'd planned it with the officers on duty.

The door opened, and a mountain walked in, escorted by two burly cops. Williams was shackled around the hands and ankles. He gave Ben a look that was intended to intimidate. Ben guessed it had worked many times before. He made sure to look back like he didn't give a shit. It wasn't easy.

The cops leaned on Williams's shoulders and pushed him down into the seat. He didn't take his eyes off of Ben. He sat, and they linked the wrist and ankle shackles to a single chain and locked it to an industrial-looking bolt on the floor. The cops stepped back with arms crossed on their chests. Ben opened a folder.

"You can go, guys, thank you."

They looked at each other and then back at him. One of the cops, the senior man, gave Ben an "are you fucking kidding me?" look. Ben smiled. The guy was a natural actor.

"It's okay. Go ahead. Mr. Williams and I are going to have a chat."

They turned and walked out.

The moment the door closed, Williams jerked as hard as he could against the chains. For a second it looked like they would snap. His arms were enormous. They flexed, and Ben noticed a tattoo of a Chinese character under his bicep.

"What's the tattoo say?"

"It says, 'fuck you.'"

Ben couldn't help himself; he snorted a quick laugh. Williams didn't look amused. He tried to pull at the chains again, enraged by Ben's laughter. He let up and leaned back in his chair. Ben looked down at his notes.

"You left the safe open. How stupid was that? All that coke in there, and you didn't think to close the safe behind you. You could have danced around the money, got yourself a lawyer who would have said that Guzman was your buddy. That you were just picking up some cash, say that you didn't know he was dead. Hey, you have a key. No one saw you smash his head against the wall except for your pal Vinny down the hall."

House looked up.

"Oh, yeah. We have Vinny. I'll tell you, that guy likes to talk. He says he saw you do it. He was shocked. Shocked by the violence."

House stayed back in his chair and rolled his head back then around. "That motherfucker must be high. Coming up with that shit."

"Yeah, maybe he is. It doesn't matter, though. The safe. That one little mistake is going to cost you thirty years. Stupid."

House glared at him. Ben glared back dispassionately and looked down at his file. "What do you know about Vinny?"

House didn't answer. Ben flipped some pages for effect. He pretended to read from the third page.

"Vinny Castlenni, alias Mr. Castle. Five arrests, armed robbery, assault, the usual rap sheet. Lately he's been moving up in the world, working for some high-profile clients. He's big league now. I'm wondering what he's doing running with the likes of you and Guzman."

"You ain't a cop."

Ben ignored him. He turned back to the top page of his file. "The police here don't care that much about your usual victims—the drug dealers, snitches, small-time hoods who have disappeared over the years. They know all about the noose, the hangings. Hey, some of them would like to pat you on the back. Let me ask. Did you purposely hang only the guys that you knew the cops wouldn't give a shit about?"

House leaned forward and picked up the glare again. "What the fuck are you talking about?"

Ben picked it up. The smile of gratification. Williams was proud of it; he did only kill the guys who the cops wouldn't care about. He knew what he was doing. Then an idea hit Ben like a slap.

"Do you have a friend in the Miami Police Department?"

House smiled wider and answered gently, "I have lots of friends. I'm an independent contractor, says so right on my business card."

Ben chuckled, crossed his arms, and leaned away from that big head. "That's why you're so cool, sitting here like you have it all figured out. Yeah, I see. There's a problem, though. You're right; I'm not a cop. No one is going to save you from me. You see, you should be more careful about how you select your friends. This Vinny, he's not that smart. He sent a text with a photo attached. The photo was of Guzman stuck in that wall. I know what you're thinking, and you're right: there's no sign of you in the shot, but you have a problem that no one in this police department is going to help you with. I'm here because of the man who received that photo."

Williams sat back and for the first time had a look of concern on his face. Ben stood up and walked over to the door. He banged on it twice. The two cops came back in.

Ben turned to House and spoke with his back to the cops. "One of you, I don't care which, take out your service revolver and put it in Mr. Williams's mouth."

There was silence.

"Do it now!" Ben screamed.

House jumped in his seat. One of the cops walked past Ben with his gun drawn.

House said, "Man, you gotta—" and the gun went in his mouth. The sound of his teeth scraping against the metal was like nails on a chalkboard, and House winced. Ben walked over to the table and put both hands on top, spread wide.

"You think your bullshit badass act is going to work here? With me? You'll do as I ask, and you'll like it. Or I'll have your fat fucking head blown off. Do you understand?"

House nodded slightly. The room was silent, and the cop with the gun turned to his partner, asking with his eyes what to do. Ben was counting to ten in his head. He looked at Williams and saw every stupid bully of the past, all the big Italians and Irishmen. At the silent ten, he turned to the cop at the door.

"You guys can go."

The cop with the gun let out a sigh and walked out quickly. He didn't wait for the other, and the door slammed.

Ben looked at the remaining cop and said, "It's okay."

The cop stared at him and waited then turned out.

"What the fuck?" House bellowed.

Ben sat back in his chair. "I'm not a cop. I don't care about the drugs or the money or Guzman. The man who received that text with the picture is going to kill you if I don't. You were put in solitary for your protection. You're as good as dead if you're outside that cell. I'm the only man who can save you. As you can see, I run the cops. I run the mayor. You're not getting any help from anyone. You're on your own now. You've gotten yourself into some very heavy business. This isn't a job for an independent contractor."

"What do you want?"

"I want the location of John Leandro, the man that Vinny was looking for. Now don't think about bullshitting me. I read your file. You know every dirt bag in this town. I want to know where he is. I want to know before I leave this room. Or I'll put you with the rest of the population. The man who got that text is going to have you killed today. Someone in this jail knows who you are and has a shiv or a knife with your name on it. Vinny is as good as dead also. But fuck him. He doesn't have the information I need."

House shifted in his seat. Ben could see that the thought of ratting was hard for him to get his head around but not as hard as getting a gun shoved in his mouth. Ben had been right about him; he was a survivor.

"If I know and I tell you, how do I know that you won't let me die anyway?"

"You don't have much of a choice. I will find Leandro eventually. It may take time, but I will find him. You have no leverage. I just want to get this over with and move on to other business. You let me know, and I'll take care of you."

"This is bullshit, man. I tell you, and you have what you want. Where does that leave me?"

"I gave you my word. I'll take care of you. You give me what I need, and I'll have you put back in solitary until I can track it down. If I get my man, we'll talk then. That's your deal. You talk, or you die today."

House slumped his shoulders and put his head down. He took three very deep breaths.

"Your man was shot. Got his ear blown off. There's a doctor, a dentist really, that guys go to when they get fucked up. He's got an office in a house."

"Where?"

"I don't know the name of the street. Get me a map. I can show you."

After gathering the information, Ben left the room and called Kat. She put him on hold and called a number to send a team to check out the place. Ben wondered if he would ever have access to all these resources but instead asked if he should stay down there. Kat said to get back home to cover the office because she would have to make a trip the next day. She didn't say where, and Ben got the impression that he shouldn't ask. He assumed that as he headed to New York, she would be heading down to Miami. He went back to the interrogation room to give Williams his final instructions.

"I'm going to put you back in solitary. Don't speak to anyone. I'll get word to you if the information pans out. If not, you're on your own."

House nodded, and as Ben turned to get the officers, House asked him, "What's your name?"

Ben looked down at him and smiled. "It says right on your tattoo. My name is Fuck You."

CHAPTER 27

The house was on SW Second Street in Boca Raton. Kat sat in her rental across Ninth Avenue with the gun in her hand. The team was parked along the side of the house. They were in a white van. Three men, professionals from North Carolina. Frank had given Kat their contact information. These men weren't in her files. Kat had called them while she had Ben on hold the other day. They could have taken Leandro out the previous night after getting the keys and alarm code from the owner. Kat didn't ask how they got them, only that they wait for her to make the move. They agreed to be her backup but gave her a short leash. Kat had the impression that they liked to do things on their own and weren't thrilled with having a woman give orders. She had two minutes to get in and out. Then they would enter.

The men didn't get the information until late the night before, so Kat got the briefing around 2:00 a.m. She had been awake since. The men had staked out the location that same night, and they agreed that four-thirty in the morning would be the best time to move. There was no street traffic and no city cameras in the area.

The car clock read 4:28. Kat picked up the gun and balanced it in her hand. It had been a while. She had been a cop in Telluride, Colorado, for ten years. She had grown up in the town and never wanted to leave. After four years at the University of Colorado, she'd returned to Telluride and signed up for the only open job she could find. She started in administration at police headquarters. After she had hounded the chief for over a year, he let her enroll in the academy in Denver. She graduated with top honors.

The gun was a Glock 17, lighter and more powerful than the Smith and

Wesson she had used on patrol twelve years before. She had used a similar gun during her practice rounds in the shooting range in the basement of the townhouse before she left. She was comfortable with the piece. This would be the first time she would enter a hostile environment since she got the scar. That time she walked in unprepared with her gun holstered. The mistake almost killed her. It wouldn't happen again.

Kat got out of the car and gently closed the door. She walked straight across the avenue with the gun lowered at her thigh. There wasn't a car in sight. It was dark, but morning was coming. Kat had adjusted to the light while sitting in the car, so she maneuvered with ease. She walked along the sidewalk next to the house. The dentist's office was in the back. Kat walked through the small parking lot behind the building and went up the stairs to the back door. She turned toward the van and assumed that the count had begun. Two minutes, no time for second thoughts.

Kat took the key out of her pocket, put it in the lock, and turned. Nothing happened; the key didn't budge. She jiggled it and pinched her fingers to lift the key within the slot, as she was told, and it turned. She swung the door open slowly and went immediately to the alarm. Its green light was blinking slowly and making the keyboard light up intermittently. Kat punched in the code in rhythm with the flashing light. It went out.

She raised the Glock to shoulder height, with the barrel pointed up, and stood silent. There was nothing to be heard. She didn't have a layout of the office but knew there was only room enough for a small reception area and two examining rooms. The dimly lit reception area was ahead of her, and there was a hallway to her left. She looked left and saw that the hallway bent to the right, likely circling back to the reception area. The rooms would be interior since the hall had two windows looking out to the parking lot. She started down the hallway with one silent step in front of the other. The doors to the rooms were around the corner, so she was going around the corner blind. The hall got darker as she walked, and Kat started to get anxious that Leandro could come at her out of the dark. Once she turned the corner, there was a little light seeping out of the doorway in front of her. She ran her hand along the wall as a guide, and she approached the first room. The light under the door seemed to be dimmed as if it were from a child's nightlight. She took a breath and held the gun up to her face, finger on the trigger. Kat turned the knob and gently pushed the door open. The room was empty. No dentist chair, nothing.

Kat left the door open and quickly rushed to the second door. There was no light underneath. She opened it quickly and squatted down with her arms extended, gun pointed forward. She heard movement and reached up with her left hand to find a light switch. The first side of the door had no switch, and the movement in front of her accelerated. She could make out the shadow of a body on a dentist's chair. It started rolling away from her toward the back wall. The other side of the door had a switch, and Kat flipped it. The light was bright and shocking. There were purple dots before her eyes, and she squinted like she were driving into the sun. The body moved toward her, and she shot. He went down at her feet.

Kat adjusted to the light and looked down. Leandro was lying at her feet, curled in a ball. She had hit him in the gut. He had gauze wrapped around his head. A large bloodstain was spreading out on the right side. He must have banged his head on the floor. Suddenly he started pulling at her left ankle, trying to take her down. She kicked him in the stomach with her right foot, and he screamed and writhed away from her. Kat held the gun out toward his bloody head.

He gurgled to her, "Handley, that fuck. You're from Handley, right?"

She didn't answer.

"Who sent you? I want to know. Who sent you? You fucking cunt."

"A little old lady named Esther sent me." He looked at her puzzled, and she shot him twice in the face.

Kat turned out of the room and headed back down the hall toward the exit. As she opened the door, the men were heading toward the stairs. As instructed, she handed the gun to one of them and walked back to her car. She got in and drove off. She had a flight to catch. She was having tea with Esther Landsman that afternoon.

CHAPTER 28

Pap wondered why he had bought a hot cup of coffee at Starbucks since it was such a blazing hot morning. He tried to walk smoothly as to not sweat in his new shirt. He had taken to fashion quickly since he met Caitlin. She worked for a young designer and was on him constantly to upgrade his wardrobe. Until a few months before, his idea of a fashion statement was a new Brooks Brothers button down. He wasn't quite ready for some of the things she threw his way, but he could see that changing. Damn, he loved her. He knew it, and it scared him. Pap wasn't sure how much to tell her about himself and the things he did.

Lost in thought, he didn't notice the black Mercedes van slowly crawling alongside him. Pap was walking east on Twenty-Third, heading into the office. Two men approached him straight on. Both were wearing black suits with white shirts and black ties. They had sunglasses and were Asian. Pap stopped since they were blocking his path. He adjusted his stride to try to walk around them, thinking that this was one of those odd New York moments when you practically dance with a fellow pedestrian, trying to walk around him. He moved, and they did. This time there was no awkward chuckle as they almost collided. The men stepped up tight into him. Was he getting mugged?

"Hey."

One of the men spoke. "Mr. Martinez, would you please come with us?"

They knew his name. For a second Pap was panicked. Before he changed his identity, he had had extensive training for such a matter. He was sure that they were going to take him.

He relaxed his shoulders and smiled at the men. "I'm sorry, gentlemen, but

I have an appointment."

"Please, I must insist."

The man took him by the arm and squeezed his elbow. Pap tried to shake him off, unsuccessfully. He thought about making a scene. His training kicked in, and he calmed himself, knowing that his phone and the chip embedded in his hip would help his security team track him. Now he regretted letting his security man go. It had been four years since he changed identities, and he hadn't seen the need for him—until now, of course.

Pap started thinking analytically. Only Sheng could have found him. There wouldn't be a ransom demand. Pap reasoned that this would be political, or there would be some kind of business angle to this. Sheng was deeply committed to the communist cause. He was into the whole "world domination" thing. Pap had met him once at a gaming conference in Orlando. He was a nasty little shit. Pap decided to cooperate. His thoughts immediately went to Nube, his startup. Years of work might have been flushed down the drain as he stood there. Fucking Sheng, he had the ability to wipe Pap's database clean. Pap took a deep breath and tried to settle his mind. The last thing he wanted was to panic. His trainer compared these moments to getting lost in the woods. If he panicked, he would only get lost deeper in the brush. If he remained calm, a path would appear.

"Okay, guys. Where are we going?"

One of the men took his coffee cup and tossed it perfectly five yards into a can. They walked him over to a black Mercedes van. One of the men banged on the side of it with his fist. The back door opened, and they walked Pap over to it. As well trained as he was, Pap couldn't help but be a little scared. Something about being thrown into the back of a van didn't sit well with his idea of how this would go. Maybe he had seen too many movies, but he had thought that if something like this ever happened to him, he would be whisked away in a limo that led to a private jet, where a man with an eye patch and a scruffy gray beard awaited him.

He was helped up into the van, and it took off quickly. The back of the van had been refitted. There was a padded bench facing outward toward the back doors, where two men sat. One had on the same suit as the men in the street; the other had a white lab coat over his identical suit. Pap was nudged up to one of the side benches with a man at his side. The other, who had spoken on the street, sat across from him and addressed him again.

"Please remove all of your clothing."

"What? My clothing? What are you talking about?"

"Please, sir."

Pap was about to get loud, when he was nudged on his side by the man next to him. He turned toward the man.

"What the hell?" Pap shut up. The man was nudging him with a gun. For a second Pap got lightheaded, and his back was immediately soaked with sweat. "What is this? What is this about?"

"Your clothes, sir."

Pap stripped. When he got to his underwear and socks, he stopped. "That's it. This is all you get." He said it not out of vanity but to keep covered the scar where the chip was embedded.

The man with the gun put it up to his head, and Pap noticed the one on the bench, with the lab coat, pull stretch gloves out of his pocket. There was a box in front of him, and he reached down and opened it. He spoke in Chinese to the man who was doing the talking as he pulled out a hypodermic in a plastic sleeve and what looked to Pap like a thin, long-bladed knife. The man next to White Coat reached down and picked up Pap's clothes and was sure to separate his phone and watch. He put them into one bag, the clothing in another. The van came to a stop, and the man with the bags handed them forward to the passenger. The passenger opened his door and walked away with Pap's clothes and belongings. The van started moving again, and the designated speaker spoke again.

"Please lie on the bench."

Pap was very scared then. He knew exactly what White Coat was going to do—cut out the GPS chip. Sheng must use the same technology. He only hoped that the man knew what the hell he was doing. Pap also knew that he would be on his own. He assumed he might be in China before too long. His staff knew what to do in such an emergency. Everything would be wiped out, the last dozen years or so wiped away. It was the only thing to do, of course. He wondered how many millions, maybe billions, this would cost. He didn't care, really, about the money. It was the data that he regretted losing. The data, his freedom, and Caitlin.

White Coat knelt down next to Pap, who was staring up at the ceiling, rocking with the motion of the van. He felt a needle stick in his arm and his stomach shot up to his throat. There was a big bounce, and Pap figured it was a pothole. Then he went out.

The couch smelled like cat piss. That's what woke him, the smell of piss. What made Pap stand was the pain in his right hip. He also felt like the skin of his head was somehow too tight for his skull. His head felt like an overinflated balloon, and his forehead hurt when he touched it. It was the hip, though. He looked down to see he was wearing blue hospital scrubs. He had no underwear or T-shirt. Scrubs and bare feet, that was all.

He pulled back the side of his pants and looked to the pain. There was a gauze bandage that was starting to show signs of red. He figured that he must have rolled over onto that side. Pap didn't notice anyone else in the room until he heard a static sound to his left. He turned around to see the man who had sat next to him, with the gun, on a chair in front of the door. He put a walkie-talkie to his mouth and said something in Chinese. It was dark. He must have been out for a long time. Pap tried to speak to the man.

"Where am I? What do you people want? You know I have plenty of money. Is Sheng behind this?"

At the sound of the name Sheng, the man stood. He walked over and punched Pap square in the nose. Pap was shocked by the sudden act of violence. As he fell to the floor, he realized that this was the first time since childhood he had ever been punched. He didn't like it. He went down on his side, the cut-hip side, and yelped with pain. His face felt hot like the time he turned his ankle and needed a cast for a month. Just like that time, in a second or so the heat dissipated, and pain hit him full force. His eyes watered as if they had been splashed with a bucket. Pap felt his nose and found nothing but mush. The pain was debilitating. He went to his back on the floor and vowed to keep his mouth shut. He also had the first violent thought of his life. More than anything he wanted to hit this guy. He chuckled aloud since he had spent his entire life eschewing violence. He had spent many hours debating and arguing with Ben Hirsh and others about how useless and immoral violence was, how it reduced men to animals, and now here he was, after having been punched for the first time since he was in grade school, wanting to beat the shit out of someone.

He heard footsteps approaching. Pap looked up through his watery eyes and saw the man with the white coat kneeling over him. He reached down to his nose and twisted it. Pap heard a crackle, and his head felt like it had exploded. Blood poured out and ran into his mouth. He spat up at White Coat, but he turned away to his bag. He took out another needle.

Pap muttered, "Oh, no, man, no" and felt the pinch of it again. This time he went out right away.

CHAPTER 29

Lefty had twenty-three months to go. He'd found a way to make this time inside easy. The first few months were tough, of course, guys getting up on him, trannies looking to make him a bitch. Once he got in with the Italians, he was okay. It turned out that one of them knew Vinny Castlenni from the old days when they both worked around Belmont Racetrack.

Lefty had paid his way into the Italian crew by pledging his 10 percent that Castle was setting aside. It seemed that they trusted Castle, which surprised Lefty. It didn't matter, though, since the money was gone for him. Either Vinny did the right thing and held the money for the Italians to take, or the Italians would take it out of his ass. Lefty was hopeful that at least he could take back the job from Vinny when he got out. For now he had a nice setup. All he had to do was shuttle some of the food they shipped in. He had a guard to deal with and some bullshit from him from time to time, but for the most part it was cake. He had a nice cell to himself and no one trying to bust his face or stick anything up his ass. Twenty-three months.

Lefty knew that morning that it all was going to come to an end soon since the top scumbag of the skinheads sat in front of him at the table. Lefty looked around for his buddies, but they walked away without turning. As the guy sat, two more came up behind him and sat on either side. They leaned in on him. The skinhead in front of him, Cale, leaned forward to whisper.

"How much time you got left?" His voice dripped with Southern anger, like a man scolding a rutty hound.

Lefty didn't want to answer, even engage with this guy. He looked around again. His buddies were standing over by the trash cans, observing. They wanted to see how he handled himself.

"Twenty-three."

"What do you do for these fucking wops that they cover your ass?"

"We have some business. On the outside."

"What about inside, in here?"

"Nothing."

"Nothing, huh? Well, I have a message from the outside that might affect your business on the inside. Maybe those wops won't be holding your hand much longer."

Lefty perked up. Could it be something from Castle? How the fuck would this redneck know?

"What? What message?"

"Shit, boy, you know you got to bargain." He smiled at his buddies, and they chuckled. "Ain't nothing in life free. You're from New York; you know that. Am I right?"

Lefty was getting nervous. He could handle this meth head hick himself, but there were the two next to him and the dozens more in there with him. If he was going to start something, it wouldn't end at this table. He tried to deal. Take the meth head by the horns.

"Yeah, you're right. Okay, let's bargain. Why the fuck would I give a shit about what you have to say? Here's my bargain. Get the fuck out of my face and bring your two monkeys with you."

Cale smiled with a rotting grin. "Cut the shit, New York. After today you won't have your wops to cover your ass. Maybe you should listen."

Lefty leaned back, trying to seem relaxed, but he couldn't help thinking that this jerkoff might have something. "Okay, let's talk."

"Here's the only deal you're going to get. You want to know what the message is, you introduce me to your friends, and I take over your job with them. I run the bread and cheese and whatever else those dagos eat over there at their private table."

It was Lefty's turn to chuckle. "What makes you think that they are going to go for that? You know they don't deal with you guys. Everyone has a slot here. Shit, you spend half your time keeping people in line about that."

Cale slammed his fist on the table. It made a booming sound throughout the cafeteria. The guards turned quickly, hands automatically going to their gun hips. Lefty sat frozen.

Cale thought fast. He yelled, "The fucking Red Sox, man," knowing that most of the prison referred to Lefty as "New York" because of his heavy accent. The guards turned back away. He calmed down quickly and leaned in. "You think I'm fucking stupid, man? You got twenty-three. I got the rest of my life. I ain't ever getting out of here. You introduce me, work me into the group slowly. I want some of that easy time."

"I don't know if they will go for it."

"Well, you better make it work, or you leave here in a black bag long before your twenty-three."

Lefty smirked, unimpressed. The shithead had gone too far. No one who ever put a man in a body bag told him he was going to do it. He might as well have asked to get shivved. Lefty would have someone put him down before long. He played along to get the information.

"Okay. I understand. All I can do is my best, right? What information do you have?"

Cale leaned back like he was a judge or something. He crossed his arms and made a show of looking back and forth. His guys on either side were eating it up. Lefty figured they'd all go back and jerk each other off after this.

"I get a visitor yesterday. Now I don't ever get visitors since my wife stopped coming about ten years ago. I think she's dead. Well, I sit down, and some guy in a fancy business suit sits in front of me. He says, 'Tell Lefty that Castle is in Miami-Dade, and he's talking too much.' That's it. He gets up and walks away. I asked if he had some smokes, but he didn't answer."

"That's all he said? Did you get his name? Who sent the message?"

"Nope, that's all. So I was thinking that you have a problem now. This Castle guy must know some shit about you."

Lefty almost shit himself. The guy he had worked for, that he gave to Castle, must have sent the message. He was the only one who had anything to fear from Castle. Fuck. This was bad. The man would have him killed, no doubt, if anything Castle said could trace back to him. The only thing to do was put Castle down, but that would mean that his access to the Italians would end. There might even be retribution. He couldn't go to the Italians for the hit. He had no play. The only choice was to find a way to silence Castle without letting the Italians know and try to run out the string for the next twenty-three months. This skinhead could probably do the hit on Castle. There was a network of them throughout the prison system, but then what would he owe this guy?

Cale grew impatient. "What the fuck, man, you gonna sit there like you have a dick up your ass?"

Lefty bit the bullet. "No, man. Listen, you got any guys down there in Dade? Maybe can do a job for me?"

Cale laughed. "Shit, man. What happened to that New York style of yours? You need me to do something for you? A fucking redneck helping you? Shit, what about your good friends over there?" He pointed with his eyes to the guys near the cans.

"They don't have to know about this. This is personal. We did a job together a few years back. The fuck is probably trying to cut a deal for himself by ratting me out. A fucking rat. What do you want for the job?"

Cale had come to the table ready to close a deal. "See that guard over there?" He pointed again with his eyes, and Lefty turned. The guard nodded on cue. "You're gonna start running some stuff for me like you do for the Italians. You're still going to get me in good with them, by the way. This will be business, and the Italians will be my pension. You understand?"

Lefty understood. He was going to start running drugs for a skinhead meth addict—the one thing that he should never do while dealing with the Italians. They didn't want anything to do with drug running or the person running them. This was the one thing that was sure to get his throat cut if he was ever caught. He understood that he wouldn't make it the twenty-three months, not in this place. He would have to find a way to get a transfer, maybe hit a guard and end up with more time at a harder jail just to save his life.

"Yeah, I understand. I want this guy, Vinny Castlenni, taken out today if you want me to be your mule. When it is done, I go talk to your guard."

Cale stood up. "I've already made some inquiries. We'll get him tonight after dinner. Pleasure doing business with you, New York." He smiled, and his piss boys cackled.

It was then that Lefty decided how he was going to get to another prison and get away from the Italians. He had a straight razor inside his mattress.

When Cale confirmed the kill, he was going to slash the motherfucker's throat.

The walk to the yard from the cafeteria was no more than twenty yards. It was a bad setup as there was not enough room for inmates to pass in both directions unless they were single file. Miami-Dade wasn't the best-run prison. It was mainly used as a temporary holding facility for inmates being transferred from one prison to another. There were also a lot of men who were local citizens of the county, awaiting trial. The crowding was a result of the glacial pace of the administrative end of the penal system. There were simply too many men to process and too few places to put them. This led to the unfortunate circumstance of having a mix of hardcore felons and regular run-of-the-mill shitheads in the same building. It wasn't unusual to have a killer and a stoner who fell asleep in a park in the same cell.

Vinny Castlenni had just finished the brown mound they called meatloaf and was heading out to the yard to walk around a little. He still hadn't heard anything from anyone. No lawyer, no nothing. He was getting a little pissed off. He knew that he was in some deep shit. He wasn't worried about the Guzman thing. They didn't have anything on that. He didn't rat out House, and he was pretty sure House would keep his mouth shut since he was the guy who had crushed Guzman's head. It was the guy on the phone who he left the texts for that he was worried about. Vinny wasn't sure that the man believed the text he sent him and the photo. That and spending most of the money. *Shit,* he thought. *That fucking ass, that's what it was.* He'd gotten himself some of that fat booty and lost his head. He'd have to find a way to make it right with the man, get out of there, and find this Leandro guy for him, shoot him in the face like the others. Shouldn't be that bad.

The skinny guy stepped out from the line on the other side going to the cafeteria. The guy was right in his face. Vinny could smell the cigarettes on his breath.

He looked straight in Vinny's face and said, "Pop, pop, pop, pop."

Vinny felt a sharp pain up under his ribs like a bee sting. No, a wasp, a big wasp. He felt lightheaded and had to cough. When he coughed, blood shot out of his mouth. He heard a roar from the men in line. The man in front of him was gone. Something fell to the floor and rattled at his feet. He looked down, and it looked like a plastic roller that toilet paper goes on, only melted down with a sharp tip. It was red.

Holy shit, he thought. I've been stabbed.

CHAPTER 30

"It's been two days now, and we haven't heard anything. I don't like this."

"Me, neither, Ben. I don't think any of us would have thought this. How could someone get to Pap? It doesn't make sense."

"Well, someone did. They found his phone on Twenty-Eighth Street."

Kat leaned in and asked the more difficult question. "He must have had some type of tracking device on his body. Most heads of state have embedded chips these days."

"He had one, all right. They found it in a Dumpster just a few blocks from the phone, along with his clothes. There was a pretty good-size chunk taken out of him."

"And where did you get all this from? You know that I know the commissioner, and I haven't heard a thing."

"His security team has been keeping me apprised. They haven't reported it yet. I guess he named me as a go-to if something like this should happen. Just like him not to let me know, trying to keep me safe."

Ben was clearly upset. He had been pacing in the townhouse office for the past half hour. Kat tried logic to soothe him, not being comfortable enough with him yet to use any other approach.

"They're not going to kill him. He's too valuable. Someone will hear something soon. Do you have any indication?"

Ben stopped pacing and turned to Kat. "C'mon, Kat. You know who is behind this. Handley. How do I get to him? What did Pap tell you about his movements? Where will he be?"

"Ben, you know we have a plan for him. You have to trust. It is not always a smooth path to the end with these things. You have to maintain your composure and let us follow through with the plan."

"Bullshit. I think you're going to have to change your plans. Brogan is dead, Sol is dead, but Pap is alive. There's more urgency here. I want to hear how you are going to adjust to this. We both know that Handley is behind this somehow. That means that Pap is in this situation because of us, because of me. What the hell are you going to do?"

Kat had to take control of the conversation. She knew how to give Ben what he wanted and to maintain her authority over him. The fact was he was right. They had slipped up here. She should have thought about Pap. He was sitting in her kitchen a few days before, and now he was God knows where. She stood to meet his anger.

"Don't you ever talk to me like that, Ben. Maintain your professionalism. If this is the way you're going to react when we are thrown for a curve like this, maybe this job isn't for you. You think about that. Now here is what we are going to do. Frank will be calling in about two minutes. I want you on the call. He's limited to twenty minutes. You run this with Frank. You better think fast because he has plans in place for Handley. He obviously doesn't know about Pap so think on your feet. Get your head together and calm the fuck down. I'll give you room." She walked from behind her desk and started over to the other side of the room to sit on the couch. "I'm leaving this to you two. I need a complete update on what you come up with." She lowered her tone. "It'll be all right, Ben. You'll be surprised; Frank is very good at this. I'll talk to you after the call. For now there is a pen and notepaper at my desk. He'll call on that line. Just press the red button and pick up." She walked past him toward the couch.

"I'm sorry, Kat. I shouldn't have flown off the handle. Things are still moving pretty fast here. I never lost anyone ever."

"You haven't lost anyone yet."

"What happened with Leandro?"

She kept walking and answered over her shoulder, "That's taken care of."

The phone rang. Ben scrambled over to Kat's desk. He pressed red and picked up.

"Frank."

"Oh, hey, Ben. How is it going? Where's Kat?"

"She's here. Pap has been kidnapped."

Frank changed his tone immediately. "Do you have any details, anywhere to start?"

"No, we have nothing. There hasn't been any word. It's Handley."

"He must know that Pap dug into his records. Do you have enough information to put him away?"

"Yes, but if it came from Pap, how could he possibly know?"

"Well, he does. He's going to want to deal."

"No deals, Frank. This is Pap. I can't make a deal unless I know he is safe. I mean eyes-on-him safe."

"I said he is going to want to deal. I'll determine what he gets or doesn't get. Ben, we'll get Pap out of this. You have my word. You have any ideas?"

Ben told Frank about House and his idea of getting Handley down to Florida to meet the man. Frank seemed to like it.

"That's a good start. There's going to be more to it than that, though. Put me on speaker."

Ben looked over to Kat and shook his head and raised his arms. She walked over and pressed a button. "You're on speaker, Frank."

"Okay. Kat, is D'Amico still the superintendent of the state troopers?"

"Yes."

"Good. Transfer me to his private line after we're done here." He paused for a few seconds that seemed like an eternity to Ben, who was about to interject. Kat put a hand on his arm and shook her head. They waited a few seconds more. Kat had a pen in hand, hovering over the legal pad.

Frank got back on the line. He rattled off a seven-step plan. It involved multiple government agencies, Commissioner Marshall, House, the New York State troopers, the NYPD tactical team, the men Kat used for the Leandro "thing," and the Miami police chief. He gave them the places to be and the times to be there. He suggested what equipment to use, down to the communication units for the tactical team. When he finished, he asked if they had any questions. Ben was dumbstruck.

Kat said, "Got it. I'll transfer to D'Amico now." She pressed a button and dialed a number, waited for a connection then said, "Talk soon, Frank."

Ben walked over to the couch and slumped down into it. "What the hell just happened?"

Kat was already deep into her tasks, writing furiously. She looked away from her pad and glanced at Ben.

"What, Frank? Yeah, well, get used to it. He thinks fast when he's sober. Now let's get to work."

CHAPTER 31

Carter Handley finished nine holes around nine in the morning. As he waited for his car to pull up, he looked out toward the front gate to make sure his security guys were ready. He had brought them on after the Martinez pickup. He didn't like the way things ended with Huang, and with Sheng involved it was better to play it safe until the Martinez matter was cleared up. They were there.

His Maybach rolled up, and he got behind the wheel. He idled as the attendant put his golf bag in the trunk. He made a left out of the Winged Foot lot and headed west on Fenimore to get to the Hutchinson River parkway. The security car nuzzled behind him, and they made their way back to Manhattan. Before he got to the Hutch north ramp, he saw flashing lights, two sets, from two police cars. Handley glanced into his rear-view mirror and saw that his security car was being pulled over. He continued a few yards then thought it best to pull over. The second vehicle, a state trooper cruiser, roared into the space between the Maybach and the Mercury the security men were driving. A man in high boots and a Mountie hat stepped out of the cruiser. He walked over to Handley, who sat patiently. When the man got to the side window, Handley pressed the down lever, and it opened silently. He could feel the rush of hot air enter the vehicle.

"License and registration, please."

Handley reached over to the glove box and pulled out a leather booklet. "Is there a problem, Officer?"

"Please remove your license and registration and hand them to me." The trooper leaned into the car as if he were checking for contraband. He had mirrored sunglasses and a chin that could break a baseball bat.

Handley fumbled through the booklet, pulled out the items, and handed them over.

The trooper read the documents and turned back to the patrol car. From the mirror, Handley could see another trooper get out of the cruiser. The officer approached the Maybach from the passenger side. Handley noticed that the trooper had his hand on his gun. He knew then that they were there to take him in. Handley wondered what it might be for. Martinez had been secured, so he was not a threat at the moment. He was sure that his apprehension couldn't be traced to him. He had been waiting for someone to contact him about a settlement or a payment to get his data back. *State troopers?* he thought. It couldn't be Leandro, certainly not the Chinese.

He was deep in thought when the trooper asked him, "Are you Carter Handley of 525 Fifth Avenue?"

"Yes."

"Please step out of the vehicle."

"What?"

The trooper took a shooter's stance and shouted, "Out of the vehicle now!"

Handley looked up at him and across to the other trooper, who was standing with legs spread and gun drawn. He dropped the leather booklet and raised his hands. "I'm taking off my seatbelt. Easy now."

"Slowly."

"Yes, sir. No need to panic. Nice and slow."

He unclicked the belt and reached for the door. The officer opened it with his left hand, keeping his gun aimed at Handley's head. The door swung open, and Handley got out. The trooper immediately swung him around and pulled his arms behind his back. Handcuffs came out of nowhere and were on his wrists. The trooper pulled them tight, and they made a clawing sound. Handley looked to his right, to the Mercury behind him. Two other troopers were putting his men into the back of their cruiser. They were both cuffed, and the troopers placed their hands on the men's heads as they eased them in. There would be no arrest. He was being taken to someone who knew Martinez or Leandro. Who the hell had the power to have New York State troopers carry this out? For the first time in Carter Handley's adult life, he felt that he might be in over his head.

Kat was on hold. Commissioner Marshall was playing a power game. She tapped her pen on her legal pad and waited. She made a check mark next to this task on her to-do list. Not a line through it, a check. The task wasn't completed yet.

Marshall came on the line. "Ms. Wells, what a pleasure to hear from you. Is there some sort of emergency that you felt the need to contact me on this line?"

"Why the hell are you calling me?" was what he meant. Kat smiled to herself. Men. Jesus. "I'm sorry, Commissioner, but this is an urgent matter."

"Please, please, call me Brendan."

Somehow he made a friendly gesture sound creepy, but Kat stayed in character. "Okay, Brendan, I have information for you that I think you will like."

"Information about what exactly?"

"Do you know Carter Handley? I mean personally."

"We've met, but, no, I can't say that I know him."

"Has he made any donations to you or anyone with whom you are affiliated?"

"Not that I'm aware of. What is this about?"

Kat ran a line through this task on her legal pad. "I'm sorry, Brendan, but I'm going to have to ask again. Is there any relationship with you or anyone on your staff that can come back to bite you?"

"No, Kat. To be honest he doesn't seem to be a big fan of mine. I don't like him much either."

"Good. We have information that is going to put him away for a very long time."

"What information are you talking about? Where did you get it?"

"Insider trading, money laundering for watch list countries and individuals, extortion, bribery—there's a whole list."

"Can it stand? Not a guy I want to go up against without facts."

"Brendan, there is so much more. The information came from Pap Martinez. It's all good. I just rattled off a few things that I think would hold up in court. There's much, much more. He's a real bad guy. This will be the biggest Wall Street scandal maybe ever. It's real, all right."

"Why do you have this? What is Martinez doing involved with you? I can't just take your word on this. No offense, but Axis is one of the biggest financial companies in the country."

"It's the biggest."

"What is this really about? I know you're looking into the Landsman killing. I have sources. McGinley has had a number of guests at his little retreat, someone from the NSA. C'mon, Kat, don't bullshit me here."

He played into the script like an anxious understudy. Kat leaned back in her chair.

"Okay. Here's everything we have. Handley is the man behind Sol's murder. When Brogan died, he left a brokerage statement with Sol that had Handley's name on it. I have it now. I can send it to you if you'd like. We started looking into it when Sol was killed. After a little digging we found that Handley hired a man named Leandro to kill Sol."

Marshall interrupted. "The same Leandro that was on the most-wanted list of three different countries? I know fucking Leandro. He was our number-one suspect. They found him with two bullets in the head a few days ago down in Boca Raton. Don't tell me you were involved in that. You were. Motherfucker. This is the kind of shit that I'm talking about. Fucking McGinley, he ordered the hit, didn't he? Listen, Kat, I'm going to have to walk away from this. I'll pull a subpoena on Frank and pull him in. I don't need to hear some kind of bullshit story so you can cover your ass on the Leandro hit. Goddamn you people. Landsman gets killed, and you have Leandro murdered. What the hell?"

"We don't know anything about that. Thank God he's off the street, though."

"Jesus Christ, you people. Where's Handley now? Did you kill him too?"

"We don't know where he is. That's why I'm calling you. We need your help."

"I'm not even going to go into the fact that you should have called me first, before anyone. I'm sure you've covered your ass every step of the way. What are you trying to do here? You think you run this city?"

Kat heard something break against a wall on his side of the line. She waited a moment to allow him to settle a bit.

"I'm calling because we think you will be running this city before too long.

I'm calling because I need your help. As for Leandro, you're happy he's dead. We both know that. He did Landsman; it's irrefutable." Kat went straight to his ego, his most vulnerable spot. "What I'm going to send your way has enough evidence to put you on the nightly news, front and center. This will run for weeks. It's that big. I'm talking about evidence that Handley had Walter Peterson killed. He planted a story in the *Journal* ahead of time to be sure that his stock would rise. We have receipts of payments in Las Vegas for liquor and gambling debts on behalf of the Chinese minister of finance. There's so much more. Handley, along with Peterson, has been running a legitimate criminal enterprise for decades. Money laundering for Iran. I mean c'mon; this is a national story."

There was silence from Marshall's side of the line. Kat could sense the political calculation through her handheld. She could feel him spinning it in his head. Who would benefit most? How could he use this to make his run for mayor, maybe governor?

"What about media coverage? I have a guy at the *Times*."

"No, we're going to drop this with the *Journal* tomorrow. You have a day to go over the material. I would suggest holding a press conference very early the day after tomorrow to sync with the morning papers. You'll be named as the source, the guy who broke it, in the paper."

"What do you want?"

"What do you mean?"

"You drop this in my lap? What's the price? Let's be straightforward about this, please. No more intrigue. What's the fee?"

"First we want to have a better relationship with you. I don't know what happened between you and Frank, but I know he wants to get past it. Face it; I could be making this call to a friend at the FBI or Homeland Security, with the Chinese connection. We think that you are going to be the next mayor. You have the real estate guys and the financial people behind you, and we both know that is all that matters in this town. We would like to work with you in the future. I think we both want what is best for the city. Hopefully, after you settle in at Gracie Mansion, Frank and I can send more your way, and you will let us do things our way even if our methods may step on your toes from time to time. I can assure this. We will have your back if need be. We don't let our friends down."

Marshall calculated some more in silence.

"What else do you want? If this is as big as you say, you can ask for more, so I figure you will. Ask now."

Kat smiled. He was walking alongside her now. "We will need your tactical team to release a hostage in a day or so."

"A hostage? What the fuck?"

"That's all I can say at this time." Ben had told Kat the night before about Pap's security people's theory that Pap was being held close by. Kat agreed. He would have to be nearby for a quick release since Handley must know how much information Pap could have pulled. Handley would be desperate for a fast resolution.

"Jesus Christ. I can't make that pledge until I see the material you're talking about."

He wanted to see if it was worth it. To Kat, it was the logical response.

"I have a guy in a UPS uniform in your lobby. Call down and have him sent up. He has a flash drive for you along with an RSA security ID key. When the program opens, your username is Kat Wells, no caps, no spaces. Then enter the number that flashes on the security key for the ID."

Marshall laughed. "You're pretty confident, huh?"

"Not really. FBI headquarters is right down the block. Happy reading and please confirm the other matter before the end of business today."

Before hanging up, he asked the only question left worth asking on this matter. "Handley isn't going to be around to muck this up, is he? I don't want a show trial where any of this material you have may come back to haunt me. I'm sure he'll have top attorneys."

"You won't hear from him, no. I'll talk to you this afternoon."

Handley had asked the troopers at least a dozen times where they were taking him. After getting silence in return for an hour, he relented. He'd been thrown in the back of the cruiser, cuffed, and taken north on the Hutch. Before long they were in upstate New York. Going up the Taconic, he gazed out the window and tried to make sense of what was happening. The drive gave him time to think. He'd been reacting to events those last few days, not being proactive. He had hoped the round of golf would give him some peace and clear his head. He was going to go back to the city to strategize, when the troopers nabbed him. Again he had to react, not act. Things were happening to him; he wasn't making things happen. He didn't like it.

As he watched the green rolling hills in the distance, he tried to focus, funnel down his thoughts. Who could be behind this? He laid out the pieces in his mind from the beginning: Brogan, Landsman, Leandro, Castle, Huang, Sheng, Martinez. From there he made lines to each of the pieces in his head and connected their associates to them and the most recent events.

Brogan's associates were Kat Wells and Frank McGinley. He knew their reputations, of course. He didn't believe most of it, though. As a man who spent most of his time influencing or intimidating people, he knew the value of a trumped-up back story. Handley had known from the start that they would look into Landsman's death. There was no link between them and Martinez. He'd had his people dig deep on that. As for the brokerage statement, their files and Landsman's were completely clean of any trace of it. Homeland Security had seen to that. They couldn't be the ones; he was too advanced for them.

This was extortion. There must be someone involved in this matter that had a link to Martinez. Maybe it was an internal leak? Fortunately, he had acted faster than whoever it was before any money could be asked for, before threats were made. These were amateurs. Something was missing here, something...the funeral. He had gotten the attendee list from a police contact. McGinley, Wells, Landsman, who else? There was one other, Hirsh. That was it—Hirsh. It came to him now. He had worked with Landsman, former SEC investigator. Handley had assumed he was a nobody. Who the hell was this Hirsh guy?

The cruiser turned off the highway. It was a sharp exit, and they took it fast. Handley slid across the bench seat and lost track of his thoughts. They went through a small town. It had its charms, but it was the fucking country. Anything that far out of Manhattan that wasn't the Hamptons was a back wood to him.

They continued through the town until they got to a dirt road past a water-treatment plant. The cruiser followed the road until they got to a one-lane bridge. The trooper on the passenger side got out, opened the back door, and leaned into Handley's face. He had a green cloth sack in his hand.

"Please close your eyes."

"What? What are you doing?"

The trooper roughly jammed the sack over Handley's head and got out to sit back in the front. The driver flipped on the siren for a burst, and it made Handley jump. They waited in silence. After a few minutes Handley couldn't take it anymore.

"Where are we? What is going on?"

No one answered, but he heard footsteps approaching. They were echoing off the wood bridge. One set was heavy and plodding, the other sharp and taking more steps. *One big, one little,* Handley thought. The door opened, and a big hand grabbed him on the bicep.

"Let's go." The voice was rough, a city guy. Bronx, maybe.

He slid out and got up to his feet. Before he could balance himself, the man pulled him along. Handley lost his balance and fell. He had no sense of the ground with the sack on, so he hit hard. The ground was soft, and he could smell water somewhere close. He was lifted to his feet like a doll. He heard the little steps going across the bridge again. In a stride, he was on the bridge also. They hurried him along. They were walking on soft dirt or sand, and the smell of water was fresher, closer. Handley assumed it was the Hudson River. He could hear the movement. He no longer heard the small steps and lost track of how far they had walked. It wasn't far, maybe a football field. He was brought to a halt, and the arm swung him around. He was facing the water; he could feel it on his skin. He immediately thought they were going to throw him in. *Shit, shit, shit,* he thought. It was his worst fear. Drowning. The darkness of it.

Suddenly he was pushed down. He sat hard on a bench. He heard lightweight keys rattle in front of his face. Handley felt his hands release from the cuffs, and then the sack was pulled off. The sun was in his face, and he couldn't make out much. He turned to his right, and he saw a large man in a suit walking away, waving the sack at his side. He turned in front of him, and there was a man with his back to him, facing the river.

Handley shouted over to him, "Are you Hirsh?"

Frank took a deep breath and looked at the water meandering past him. *Let him wait,* he thought. He had spent the past half hour watching the Hudson and thinking that the water in front of him could be seen from the window of his apartment on the West Side. It was soothing somehow to feel connected to his outside world and, at the same time, be so removed from it. He had made a deal with the staff and Dr. Delphi. No violence or he was out. The fact was he wanted to stay. For the first time in his life, over fifty years now, he felt like he was learning something about himself. Frank let himself believe that the people there, the doctors, were smarter than him, wiser. Frank liked it there. He liked himself there.

"Hirsh?"

Frank closed his eyes and thought about the old man, Brogan, and how happy he would have been to be in Frank's shoes right now. He loved this stuff, breaking guys down. Fucking Brogan. God, he missed him. Frank turned and walked toward Handley.

"No, I'm Frank McGinley. Where is Pap Martinez?"

Handley immediately put it together. McGinley must have the brokerage statement. It was the only reason he would be involved. Brogan might have given it to him years before, told him the whole story. Jesus, the day he set up Brogan was so long ago, and there had been so many others since then. He realized now that he had slipped up badly on this. How could he have been so careless? He never assumed that Brogan would tell anyone with his brother and sister still alive. He must have known that he would act on the threat even now. Handley cursed himself for not going after McGinley instead of Landsman. There was no use putting on an act. It was time to negotiate.

"McGinley. I must admit I'm surprised." He looked around. "What is this, some kind of compound?"

"No, it's rehab. You should have killed me, not Sol. Where's Pap Martinez?"

"Surely you must know that you're going to have to try a little harder than that. Where is my data? What do you have? Let's talk about that before we talk about Mr. Martinez."

Frank smiled at Handley then walked closer and stood over him. "I was out with my friend Eddie O the night before Brogan's funeral. Shit, I drank up a storm that night. He told me a story, though. I was thinking about it this morning before you got here. There was a guy when I worked on the floor of the American Stock Exchange that ran some kind of scam. Seems crazy now, but it worked. He would flip a coin. Heads or tails, you know. Anyway, what made it interesting was that there were people on the floor that lost thousands of dollars to him. I mean I know for a fact that one guy was into him for over forty-five grand. Could you imagine, on a coin flip? I don't know what he did. My guess would be a sleight of hand, but these quantitative guys fell for it. Man, if the odds were in their favor, they would bet millions. I remember when I heard about the guy down forty-five grand, people were talking about backing him, putting up serious money. They figured he was due to start winning, with the odds and all. I knew it had to be a scam as soon as I heard it. When you grow up in Queens, you can smell bullshit from around the block. After a while the scammer leaves the floor, probably wore out his welcome. That's the last I heard of it for years until the night with Eddie O. We're talking about whatever, and this guy's name comes up. Eddie tells me he was killed. They found him floating in the Chicago River."

Handley had gathered himself and adjusted to the light. He shifted in his seat and looked up at Frank.

"Why would I give a shit about all of this?"

Frank had an excited look and an even broader smile now. "Oh, you should because there is a lesson here for you to learn. You see, this guy eventually fucked with the wrong person. Somewhere in his travels he scammed the wrong guy. He ran into someone who didn't try to figure it out or try to outsmart him. The last guy just killed him and threw him in the river. That's what you've done. You tried to intimidate us and wipe out anyone who might be a threat to you. I'm guessing that it worked for you for many years, but we're the wrong people to do this to. You should have called your lawyers and waited and then just denied everything. You're right that we would have wiped you out, but at least you would have lived. We're the ones who are going to kill you and throw you in the river. Only I think we'll have you thrown off a building. As for your data, it's with Police Commissioner Marshall. We have everything, and it's going to be on the cover of the *Wall Street Journal* tomorrow morning. Where's Martinez?"

Handley felt like he had been smacked with a board. Everything? A wave of anxiety crashed into him, physically pushing his back against the bench. He thought he was going to throw up, and he burped a little bile into this mouth. He leaned over and spit it out with his head between his knees. Still, he kept up the bluff.

"What are you talking about?"

Frank grabbed his leg and pulled it up behind him to stretch. He was wearing running gear and had a sweat mark under his neck running down in a half circle to the top of his stomach. He ran his hands through his hair and paused to squeeze the side of his head with both hands, focusing his thoughts.

"Before Brogan died he left a brokerage statement with Sol Landsman. The statement was account number eight-seven-four-three-zero-nine-five-two. The balance was two hundred and three thousand and forty-seven cents. There was one transaction, a dividend payment on a T-bill. On the statement Brogan wrote your name, Handley, across the top. He must have slipped it into his file shortly before his death because Sol didn't know anything about it. You moved too slow. The demand for our files came a day late for your purposes. The Mr. Hirsh that you mistook me for had the statement in his pocket when the Homeland Security people seized everything. Using Senator Marche was your undoing. Never trust a politician, huh? His staff was tweeting about the raids before they even happened. We didn't pick up on them at the time, but they're part of the public domain, so they are going to be cited in the indictments. I'm sure Marche will squeal like a pig. There are other things, of course. The money laundering can be traced through public documents. I'm pretty experienced with that. I'll follow up on it. This will be bigger than Madoff. There'll be a number of arrests. My partner, Kat Wells, has gotten our clients out of your stock. I don't expect it to fare well tomorrow. I could have gone short your stock, but that wouldn't be honest, would it?"

Handley thought he was having a heart attack. The wave of anxiety was so strong that he started to sweat profusely. He had to gather himself. He had dealt with extortionists before. Never with this much on the line, but he had done it. He could get himself out; he knew it. He sat up straight and cleared his throat.

"That's a nice story. Maybe you can tell it to Martinez's widow or parents, whoever he is going to leave behind. Tell them at his funeral how you took down the big bad Wall Street banker."

Frank sighed then smiled again. "I should have known. I should have done a better job protecting the people around me. That is what has been bothering me the last couple of days. I should have known that you were a corrupt motherfucker. There is a reason that you don't know me that well. It's funny that you took me for Hirsh. I told him just the other day I work for the clean Wall Street people. He was at the SEC; he knew all the dirty ones. I've worked with every major firm on the street except for yours. You didn't want anyone on the outside poking around. You're the guy that never takes a vacation, worried that someone else may see your files. The diligent worker who's really a crook. Yeah, it makes sense now."

Frank walked close enough to be standing over Handley. "I want to sit down. Get on the ground."

Handley looked up at him. No one had given him an order since he was a child. He responded the only way his instincts allowed. "Do you think—"

Frank slapped him in the face. Handley was more shocked than he was hurt. Someone had actually struck him.

Frank glared at him. "I promised the people here no violence but don't fuck with me." He grabbed Handley by the hair and pulled him to his feet. Once he was standing, Frank pushed him in the chest with both arms as hard as he could. He wanted desperately to beat the shit out of him right there. He knew he couldn't; he needed Handley alert. Once he was on the ground, Frank made a slow kicking motion like a man shooing a cat. Handley moved back a few feet, and Frank sat. He let out a deep groan. "I'm up to three miles now. Not bad." He leaned his elbows on his knees and looked down at Handley. The smile was gone. "Listen, this isn't a negotiation; you're not going to get out of this. We killed Leandro the other day, and we're going to kill you. We know you had Sol killed, you made Brogan miserable—that would have been enough for me—and you had Peterson killed. Your own buddy. Jesus, you're a shitty guy. Yeah, we're going to kill you. I was planning a shot to the head or the building toss. Suicide because of the scandal. But then you picked up Martinez. So now we are going to have to hurt you first. You'll tell us where he is. I'm guessing you're going to think I'm bluffing, so you're going to hold out, hoping for a break. You have money squirreled away somewhere, I'm sure. You think you'll be able to get to it. Sitting there weighing your options. I know this drill, believe me. This is no bluff. The news will be released, and you're going to die; those are facts. This is what it is. You've lost. It's done."

Handley looked up at him. McGinley was so calm about it that it made him furious. *He can't actually think that this is going to work for him,* he thought. He would let Martinez die because of this? It didn't make sense. McGinley had nothing to gain from letting Martinez die. Where was the benefit? It had to be a bluff. They must need Martinez. He was the brains behind this. He recalled now. McGinley, he was the drinker, the Irish hood. That was it. Brogan had all the contacts; he was dead. McGinley, with his Queens accent, sitting there in a glorified drunk tank, he needed Martinez more than he was letting on. With Brogan dead, who was going to do business with a man who had a reputation as a hothead and now a drunk? Then he remembered the nickname that he had heard.

"They still call you Brogan's bitch?"

Frank busted out laughing. It wasn't the reaction that Handley expected, and he unconsciously slid away from Frank and the bench a few feet. McGinley seemed unstable. Frank finished with an "oh, God" and turned serious.

"How old are you, man?"

"Seventy.."

"Jesus. Seventy years old, you have more money than you can count, and here you are, sitting in the dirt. You thought you had it all figured out, didn't you? You thought that you had Brogan, that he was in your pocket all these years. He just sat on the statement to protect his family. I don't think we would have even acted if you didn't kill Sol. You overplayed everything. What kind of pompous ass are you? Jesus, I'll never get guys like you. Is it just that you don't care about the rules? Does it make you feel powerful? I don't get it. I really don't."

Handley sat up and straightened his back. "Yes. I'm seventy years old, and I have done whatever the hell I've wanted my whole life. You see, I have my own rules. I don't recognize any others. I do what I want when I want. Seventy fucking years old and I have never once been in fear of anyone. Never. I have amassed a fortune, and I have done things you could never imagine. Women, money, I've lived at a level that very few men could dream of. I've had men killed, and I have held entire governments in the palm of my hand, and never once has anyone seriously challenged me. Never. Do you know why? Because everyone has a price. Look at Wall Street now. My own firm, we stole and misled our own clients and traded like drunk sailors. What happened? We paid a fine. A fucking fine. Shit, I'd do it over again a thousand times. You're going to psychoanalyze me? Why do I do these nasty things? Grow up. I like it. I like drowning puppies, taking candy from little girls; I like it, and it pays well, and I've had a great life. You can do whatever you want to me at this point. I have beaten the system many, many times over. Someone should have killed me years ago or sent me to jail. So do or say whatever you want but don't judge me. I don't give a shit what you think. Fuck you, you drunken Irish prick."

Frank smiled. "Are you a college football fan?"

The question seemed out of left field to Handley. "College football? Why?"

"It doesn't matter. There's a guy; he was a tackle for the University of Miami. His name is something Williams, but he was known as Big House. The Big House, whatever. This was maybe ten years ago. He was going to the pros, but he blew out a knee. The only reason why I remember him is because of the injury. It was, I think, on the last game of the season. Some defensive lineman rolled up on him. The only thing noteworthy about the play was after. I saw this on YouTube once. There's this collection of gruesome injuries—you know, Joe Theismann and all. This House guy, his leg was bent in a forty-five-degree angle the wrong way. I'm talking about his foot was out over his kneecap. The knee just snapped backwards. Man, when he tried to get up, the bottom of his leg just hung there from the skin. Fucked up."

"Why would I care about any of this?"

"Well, you're going to meet him. He's down in Florida. Worked for a local hustler, put his head into a wall. You must remember; you got that text. We intercepted that also. Yeah, you know House's work. He doesn't just bust heads, though. He's pretty creative. He set up this pulley system in a warehouse. Puts a guy's head in a noose then he pulls it up in increments until the guy says or does whatever he wants. It's pretty smart. I'm told it has a similar effect as waterboarding. That feeling like you're going to choke to death is a lot like drowning I'm told."

Handley didn't respond. He thought about the picture of the man's head in the wall and thought of the force that must have been used to leave him stuck there off the ground. Then he thought of drowning and gasping for air in the dark. As terrifying as it was, he felt that he had no choice but to play this bluff. He had nothing to gain by giving McGinley Martinez's location. If it wasn't a bluff, he could give the information before the torture started. He decided that now was the time to stop talking.

Frank stood up and stretched. "I don't have the bench for much longer. Let me know where Pap Martinez is now, and you can avoid all of that. We will make it fast and easy. One shot to the temple. There's nothing left to fight for." He looked at Handley and gave him a chance to answer. "No? Okay. There's a van at the end of the path. Head out, and I will follow. The fence on your left is electrified, and there's a ten-foot-high wall behind the bushes on your right, and also, if you try to run, I'll kick your ass. Once you get in that van, it's out of my hands. The men will take you to House no matter what you tell them. There's no turning back once I hand you over. C'mon, get up."

Frank kicked him on the side of the leg, and Handley slowly got up to his feet. He looked at Frank for an instant then turned his back on him and started walking up the path.

Marshall called at three. Kat was drafting a cover sheet for the *Journal* reporter when the phone rang. She checked the caller ID then picked up.

"Commissioner, what do you think of the data?"

"I have the legal guys going over it now. This is the mother lode. Was it Martinez got you all this? I know he's pals with Hirsh. Hirsh has been going back and forth to the townhouse the last few days. It has to be Pap."

"Yeah, most of it was from him."

"I had no idea he was part of your organization."

Kat could sense the respect in Marshall's tone. She wanted to dispel the association from the start while retaining a little bit of gravitas.

"He's not. We needed a favor, and he was gracious enough to help out. You're right that he is friends with Ben. Mr. Hirsh has joined our group."

"He's okay with the Shake Shack thing?"

"I explained that it's part of the job. No hard feelings. Can you bring indictments with the data?"

"It's early, and the legal guys are being careful since it is Axis Financial we're dealing with, but, yeah, Handley's going to get indicted. This is our Madoff. I haven't practiced law in quite a few years, but most of this is ironclad. We just have to frame it to pass certain legal thresholds. We could use a few more days with this."

"Sorry, Brendan, we can't wait on this. I'm using it to put pressure on Handley. It pertains to the tactical team I mentioned. We're going to need that in a day or so."

"I thought about that. I can't be putting together a team without something from you. There's a mayor in this town. Control boards, oversight. It's not like rounding up a posse. I need a reason."

"Pap Martinez."

"What?"

"Pap Martinez, that's who we'll need you to extricate. His security team believes he's in New York City."

"Handley has him?"

"Yes, he figured correctly that Pap must have been behind the data capture. He had him picked up on Twenty-Third Street. The job was carried out by Chinese nationals. I viewed the tape this morning. Professionally done. Handley has a known associate in the Chinese government."

"Huang Jao. We've known that for a while. Nothing to go on with that until now, I guess. You think this is international?"

"No. I think Handley knew he had been breached and called Huang for help. He had Martinez taken as leverage to negotiate his data back."

"So why give it to me? How does this help Pap?"

"We took away Handley's only chip. He has nothing to deal with."

"Why would he deal at all then? Wait. Shit. You have him, don't you? Wait up now. Things have changed. We think the material you gave us is strong enough to warrant bringing Handley in. We want him."

"I need Martinez's location before that can happen."

"Fuck, Kat. Once he gives you that information, you're going to kill him. Stop the games here. How do you plan on getting anything from this guy?"

"We'll get it. Once we do, you will get it. Put together a small team, four or five guys. Have them ready to move fast. Another thing: no publicity on this. It is Pap Martinez. We can't have the press on this."

"I agree. I know that you have given me this case, and I appreciate it, but I can't put men in harm's way without a chance for a collar. I can't have a shootout in my streets without a substantial reason."

"Pick up the Chinese. I'm sure at least one of them will be dirty. No one will notice if you release them a few days later. Listen, there's something else. I spoke to one of my friends on the national level. We're thinking it may be good to back off the mayor's race."

"What? You're backing off now? Bad timing, Kat. I haven't done anything yet."

"We think that you put all of your backing behind him, be a team player. The governor's term is up in two years. With a few years of goodwill, I'm sure you'll be able to use the Handley thing to your advantage for at least two years; you'll be ripe for a run. We'll put a lot behind you."

"What if the mayor runs?"

"He won't."

"I'm going to have to stretch the indictments out a little longer. We have paperwork on the CFO and a few market research guys. Man, there's some dirty shit in here."

"Heh, work it any way you want. Are you with us here? Pump up the mayor, and we have you backed in two years."

Marshall paused to think. He was in the big leagues now. He had a couple of guys he could use for a raid. The Chinese might be well armed. It would require some work, but the reward—governor. He could hardly imagine it. He decided.

"Two days, tops. I'll put together a small team for this. I need to produce Handley in two days or at least his body."

"You'll have it. Brendan, thanks for your help with this." She hung up.

Marshall caught that she said "it" and not "him." *It's better off,* he thought. *Makes for a neater package.*

Pap was dreaming that he was standing over a stream, looking down from the bank. He felt like he was slipping, the mud beneath his feet giving way. He jumped awake as he was about to hit the water in the dream.

He had to go to the bathroom. He sat up quickly, thinking that he might go in his pants if he didn't hustle, prepared to cut over to his bedroom bathroom. He slipped on the wood floor, having expected expensive carpet. He fell to his side, and then the nose hurt, followed by the hip. He remembered where he was.

Not by a stream or in his bedroom. He was captive. He also still had to piss, or he was going to go in his pants.

He stood up, and across the room was a card table with two men sitting and smoking. He hollered, "Bathroom," and one of them stood. The one that remained seated whispered in Chinese, and they both chuckled. Pap hollered, "Bathroom" again and bent down in a cramp. The standing one pointed down a hallway on his side of the room. Pap waddled over, holding his penis like when he was a little boy running to the toilet. The men laughed.

As he stood over the bowl and relished the relief, he looked in the mirror. His face was a mess, and no one had bothered to repair it. His nose was crushed, and his cheeks were puffed and purple. The whites of both of his eyes were bloody. It was dark outside, so he must have been sleeping a long time. He wondered what it was that they were shooting him up with. The funny thing was he felt rested for the first time in a while. This was probably the first time he had gotten over five consecutive hours of sleep in years.

He finished and went to wash his hands, but there was no soap. He rinsed his hands and gingerly splashed a little water on his face. It wasn't until after he did so that he noticed there was no towel. He walked out of the bathroom and tried to wipe his face with his shirtsleeve. It didn't quite make it.

He spoke to the men. "Towel. Is there a towel?"

Neither of them bothered to look up at him. He was sure they didn't speak English, and he knew that he didn't speak their language. He tried something else.

"Food." He made a shoveling motion toward his mouth.

One of the men barked at him and pointed to the couch. Pap went back to the couch and looked around. The apartment was empty of furniture except for this foul-smelling couch and the card table and two chairs the men were at. There was no phone and one lamp on the table. He noticed now that they had money on the table, and there was an overflowing ashtray. He could hear street noises outside; he was clearly in New York City. He sat still and heard someone shouting in Spanish and a siren blocks away.

Pap sat back on the couch and tried to breathe in through his nose. All that happened was a gurgling sound and a shot of pain up through his eyes.

For the first time that Pap could remember, he didn't know what to do. He thought that he just had to wait. The feeling was a shock to his system. He couldn't think of a time when he had just sat with nothing to do, nothing he could do. Not having any control was the one thing that could make him panic, and he never panicked, ever. But then, until this moment, he could control his environment. He closed his eyes and thought about his father, something he had done a lot lately. Pap's work made it difficult to stay in contact with his loved ones. He was closer to his dad than anyone on this earth, and he missed him more and more each day. He thought about this predicament and what his father would say about it. His father was an IBMer. A lifer. White shirt, black tie. A brilliant man but a company man. It was this mentality, this conformity, that Pap had pushed back against his whole life.

God, how they fought. It was frustrating to no end to Pap. How could this man, this great man, kowtow to his boss? Some Eastern regional manager or something. He would tell his father it was because he was Puerto Rican and the boss a white man; that was why he was over him. How could his father not see it? It wasn't until later in life, times like these, when Pap would allow his father's words to sink in.

He spoke about commitment and taking care of your own. This was a man who had lost his wife, Pap's mother, when Pap was only nine years old. Pap knew then what his father was saying—he had to listen to his boss; he couldn't take chances. He had a son to raise, a mortgage to pay, college to save for. Pap knew what he was saying, but he was a kid. Therefore, his father was slow and old and behind the times. This was why Pap could never settle down, never stick to a job. He was an entrepreneur, a man who created things. He didn't settle. There were no regional managers in his life. He realized now that there wasn't anyone else either. Sure, he had a girl he liked, maybe even more, but he would have to leave her now. He wouldn't be able to see Ben for who knows how long, years probably. He would have to sell the business, if there was a business to sell; he had been breached. It was Sheng, no doubt from the company in the room. Besides, no one else could have gotten to him. It was all because of this Handley thing and his ego. His fucking ego that had led him to believe he could take down anyone. The great Pap Martinez, he thought, the legend, sitting alone on a couch with a broken nose and no idea how he was going to get himself home. Yeah, he thought, he was some fucking genius. He had outsmarted them all, hadn't he?

If he got out of this, he knew he would have to disappear for years. He made a vow to himself. It was time to start living a life of substance, to stand for something. How many years had he spent looking into other people's lives without examining his own? He had everything and nothing. He had so much money that he'd lost track of it. The money would buy him anonymity and a good life for years to come, but it wouldn't buy him the one thing he wanted the most: an evening sitting in the backyard, drinking a beer with his dad.

CHAPTER 32

Ben dialed the police chief as his cab was nearing the Miami-Dade Correctional Facility, not wanting to give him a chance to change his mind or come up with any demands or restrictions. The chief picked up right away since Ben had said the night before that he would confirm his arrival.

"Hirsh?"

"Yes, Chief. I'll be there shortly. Is Mr. Williams ready?"

"Yeah, but there's been a development that you should be aware of."

"What's that?"

"Vinny Castlenni is dead."

"Dead?"

"Yes. Yesterday afternoon. I just got word this morning."

"Jesus, do you know how?"

"Fucking skinheads. They've been feuding with the Italians throughout the entire prison system. Been going on for years now. Castlenni should have known better than to put his head down when he walked past one of those fuckers. Shivved him right up under the ribs."

Ben had barely slept. He was concerned about Pap. Randi had asked what was wrong, tried to soothe him, but he couldn't tell her. He was having a hard time with it, keeping things from her. He wondered if this would be his way. Was he now a guy who lied to his wife?

Ben answered the chief without thinking. "Good. I can use this as leverage with Williams. What's his street name again?"

"House. Are you kidding me here? Leverage? What kind of fucking game are you running? I have a shitload of paperwork in front of me because of this.

This is it, Hirsh. Get House out and take him wherever you want as long as it isn't in my county. I don't care how many connections you have up the chain. Get this guy out, and I don't want to see you or him back in my precinct. Got it?"

Ben didn't even listen to the last part of the chief's response. Cop talk. He'd heard hours of it over the years. His cab pulled up in front of the jail.

"Have all of my instructions been carried out, the money?"

"Yes, it's all ready. Just get him out of here today."

"Thanks. Got to go, Chief." He hung up before the chief could respond.

Williams was waiting in the interrogation room. Ben entered and nodded to him. He was relaxed and just about to nod off. He wasn't cuffed. It seemed to Ben that the chief was fucking with him because of his wise mouth. Ben knew he had to establish authority immediately.

"Sit up. I'm getting you out of here."

House sat up. "What the fuck, man? You got me sitting in that fucking hole. Shit, I haven't seen the sky in days. This is some kind of bullshit."

Ben ignored him and carried on. "Vinny Castlenni is dead. He was shivved by a skinhead yesterday. The man I want was behind it. You have been kept in solitary for your protection. You would be dead right now if it wasn't for me. I'm the best thing that ever happened to you, so cut the bullshit, or I let you stroll out onto the courtyard, see who comes at you."

"I ain't scared of no fucking cracker."

"Maybe not, but he won't be the only one. Don't you see? The word is out. There's a price on you. How many you think you can take?"

House just leaned back again and said, "Shit."

"The good news is I have the man. He'll be down here in a day, and I want you to help me take care of him."

House laughed. "What is this, some kind of James Bond caper? You tell me you're going to let me out so I can help you with a motherfucker that you're protecting me from? Shit, if you have him, leave me the fuck alone."

"It's not that simple, House—can I call you that? I have the man, but the hit on you still stands. He isn't going to call that off."

"You can call me House as long as I can keep calling you Fuck You."

Ben smiled briefly then continued. "My attorney worked with the Miami

Police Department, and I've had all the charges dropped. You're going to leave with me. I'll get you back to your apartment. I'll have some men there to watch you. You'll get a good night's sleep. Tomorrow you will go to the warehouse where you have the pulley-and-rope setup. The man will be delivered to you. You're going to work on the man until he gives me the information I need. If I'm not there, you can get started with him. Don't kill him."

House stood up and banged both hands on the table. Despite seeing it coming, Ben still winced. The sound was that loud. He towered over Ben.

"You got some balls, little man. The charges are dropped? Fuck you. I'm out."

He waved both his arms at Ben as if shooing away a pest and headed to the door.

"Two hundred and sixteen thousand dollars."

House stopped at the door, his hand on the knob. "What you say, little man?"

Ben didn't turn his way. He spoke facing where House was seated previously, summoning him back. "In Guzman's safe. Two hundred and sixteen thousand. That's how much you had in your hands when the cops took you."

House slowly walked over to his seat. Keeping a defiant attitude, he stood over Ben, crossed his arms, and leaned back slightly in a cocksure stance. "What's that mean to me?"

"I told you I had my lawyer talk to the police about your case. It turns out they have no reason to believe that you stole anything. The safe wasn't broken into; you had the combination. No drugs were taken. My lawyer said that you were collecting on a debt. Guzman gave you the combination. You didn't steal anything."

House sat down but kept his arms crossed. "That's right. It was payday. I was collecting my pay. That's all."

"Yeah, that's all. Only you work for me now. Payday has been pushed back. You get your pay once you take care of the man. You understand?"

House lowered his head and shook it slowly. He looked back up at Ben with a broad grin. His teeth were shockingly white. "You have this whole fucking thing figured out, don't you? Shit. Did you have me picked up from the start?"

"No. We called the police to pick up Castlenni. He gave you up before they even got him to the station. They followed you to Guzman's place. Think this through, House. You're free of Guzman, Vinny is dead, and you get paid two hundred grand. You just have to move out of Miami. That's the deal I made with the police chief—get you out."

"I was moving anyway. Hey, wait, I thought you said two hundred sixteen?"

"I did, but I don't like being called 'little man.' That will cost you."

"Shit, man. What the fuck do you want to be called, James Bond or some shit?"

"Call me Ben."

House stood. "All right, Ben, we out of here?"

Ben stood and walked to the door, opened it, and walked out. House followed.

CHAPTER 33

The phone rang at seven in the morning. It was Ben. "Time to go to work, House. My men are downstairs."

House rubbed his face. "Gimme ten minutes to get my ass up. You got the money?"

"Yeah, don't you trust me?"

"Shit, I wouldn't trust my momma with two hundred sixteen grand."

"Two hundred. Yeah, I have it. I need this guy talking soon."

"Most bitches break before the rope goes over their heads. Don't you worry; I'll do my job. Always have."

"Okay. You have ten minutes. There's coffee and some food at the warehouse. The man is there. His mouth is taped shut. Don't take it off and don't speak to him. From this point on the less you know, the better. Things go right, you'll have your money, and you'll be on your way out of town this afternoon."

"Cool, man. See you there."

They hung up, and House went into the bathroom. After washing up quickly, he went to his kitchen cabinet and took the bag of weed out of the sugar bowl. He packed a wad into a green pipe he took from the spoon slot in the utensil drawer and fired up. He opened the fridge and took out a gallon of milk, sniffed to make sure it wasn't soured, and drank down about a quart. He went to the door and turned to look around the apartment he had called home for the past ten years, and didn't give a shit. The night before he had considered the chance that Ben would jack him. Once the job was done, House knew that he didn't have any value. He didn't seem to have any options, though. As soon as they walked out of the jail, his dudes were waiting. He had no choice but to trust Ben. The funny thing was he did.

By the time he got to the elevator, he was in character, the bad motherfucker that will fuck you up. He was wearing Miami Heat basketball shorts down to his ankles, a white Ralph Lauren polo, and his new Jordans—untied, of course. He rolled the Tumi bag he had packed the previous night. He wouldn't be coming back. By the time he met the dudes out front, he was already thinking about skinny California blondes.

The warehouse was cleaned up. House thought it was a bad move. The nastier the warehouse got, the easier it was to intimidate. No matter. The dudes let him in. Neither of them spoke, but House knew they were the real deal. Thin and wiry, dressed in all black. Shit, he thought, Ben had gotten himself a couple of white ninjas. They got in the car and took off around the corner. House figured they wouldn't be far.

He walked over to the table. On the far end of the warehouse was the pulley and the rope. The man was lying under it. He was sleeping and naked. He was in a puddle of water. They must have hosed down his ugly ass that morning. House bent his knees and looked over at the man; shit, he was old. *This is some fucked-up shit,* he thought. He looked over at the table. All that was on it was a box of coffee and a box of donuts. *Motherfucker has sixteen thousand dollars of mine, and he can't buy an egg sandwich?* House filled a Styrofoam cup with coffee and looked around for some milk. Nothing there. He sipped the coffee and opened the donut box. He grabbed a glazed and ate it in two bites, then a chocolate frosted, then another. He took another sip of the coffee, put down the cup, and walked over to the rope and pulley.

Someone had strung it and tied a noose. House took the noose in his hands. Not acceptable. He pulled the rope out of the pulley. It fell down in a thump at his feet. House started untying it, and it came loose easily, as he expected. He wasn't going to let someone else set up for his job. Shit, what kind of professional would he be if he didn't prepare his own tools? He didn't like people touching his shit. All of this—the Styrofoam, the shitty breakfast, people touching his shit—put him in a bad state of mind. He stepped over and kicked the old man.

"Wake up, motherfucker."

The old man groaned and opened his eyes. House could see the fear. He bent down closer.

"I'm not supposed to talk to you. So let's keep this our little secret. I don't like old white men. Best I can figure it, men like you been fucking me my whole life. I want you to know how much I'm going to enjoy this. You see here?" He held up the rope. "I'm going to tie this into a noose. Then I'm going to lift you up and choke your skinny ass."

House started laughing to himself. The weed was kicking in nice now. He started doing a little sway back and forth as his enormous hands tied a fresh, tight noose. He went into a white plantation owner accent.

"Get me a Neeegro from the field and bring him to the hangin' tree." He dropped the accent and bent back down within an inch of Handley's face. "No, Massa, I think I'm going to hang your white ass from a tree. Yeah, boy, I'm going to lynch your bitch ass."

As he put the noose over Handley's head and snapped it tight, Handley started squirming and wiggling on the floor. House walked over to the side of the warehouse and grabbed the ladder. He lifted it with one hand and set it up under the pulley. Up he went. House strung the thick rope through and pushed it until the untied end reached the floor. He had plenty of slack. The old man didn't do shit. His hands were tied behind his back as House had requested. He wasn't going anywhere. Handley started screaming under the tape. House couldn't make out anything except panic. He left him there and walked over to the other side of the rope. He pulled it slowly. The old man started turning. He was gurgling, and his legs didn't catch ground. He was spinning from his tiptoes. House pulled a little harder, and he heard a short, startled scream inside the tape. The old bastard was too weak. House walked over with the rope in his right hand. He pulled the old man upright with his left. Finally the man stood. House waited a second to make sure he didn't fall and snap his neck. He put a hand on the man's chest to steady him. His heart was beating so fast that House was sure the man would die on the spot.

He didn't die, so House went over to the other side of the warehouse, rope in hand, and tied it to a large bracket on the wall. He tightened it just enough to make the man stand on his toes. He walked over to the table and took another donut. This one was some kind of pink thing. House folded it and tubed it into his mouth with his forefinger. He sat on the table and waited.

Ben was running late, and he hoped that House hadn't killed Handley. He had spent over an hour filling Kat in on the latest. She gave him the update from the New York end. There was no need. Ben had the *Wall Street Journal* dropped off at his room and was well into it at the time of the call. The headline said it all: "AXIS FINANCIAL A CRIMINAL ENTERPRISE."

Ben knew the bulk of the story and noticed that a few things were left out. Having dropped information to the press many times in the past, he knew it was a combination of verifying data and bleeding the story out for maximum attention.

He unconsciously put his hand on the briefcase next to him in the car. The case had the bank receipt, a new passport and driver's license for House, along with a new Social Security card and plane tickets to LAX. Ben tried to focus on the job in front of him. Kat had urged him, demanded really, that he keep his cool. The only thing needed from Handley was the address of where they were holding Pap. If he "overplays his hand," as she put it, they would lose Handley and maybe Pap. "Keep your wits about you," she said. Ben knew she was right, but he wasn't confident he could do this. How could he keep his cool when facing a man who had killed such a dear man as Sol and took his friend, who must be going through hell right then? How did he do this? He had never lost anyone, ever. His family was happy and healthy; Randi was great. He'd had everyone he loved around him his whole life—until this man came into his life. Jesus, he thought. It had started as just another financial investigation; now he was pulling up to a warehouse where a killer was likely hanging from a noose held by a mountainous street thug. He parked and got out of the car. Ben took out the case, went to the back of the car, and put it in the trunk. He lifted the floor panel in the trunk and pulled the spare tire out of the well. Underneath he found what he was looking for. The tire iron was smaller than he remembered it being, but it would do the job.

He knocked, hoping that House had remembered to lock the door behind him. He did. Ben could see House's massive shadow behind the beveled glass in the door. He heard a bolt turn, and he stepped in. House got in his face immediately.

"What the fuck is with this breakfast? Don't you know how to run a job? Man, you got to take care of your people. Shit, a fucking egg sandwich or something."

Ben was so surprised that he said sorry. House grumbled and walked back over to the table and poured himself more coffee out of the box. Ben dropped the tire iron on the cement floor, and it made a loud rattle.

Ben walked over to where Handley was. His eyes were closed. He turned back to House.

"Any problems? Is he okay here?"

"You got tire trouble?"

Ben didn't answer.

"Yeah, man. Just slap his face a little."

Ben did just that. Handley stirred and opened his eyes. Ben held up the paper, headline facing him. He could see the shock register on Handley's face, and just for a second Ben felt good.

"Where is Pap?"

Handley mumbled a "fuck you" under the tape. Ben turned back to House.

"Want to grab the rope?"

"Sure thing, man. You got my money?"

"Yeah, it's in the car. Can we get to this, please?"

He walked over to the rope, and Ben could make out the words "egg sandwich" mumbled under his breath. He got into position and untied the rope. It went slack for a second, and Handley's knees buckled. House pulled the rope up slowly to create tension.

He asked Ben, "Do we start hard on this bitch or easy?"

Ben stared into Handley's eyes as he responded. "Start hard but not too hard. I want this to last."

House pulled up fast, and Handley went up three feet off the ground. He made a screaming gurgle under the tape. House let him down slowly while jerking the rope up intermittently. Each time, Handley squealed. It sounded like a balloon being choked of its air. House let him down, and Handley crumpled to the floor. House walked over to Ben with the rope in his hands.

"Shit, man, this isn't going to take but a few minutes. He's too weak for this shit. Take the tape off. He can't breathe. You're going to lose him. There's a hose over there. Get it and spray this motherfucker down. He's going out on us."

Ben hustled over to the hose, and House tore the tape off. Ben could hear the rip from across the warehouse. Handley yelped. Ben walked over with the hose and sprayed the old man. He squirmed on the floor like a bug trying to get away but got the taut end of the rope and stopped. Ben dropped the hose and walked over to him. He leaned down.

"Where is Pap?"

Handley gathered all his strength and looked up. "He's dead. I had him killed. You killed him, you little putz. I know you; you're a nobody. I know you."

Ben knew he was lying. He had to be. He couldn't have had any contact with his people in the past couple of days. Still, the words stung. He looked at Handley and could tell he was trying to recall Ben's name. Before he could, Ben turned to House.

"Again. Pull him up."

House pulled, and Handley went up, four feet this time. His face turned bright red, and his feet danced in the air. House waited until the red started turning blue and Handley's eyes were bulged then he dropped him. He went down in a heap, and Ben heard his shoulder crack.

"Where's Pap?"

"I have money."

"Pull him!" Ben shouted it this time.

As Handley was about to go up, he shook his head. House lifted. Handley went up and didn't kick this time. He went blue right away. House got the feeling again. Wasting a motherfucker. Fuck, yeah, it was good. Pulling the breath out of him. This time a rich white guy, not one of those smelly little Puerto Rican punks that Guzman dragged in. He was killing a serious man. This was nice.

House called over to Ben, "Got to let him down. We'll lose him. You want me to kill him now, I just have to tug the rope. You want some answers, you better let him down. We got time, brother. No need to fuck him up so quickly."

Ben turned again and spoke, staring straight at Handley. He wasn't sure that he could even see him back, but Ben couldn't take his eyes off of him. "Get him down to his feet but leave him standing."

House lowered him, and Ben walked over to where the tire iron was. Ben heard House chuckle as he lifted the iron. He took it and shook it in his hand and felt the weight of it. He walked over to Handley and poked him in the stomach with it. Handley roused and looked down. Ben held the iron up to his face.

"Where's Pap?"

"I can't. I can't."

Ben swung. The tire iron hit Handley square on the kneecap. Ben heard it shatter. Handley screamed, and House yelled, "Damn!" from across the room. Ben looked down at the knee. He couldn't believe that he had just done that. He tried to calm down, but he felt as if Pap was slipping away. The more Handley refused to talk, the more anxious Ben became. He had to know.

He slid over, took a batter's stance, and looked at the other knee. Without looking up, he asked, "Where is he? I can do this all day. Where is Pap?"

Handley was crying. He couldn't speak.

Ben shouted, "Where's Pap?"

Handley mumbled something. Ben pulled back the tire iron.

Before he could swing, House shouted over, "Wait, man! I hear something."

Ben stilled and listened. He got out of the stance and leaned in close to hear.

"Five eighteen West One Sixty-One."

"I didn't get it."

Handley mustered his strength to yell the words. "Five eighteen West One Sixty-One."

The words snapped Ben out of his lunatic trance. He took a second and looked down at the tire iron in his hand. He dropped it to another clatter and reached into his pocket for his phone. He dialed the number; Kat picked up.

"Five eighteen West One Sixty-One. Hurry."

Kat wrote down the address. "Are you sure? Do we have to wait to confirm it?"

"I'm sure it's right, but I'll wait."

"Okay. Good work. I'll call Marshall. Ben…Ben, are you there?"

Ben was staring at the back wall of the warehouse. He heard a voice then realized it was coming from the phone. He put it back to his ear.

"Ben…Ben. Are you okay?"

"Yes, yes. Sorry, a little distracted."

"Listen to me very carefully. Don't try to clean up. The men are around the corner. They'll be there in less than five minutes. The tactical team is ready to move. The address is uptown. It may take a few minutes. The confirmation should come soon. Go outside and wait. I'll call as soon as we hang up. Are you okay with that man there? It could be a half hour or so. The men will clean up the scene. Ben?"

"Yeah."

"You did a good thing. Pap will be fine. You did a good thing."

"Okay. I got it." He hung up.

House walked over to Ben. As he approached, Ben heard Handley screaming again. The sound of it was whitewashed out for a minute. The first thing he thought was that Kat must have heard him through the phone. House was right in front of him. He clapped his hands in a thunderous snap.

"Man. You are a crazy motherfucker. Little man getting all nasty. That was some crazy shit. You should have seen your face."

Ben's head cleared. The first thing he had to do was take back control of House. He didn't like the familiarity. The lines were getting blurred. He had to get outside as Kat had said. He started walking toward the door. He looked over his shoulder at House, purposely avoiding looking at Handley.

"C'mon. You want your money, don't you?"

House followed, and they went out. The air was hot and humid. It helped to clear Ben's head further. There was one more thing to deal with. Ben had to rid himself of House without incident. He went around to the trunk of the car and opened it. He took out the briefcase and opened it with the trunk door still open. He waited for House to come over. House towered over Ben and looked in the briefcase.

"Goddamn. What the fuck is this shit?"

"This is ten thousand dollars in small bills. In the envelope is a statement for a money market account. It's being held by a firm in Los Angeles. Here's how it's going to work. One month from today, you will walk into the office on the statement letterhead; you will ask for Ben. The man will transfer ten thousand dollars into a bank account which you will have set up before then.

Every month ten grand will be rolled into your bank account. No need to go back after the first time. If you stay out of trouble—no arrests, no bullshit—for six months, on the seventh month one hundred and thirty grand will be transferred, and you will be done with us. There's also a new driver's license, passport, and Social Security number. You're not Carlton Williams anymore."

"This is some fucking bullshit."

"Do you think I would give a killer like yourself two hundred grand to go party with and talk to who the hell knows? I'm not your fucking little man, understand? You keep your mouth shut and your game clean, and you get all your money. That's the only deal you get."

"So what you're telling me is that you're going to give me my money over time so I keep my mouth shut. The money that I stole from Guzman, that the cops think is mine, that you stole from me. Is that right?"

"That about sums it up."

House was pissed but not pissed enough to walk away from the money. He shook his head and laughed a bit.

"Motherfucker. What's with the license and shit?"

"I never knew any Carlton Williams, that's why. Never heard of you."

House rubbed his face. "Damn. That's all right. I don't want none of my old crowd looking me up anyway. Long as I can still be House."

"The ten grand is traveling money. There's also a ticket to LAX, one way."

"Yeah, man. How do I know you ain't going to fuck me? I could walk into that office in California and have a hundred cops on my ass, or the money might not be there."

"I told you at the start. You have to have trust. You could have bashed my head in and taken this car, but you didn't."

House smiled. "Not yet I haven't."

There was a moment between them. Ben didn't know if House was going to shake his hand or bust his head. The moment passed as two gray sedans and a white van came around the corner into the parking lot. House picked up the briefcase and held it to his chest. The cars pulled up, and two men from each car walked past them, without saying a word, into the warehouse. Two more men got out of the van, both with shotguns held tightly against their chests.

House laughed. "Yeah, trust, but have two motherfuckers with shotguns around the corner."

Ben laughed. They waited in silence. After twenty minutes that seemed like half a day, one of the men came out of the warehouse.

"We have confirmation. Your man has been released."

He waved his hand to the two men by the van. One of them got behind the wheel, and the other stayed where he was. He kept his eyes trained on House. House was getting anxious to leave.

"Man, your buddy with the shotgun is pissing me off. When can I get the fuck out of here?"

Ben handed House the car keys. "Go to the airport and park in the long-term parking area. The number of the spot is written on an itinerary in the glove box. You have a six p.m. flight. Don't stray off course. We have GPS on the car. Don't make us pick you up. Buy some clothes when you get to the airport. There's also a pass to one of those executive lounges. I forget which one; it's written down also. Stay at the airport until your flight. Be cool. Got it?"

"Shit, little man. I'm always cool."

He grabbed the keys and got in the car. He didn't turn around. He did the smart thing. House got the hell out of there.

CHAPTER 34

They gave him another shot about a half hour ago, so Pap watches it all happen through the projector in Mr. Benson's science class. The images pop and bounces on the screen in front of him, the white screen Mr. Benson pulled down from the blue case above the blackboard, which is green. Pap smiles. *That makes it a greenboard.* Pap goes behind the projector; something is broken. Just the film slipped out of the track. He smells the film, secretly leaning in to sniff the burning odor caused by the hot bulb.

The man with his back to him opens the door slowly then it bursts out. The man, with a cigarette hanging low on his left lower lip, falls back. The film stops; there's a skip in the reel. It goes bright white. Then there is a flash coming from a standing man. He's wearing a helmet and goggles—no, yellow-tinted glasses. He stands, hands pointed out, clasped together. The flash comes from his hand again, bright. There is a sharp smell in the room; the air is burning. There's no sound. No sound. What happened to the film? He can't go back to fix it. The projector is gone. The card table goes over. Is there someone there?

Pap stores away the projector after class. All is well in the closet. They gave him keys. He walks to the bus stop. Out front the kids are lined up in neat little groups. The boys are behind him. "AV squad." They're singing the words. Pap walks faster out the front door. Pressing the horizontal handle, it clicks in, and he pushes. It's sunny. She's over there on one of the lines. Plaid skirt, brown hair. She's so pretty. She'll never talk to him.

The boy shoves him from behind. It's Ben. The other boys are behind him. "Yo, Pap. What's up?"

The other boys peel away. "Yo, Pap."

There's another flash close to him. He feels the heat. He's jostled from behind. Something leaning on his shoulders. Cigarette smell. Words, jumbled words. The sound is back. Hit the side of the projector, that's the secret. The sound came back. Yelling. Piercing his ears. Flash. He falls down. Something bites him. He looks at the floor. Wood squares. He rises up. No, something lifts him. He is being dragged. A loud noise again. Feet dragging. Where is she, the girl? Ben, Ben, the bus left. He's flying a foot above the ground. Stairs going down. His toes tap each step as he flies down. Lower and lower, turning, his weight shifting with the turn.

He's on his back on the old couch in the basement, yet when he looks up, there is blue sky. Something blocks the light. A head with a helmet. Yellow glasses. There's music. Pap listens and smiles broadly. Bill Evans and Stan Getz. His father's music. "Waltz for Debby." He leans his head to one side to hear better then falls asleep.

CHAPTER 35

K at had a desk moved into the office. Ben sat at it across the room from her. It was already somewhat cluttered with his notepads and stacks of financial statements. He was trying to consolidate all the Prime Equities data into one concise file. Kat had secured the business after lunching with Esther Landsman a few times that past week. Esther was off to California to move in with her children. They'd had dinner the night before at Willy's place, a great meal. Kat and Randi had already become fast friends. Willy, well, he was a funny guy. Life of the party, and he could cook too. Jesus, what a meal. Esther had looked happy, laughing along and telling stories about her grandkids.

Kat had let Ben know about Pap's safe extraction as soon as his plane landed that day. She told him that he was pretty drugged up when they got him out. They were giving him morphine. In heavy doses. She said it might take a few weeks to clear out his system. Commissioner Marshall kept his word, and there wasn't any mention of the event in the papers or on the news. Ben didn't have to be told that he wouldn't hear from Pap for quite a while—years maybe. His whole identity was blown. Ben couldn't come near him, and Pap couldn't come near anyone. Kat explained to Ben that their part of it was over, never to be mentioned again. They all did what had to be done. No sense going on about it. The only thing to do was to let Marshall grandstand a bit about Handley. The papers were having a field day with it. The news hit the day after Ben got back that Handley had jumped off a building in Miami. Somehow he snuck into a construction site of a new condo tower and threw himself off. Ben had wondered until then how they were going to cover up the broken kneecap.

It seemed that everything was buttoned up, so Ben thought it a good time to press Kat a little. He was thinking about going out to get a smoke. It had been over a week without one. Instead he got up from his desk and walked over to her much larger one.

"I have most of the Prime data logged. I'm going to set something up with the CFO next week. I have a few ideas for him."

Kat looked up. "Anything I can help with?"

"No. I just want to get across that we are going to take a more comprehensive approach to our services for them. He probably still looks at me as an outside consultant. Even though Esther was the hand of God on this deal, I want to establish a good working relationship."

"That's smart. I have a ton of things to get to. I wish Frank was back. I'm spending half my time doing bills." She picked up a Con Ed bill and waved it in disgust.

Ben sat on the chair next to her desk.

"When is he getting out?"

"Not for two more months. He's doing the whole thing. Says he owes it to Brogan. I'm starting to think he likes it up there, and he's having a nice, long vacation."

Ben would have chuckled if he thought Kat was joking, but she clearly wasn't. She didn't like doing the bills. He leaned forward, put his elbows on his knees, and looked at the wall.

"How do you do this? Compartmentalize like this?"

"What, the bills?"

"No, Kat, all that happened. You killed a guy, a bad guy, of course, but you killed him. I tortured an old man. Is this what I'm supposed to do? Move on to filing after practically hanging a man to death? And Pap. C'mon. It's been over a week, and I don't know anything."

Kat dropped the Con Ed bill and sat back in her chair. "I've been waiting for you to calm down. You were pretty stressed out when you got back. I think it would be good to talk it out. So what are you thinking? How do feel about all this?"

"I guess I'm just in shock. I mean I go from running my safe little business, and less than two weeks later, I have one of the biggest CEOs in America hanging from a noose. I mean it's pretty fucked up."

Kat acted as if she hadn't heard him. As she started speaking, it occurred to Ben that she wanted to unburden herself, and he had given her the opening. He shut up and listened.

"I was a cop for a long time. Oh, I told you. Out in Telluride. I never pulled my gun, ever. I talked to my chief once about it. He shot two guys early in his career. He didn't seem fazed by it at all. In fact it seemed like he enjoyed telling me. I chalked it up to male bragging. Macho shit. After leaving the force I never thought I would draw my gun. I knew Frank and Brogan were into some violent things from time to time. They made sure to keep me away from it, maybe because I'm married with more to lose or because I'm a woman. It didn't matter to me. I was glad to be away from it, carrying a gun, the danger of it. But I did it. I shot him once in the stomach to get him off me and then twice in the face. I did it for Esther. I walked out, and you know what? I don't have any regrets. I mean I grew up out West. We have a different way of looking at these things, I think. Guns, violence, it's more of our culture. Telluride, my hometown, has a history of bringing people to justice with the gun. I was raised on those stories, that history. It's ingrained in my DNA I think. I never thought about it until I pulled the trigger, but, yeah, it was right. I don't feel anything at all. I don't."

"I know what you mean. That is what has been bothering me. I don't care either. I'm glad I cracked that bastard with a tire iron. I really am. I never thought I could do something like that, but I felt for Pap, you know? I felt like I let him down, and I had to get that information. What does that make me? Not caring like this."

"In my mind it makes you honest. An honest man."

They sat for a while in silence, looking past each other to another place.

Kat was thinking about her childhood in Telluride. She thought about how wonderful it was, and when she and Willy adopted their child, she was going to take him there. She smiled at the idea that she would tell Willy that night that she wanted to adopt a boy.

Ben thought about Randi. They were going to start testing that night to see if she was pregnant. It was such a delicate balance with her at these times. He would be encouraging, of course, but, God, he wished this would be the time.

Kat broke the silence. "Why don't you call the CFO and set something up as soon as you can? If you need help with the presentation, I can lend a hand."

"Yeah, good idea. Thanks."

CHAPTER 36

Frank walked up the stairs onto Queens Boulevard. He took the F train from Rock Center. It was the first time in many years that he had taken the subway out that far. Having grown up in Woodside, he had taken this line many times over the years, but now he took a car service to come out to see his mom and some old friends. Since he had stopped drinking, he thought he wouldn't be seeing the old friends much anymore. He called his mom the day before and would stop by her house on the way back to the city. It was a perfect day with high clouds and the bluest of skies. He waited at the light to make the sprint across Queens Boulevard in one shot. As the light turned, he fast walked the expanse and thought of the old *Post* headline: "Boulevard of Death." It was a wide street and used quite often as a cut through for commuters trying to skip traffic on the LIE.

Frank had come home two days before. He didn't let anyone know the day he was getting out. The last thing he wanted was some kind of welcome-home party or any kind of fuss. He went straight to his apartment and opened all the windows. He sat on his couch with the windows opened and listened to the city, the taxis and sirens, fire trucks and ambulances. He had missed the noise, the urgency of the city. That night he roamed the streets, trying to get everything back into his bloodstream. New York. The smells and sounds. He walked down Broadway from the Upper West Side and made a left at Columbus Circle and walked through the pathway at the southern tip of Central Park. He took the path to the East Side then north up to the little zoo. He walked out of the park at Sixty-Second and went up Fifth Avenue past the townhouse, his house soon. Then he cut across the park back to the West Side like he had done every day for years.

Frank was as physically fit as he had been in decades. He was up to four miles per run every other day. For months he had looked forward to running the Central Park Reservoir loop. The previous day he finally did it. He went around twice and had plenty of energy left to jog back to his place. It wasn't that long ago that he couldn't even have imagined such a thing. He didn't wear a headset or earbuds. All he needed was the memory of his dream and the image of his Danny in white, smiling with her head to one side. He thought of her advice: take the stairs. It was amazing to him what he had put his body through and its ability to recover. He was blessed.

Kat made a fuss over him when he strolled into the office. Ben wasn't there. He had a meeting downtown. After hugs and coffee, Kat gave him the envelope that she had held for him for three months. It was from Brogan's lawyer, who delivered it three days after the funeral. It was written to Frank and sealed. Frank sat on the office couch and opened it. Kat asked if she should go out to leave him alone, but Frank wanted her there.

The message was cryptic. After a quick read through and a look at the check attached, Frank looked at Kat and smiled. "Fucking Brogan!"

They shared a good laugh and then sorted through the letter. They spent most of the day putting together the pieces of the puzzle that Brogan had left them. It was one of the best afternoons Frank had had in a very long time. They both knew, and reveled in the knowledge, that Brogan had left this for them to work on so they could bond together, start on a project to get them out of the funk of mourning. They were in sync immediately, Kat looking something up before she was asked, Frank thinking fast as always. Brogan couldn't have known, of course, how much they had bonded after his death due to the events that unfolded after his passing.

Ben got back to the office at twelve. Frank reluctantly agreed to a celebratory lunch. Willy joined them. He took a moment at the meal, as they were all talking, to look around him, look at the people at the table. His life was a joy. He vowed to take in these moments, take the time to look around and see what was before him, see the gifts that he received every day. He smiled at himself and thought that a few months before he would have laughed at himself for thinking those things, but then a few months before he was only thinking about his next drink. He did learn something this time. He learned to live for the moment in his personal life and to think long term in his work life. That credo wasn't something he had been taught or that had been any kind of mantra in rehab; it was what Frank had gotten out of it. It was his credo.

After the very long lunch, he went back to the office and told Kat to take off. He wanted to finish the puzzle on his own, thinking that Brogan meant it to be that way. Once the puzzle was solved, Frank made the appropriate phone calls and went home, got a solid night's sleep, and headed to the subway that morning.

As Frank made a left onto 110th Street, he remembered that, as a kid, he always thought of Forest Hills as the rich neighborhood. There were mansions there, all the kids would say. He walked past the modest brick homes, all of which were neatly landscaped but certainly not mansions, and recalled how little he had as a kid. He could see how he thought those homes were mansions when he'd grown up in a two-bedroom with two sisters, a brother, and a mom. Maybe he'd buy one of these for his mom, he thought. She would still be in Queens and be able to see her friends. That was what she always said when he suggested she move to a nicer area, maybe the suburbs. She would gasp and say that she couldn't leave her friends, and besides, Franky, how could she afford it? Forest Hills was only three stops from Woodside. He was growing weary of fighting her to get out of that dinky little apartment. He knew it was hard for her to understand that he was quite wealthy at this point. She wouldn't take a dime from him. She lived off of her teacher's pension. Maybe she'd move here but probably not.

He came to the address, a little brick house with a new porch. The cement almost looked wet as he stepped up. He rang the bell. After a long pause and another ring, an elderly woman came to the door. She opened the inner wood door but kept the screen door closed. Frank leaned in closer to see her.

"Hello, Mrs. Melton, I'm Frank McGinley. Mr. Sterling should have called."

"Yes, yes. Can you show me some ID?"

"Yes, of course." Frank pulled out his wallet and removed his driver's license and business card. He held them up to the screen, all the while thinking that if he was an intruder, he could have pushed the screen in. She peered at the documents and then clicked the screen door lock open. She opened it with a squeak. The door's springs were too tight, and the door closed on Frank before he could move. She had already started away, so he let himself in.

The interior of the house was compact, neat, and smelled of just-sprayed Fabreeze. She was overweight and walked with a waddle and a slight limp in her left leg. Wearing a housecoat and an obvious brown wig, she turned out of the tiny living room into a dining area. Frank followed wordlessly. On the dining room table was a ragged accordion folder and two neat stacks of documents. She was ready for her meeting. From her demeanor, Frank expected her to be cranky, but when she spoke, she had a pleasant, calming voice.

"So how do you know Mr. Sterling? Are you with the firm?"

"No, I'm not. I hope he explained it clearly. I'm with an investment company in Manhattan. We discovered a financial discrepancy that I would like to correct."

"Well, Sterling said it was something about Federated Insurance. I have a life insurance policy, but I'm not dead yet, so I don't see what you need to see me about. Would you like some coffee?"

She turned into the kitchen before he could respond.

"Coffee would be nice. Thank you. Just a little milk." He heard her milling around in the kitchen. Frank sat down and put his case on the chair next to him. He opened it and thumbed through the documents to be sure that they were in proper order. He took out the envelope and put it face up at her place at the table. She was taking a while, and Frank thought he might go in to help, when she reemerged into the dining room with two cups on a tray along with a plate of Milano cookies. She put the tray down but didn't look at the envelope.

"You're not with Federated? I don't understand. How do you know Matt Sterling? He's been my insurance agent for years now. Me, my children, all of us. If you're not from Federated then why are you here? How do you know Matt?"

There was a trace of concern on her face. Frank wanted to dispel it right away. He pulled a piece of paper out of his case and put it on top of the envelope.

"I don't know Matt Sterling. I'm friends with Bill McManus, the CEO of Federated Insurance. Here is a letter of introduction from Mr. McManus." He raised the top corner of the paper toward her to bring it to her attention. She read. It was signed by hand by McManus and embossed with the corporate seal of Federated. Kat and Frank had called in some favors to get this hand delivered to them the previous night.

Francis Melton was impressed. "Do you know I was a corporate attorney for many years? I worked for the old American Can Corporation. They moved upstate, and I left." She had a wry smile on her face. "You know that, though, don't you? You figured I'd know that this letter was real. Okay, what is this really about?"

She looked ten years younger now that she was engaged. Frank sipped his coffee. It tasted like shit. He first tapped at then picked up the envelope in front of her. It read "Francis Feldman" on the cover in Brogan's very neat handwriting. She looked at it, and shock came over her face. Francis looked up at Frank with confusion in her eyes. Frank ignored the look and spoke in a calming tone.

"I'm here about the death of your first husband, Hiram Feldman."

"Harry? It's been over forty years. God, I haven't even thought of him in years. We were only married a few months."

"Yes, I know. I'm here on behalf of the man who killed him."

The confusion on her face turned to fear. She looked around her to see if her path to the door was blocked.

"I don't understand."

Frank smiled in an attempt to reassure her. "I know. I know." He pushed his coffee away to the center of the table. "It's a shock, I'm sure. I know it has been years, but if you indulge me, I would like to explain why I'm here and the financial settlement I'm offering. Will you allow that?"

"Do I have a choice?"

Frank laughed, and she smiled but nervously sipped her coffee as her eyes danced around the room—anywhere but on Frank's eyes. Before there could be an awkward pause, Frank went straight to the story.

"Your husband was not killed by a mugger as you were told. He was intentionally murdered so a man named Carter Handley could take over the company he worked for." She tried to speak, but Frank plowed on. "My dear friend was the man who pulled the trigger. He was deceived into thinking that your husband was someone he was not. Believe me, the man who killed your husband was a man of the noblest intentions. The way he was deceived haunted him for most of his life. He was unable to tell the truth because of a threat to his family if he told. As an additional way of keeping my friend quiet, Handley opened an account under my friend's name and put two hundred thousand dollars in it. It was Handley's way of blackmailing my friend with the evidence that could be considered a payoff for the murder. My friend never intended to use this money. He died four months ago and left the original account documents for me so I could uncover Handley's deception and make him pay for his crime." He let her speak.

"I saw this on the news. This is a part of all that? You are involved? You uncovered all of that? My goodness, what an awful man. He killed himself, didn't he? Just as well. Those thieves never go to jail anymore."

"Yes. I was part of uncovering it, but there were far more important people than me involved in the case. The murder of your husband started this way back then. It took a lot to unravel everything, but all along my friend had this money for you."

"I always knew, you know. I always knew he wasn't mugged. Three weeks later the company gets taken over. You know Harry had a lot of stock. I inherited quite a bit of money. I bought this house with it."

Frank smiled. "It's a beautiful home. May I continue?"

"Yes, please."

"Well, as you know, Carter Handley is dead. My friend's relatives are still alive, but with Handley gone I don't believe that there is any threat to them any longer."

"Who is your friend?"

"I can't reveal his name due to national security concerns."

She smiled as if he were joking. "Are you serious?"

"I'm very serious. I'm withholding his name for your protection. Please open the envelope now."

Francis opened it and pulled out the check for $2,107,000. Before she could speak, Frank continued.

"This check was given to me just yesterday. I mentioned what an honorable man my friend was. Around the time this blackmail account was opened in his name, he opened this account with an equal amount of two hundred thousand for Hiram Feldman's survivor. He would never have taken that money from Handley. He opened this account in a blind trust for you, his widow. Of course, no one knew about this but him, but it has been earning interest for these forty years. This is your money."

"Is this real?"

"Francis, you probably signed checks like this when you were an attorney. You know it's real."

She knew. "What would I do with this? I have the pension from my second husband; the house is paid for. I mean, this…it's too much. It was so long ago; I hardly remember Harry."

Frank reached for his coffee, thought better of it, and turned back to Francis.

"You have four grandchildren. Start a college fund for them. I'm sure Mr. Sterling could advise you."

She thought about it. "You didn't have to do this. If your friend and Handley are dead, you didn't have to bring me this. Why?"

"Francis, all I'm doing is fulfilling the wishes of a great man who thought about your wellbeing many years ago."

They talked some more. Frank told her what he could, which wasn't much. She asked him if he could speak to her son, who was a banker in New Hampshire, but he declined. He didn't have any more coffee, but he had a Milano and left soon after. He gave Francis his numbers if she should need anything. Frank would call this Matt Sterling once he got back to the office. He wanted to make sure the money was treated right. He would be sure to speak to Sterling a little about how it should be handled. Frank didn't want Francis to get screwed after all these years.

Frank walked the streets of Queens a little while. The weather was so nice he didn't want to get back on the subway or leave the tree-lined streets just yet. As he walked he had a feeling in his chest that was hard to define. He felt lifted, as though he was on a higher plane. Giving Francis that money had a profound effect on him. The look on her face. The idea that he would get to do this many more times now that he was running the charitable trusts was a bigger concept than he could fathom.

His thoughts went back to the old man and the early days, when he lifted Frank the first time. Frank had been lost then also, drinking and drugging, generally not giving a shit about anything. It had been Brogan with a hard hand. Frank remembered now. He had picked him up in front of Trinity Church and taken him in a car under the FDR. He had threatened him, forced him to tell him everything he knew. Frank had long forgotten the rest, just that he had been saved as he was being saved now. He now knew exactly what the old man had intended. From the grave he was caring for him, giving him something uplifting to spend his time on, keep him out of trouble. He roamed and thought about how he was going to start. Which charity should he turn to first? How should he begin this next phase of his life, this virtuous life that he had been given the opportunity to lead? How to make the most of this gift he had received?

He came across a playground; he thought he was near Sixty-Eighth Street. There was a pickup game going on. He sat on a bench to watch. A city symphony played out, the basket rattling, guys talking, insulting, slapping hands. The net hung loose on the rim, and a shot passed through it. The argument ensued, air ball or swish. Frank saw the swish but lost interest. He turned to the playground, small children running, chasing each other with sticks. Frank closed his eyes and listened: the laughter of the children, the barks of young men hustling, cursing each other as they chased a round ball, the sound of squeaking sneakers, and the rattle of the rim. Behind him a horn blared, and a distant radio played Latin music. He loved this fucking city.

He opened his eyes and looked over at a man sitting on a bench, reading a paper, then looking at the playground, up and down from the paper to the swings. Suddenly a little boy ran over to the man.

"Billy knocked me down."

"Well, go over there and knock him down."

"Okay, Daddy." The boy ran back to the swings.

Frank smiled. "Fucking Brogan."

THE END

About the Author

John Nuckel lives in New York City with his wife and two children. He is a longtime "student of the city." When he's not writing, he's often researching in one of Manhattan's libraries or museums.

www.johnnuckel.com

John's Novels
Rector Street Series:
> *The Vig*
> *Grit*
> *Blind Trust*

The Volunteers Series:
> *DRIVE*

John's Short Stories
> *The Garden*
> *The Victory Grill*

CPSIA information can be obtained
at www.ICGtesting.com
Printed in the USA
BVHW05s0820070918
526555BV00007B/53/P